WE WILL ALL BE TREES

a novel by

JOSH MASSEY

© Josh Massey, 2009

First Edition

Edited for conundrum press by Maya Merrick

Front cover art: "Mecca" installation and photo ©
    by Peter von Tiesenhausen

Design by Andy Brown

Library and Archives Canada Cataloguing in Publication

Massey, Josh, 1979-
We will all be trees / Josh Massey.

ISBN 978-1-894994-41-5

I. Title.

PS8626.A7989W48 2009   C813'.6   C2009-904772-1

Dépot Legal, Bibliothèque nationale du Québec
Printed and bound in Canada by Gauvin

conundrum press
Montreal, Quebec
Greenwich, Nova Scotia
www.conundrumpress.com

conundrum press acknowledges the financial support of the
Canada Council for the Arts and the Government of Canada
through the Book Publishing Industry Development
Program (BPIDP) toward its publishing activities.

This book is dedicated to all those who have turned soil.

PART I

'T was early in the spring when I decided to go,
To work up in the woods in North Ontario;
And the unemployment office said they'd see me through
To the Little Abitibi with the survey crew.
And the blackflies, the little black flies
Always the blackfly no matter where you go
I'll die with the blackfly a-pickin' on my bones
In North Ontario, oh in North Ontario.

— From "The Blackfly Song" by Wade Hemsworth

LOW LAND

*at the last
judgment we will all be trees*
— Margaret Atwood

The clear-cut reminds Grant of a dirty sheet of paper that has been scribbled upon then erased, wetted and dried, repeatedly, until what remains of the medium is a sloppy smudge. It's an alienating anti-landscape: as if Tom Thompson had been reincarnated as HR Geiger and gone to work populating Meso Ontario with freakish flora dredged from the daydreams of a freshwater crab.

Grant can feel his pulse throbbing at the joints in his ring and index fingers, which he wraps in strips of protective duct tape. He sweeps two taped fingers over the side of his head, a nervous tic. The flies haven't even hatched yet and he's already swatting. Soon they will start breeding, then emerging in lustful droves, smooching his arms, leaving little love drops of blood on his skin.

The puddle in the ditch he needs to cross is streaked with grey plasma and stuck full of pussy willows that haven't yet released their little pods of feline fur. The land looks snarly, impenetrable. He is feeling what some call *the dread*. He alone is responsible for planting this section of land. This is *his piece*.

He scratches his moist ass. He's already experiencing some SWASS — sweaty ass. He's already got itchy balls — SWALLS. And this is pre-contract work. The real work hasn't even begun yet.

Drizzle begins drooling on the baldness of his shaved head and he stands there getting wet for a minute before realizing that he forgot to back-bag his raingear. So he unbuckles the belt clip that hugs his stomach just above his hip bones, letting the frayed planting bags slide down his thighs to the earth. He spears his Workwizer speed spade into the ground and marches back to his tree cache to grab his raingear.

Wavy shocks of deep green needles stick eagerly out of the tops of his planting bags: baby spruce fresh from the nursery. He used to believe that a conflagration of pheromones created an aura of youthful potential around the infantile evergreens. That they almost shone with the green light of intelligence. Today the light seems dulled, snuffed out. Nothing has any meaning and he still hasn't planted a tree yet — he's been lollygagging all morning.

Why would the spruce's genetically duplicated and perfected offspring be any different from the veteran? Well, the cloned saplings just shine, shine with energy. The spruce is, after all, one of the masters at surviving the northern climates, and the most populous member of the boreal forest. From a certain perspective it is a triumphant and heroic tree.

Grant's shaved head resembles a flower bulb yanked from the forest floor. His smile rustles into the shape of a twisted branch. His earlobes are dangling slugs.

His boots stick and unstick at each step, accumulating clay around the soles until the sludge achieves a kind of critical mass and breaks off in ragged parallelograms. He sits on the trunk of the fallen birch next to the tubs of trees which are his to plant today. He has the sudden desire for tobacco but remembers he has quit. Just the occasional cigar. He yanks his shell from his day bag and wraps it over his shoulders. He takes out his bandana, folds it into a triangle and ties the three tips of the triangle together around the bumpy back of his skull. Erects the jacket hood.

The rain hardens, tapping on his hood, then dripping off the visor of his hood down onto his leather work boots. He watches the rain funnel through a tangle of sticks and spatter on a fiddlehead which looks like it wants to unfurl but the strokes of rain are holding it down in a shamed and curled position. The rain is smudging the big mud landscape, greys and deep greens and dark pollards and clumps of dirty grass. Frog spawn and mosquito slime wreathe the puddles and bog, and cerebral mosses bulge on slimy stumps, giving the impression of an alien breeding zone. The sky appears filled with storybook ghosts passing gloomily on by. The trees have been sheared away to reveal the whole of the sky, peeled back, exposing the forest floor, the two horizontal planes of earth and sky contemplating each other.

It took forty-five minutes of slogging to get here. As if the walk-in to the block was actually a march to the block. As if the planting shovels were rifles, the hard hats were helmets, the static of walky-talkies set to the frequency of a war zone, the clear-cut zone; the zone of disappearance.

Grant is having difficulty planting his first tree. He wants some meaning; it's as if he's waiting for a sign before entering his piece. He's tired of just surfing the landscape like a wave; he would prefer to know it like a book. He wants to know the secrets of the forest. He wants to discover the ecstatic codes etched into the earth and sky. The green of the plants seems to swell and grow visibly by the end of a rainy spring day and the land croaks with life: the scattered residual trees at various stages of toppling from snow press, all the cantankerous secondary growth — this biotic acropolis full of amphibian, floral, and faunal knowledge — wakens with a faint sepulchral murmur.

The whole crude scene is a big smile with stained teeth gleaming of money, but more than money he loves to work until he is sweaty good in the rich muck, to overcome his inhibitions out here — the laziness, the melancholy, the fatigue — to continue tucking saplings by the thousands into the earth.

Oh, Mcao Ontario, how great it feels to piss wherever you want!

And with that thought Grant finishes urinating and hoists up his planting bags onto his hips. He pulls his shovel from the earth like Excalibur. And now he bursts through the alders at the front of his piece and starts pounding trees into the muck, spacing the required distance from one tree to the next.

Every springtime involves looking forward to summer. For most people, this includes buying a new swim suit and sunglasses and making sure any job fits snugly around a certain vacation time slot. At least these are the springtime ways of normal people, otherwise known as "normals". Everyone who is not a tree planter is a normal. They plan normal things, and dream into reality a summer that would befit a normal person, i.e. a fun, good summer. The tree planter, on the other hand, is preparing for another bone-jarring season up North — a not-fun, bad summer. And yet somehow the tree planter is just as excited as the normal. As if the tree planter had come to accept pain as an inevitable fact of life. Would you descend to the "dismal forest" in the Inferno's seventh circle if the pay ratio was right? Would you confront the mythless face of raw nature for a shitload of cash? "Yes," responds the tree planter — yes, but that's only half of it. For friendship? Maybe, but there is something else drawing them back up to the northern latitudes.

The best tree planters are not "up north" in the grand scheme of coordinates — generally above the fifty-second parallel. Unless one is referring to reforestation programs in the southern hemisphere; in Australia, or Argentina. But that's another story. Like hockey, tree planting is a socio-economic system that has been uniquely mastered by people you can call Canadians. Quite simply, we are the best at it, just as we are the best at hockey and the art of maple syrup.

Every spring the tree planter prepares to joyfully head into hell, amidst the chaos of final exams, the final negotiations with anxious loved ones, the subletting of apartments — an eclectic process that involves more than a few break offs, break ups, broken wine glasses, false promises, crocodile tears, and outright lies. Duffel bags shoved full with camping gear such as water jugs, play lists, weed: everything you might need for the dark, timeless days in the bush….

The policewoman, who totes what appears to be an old-fashioned pizzle instead of a billy bat, quickly deems our bus unfit for the roads. The strips of duct tape obscuring the rear license plate has alerted her to the presence of an unsafe vehicle full of potentially promiscuous and rebellious young men and women. The normal 8V4 S1X had been changed to 8V4 SEX with three strips of the shiny grey tape. Upon inspection, she found the bus was short a tail light and crammed beyond regulation with our gear, as well as two generators, a whole stack of coping, and six boxes of bananas. The duct tape misdemeanor was an ill-conceived practical joke played by some fool employee back at the yard: one hundred percent fixable (simply peel off the tape), and excusable in the policewoman's view. The busted light is more serious, and so is the load violation. We are an unsafe operation, she tells us, removing her shades, and chewing on one of the arms. We will have to wait for a couple of hours until Tamponix can send us a van from the head office to redistribute the load. Bosso, our bus driver, who is also one of the Tamponix crew bosses, runs over to the other bus and talks to the driver of indeterminate gender. He/she nods, then pulls back onto the highway and keeps chugging north towards Kapuskasing. There is something "evil", "creepy", and "weird" about Bosso, nobody could deny that. He looks kind of like a skid, with ragged beard and purple-tinted aviators. Like he's being nice and everything but any second he could turn into a crazy motherfucker. We wait out back of a highway strip mall, under a comatose lilac in early bloom, some of us cross-legged, others kicking around a bright red hacky sack that spends most of the game idle on the asphalt. Most of us are clustered by a dumpster that smells of coffee beans and donuts, and some of us go inside Tim Horton's and buy some. After Bosso finishes settling things with the she-officer, he comes over and jokes that none of this matters — this sort of screw up is rudimentary. The thing is, we aren't beyond the radar yet; once we reach the logging roads we will be free from the law. The planting experience is like a dream — you won't really remember it very well once it's over, all the seasons blur into one. So says the only veteran on the school bus. You realize humans are all slaves in one way or another, he adds. The vet cheers up when his rookie friend brings him a donut and a coffee. He stands up and starts hacky sacking like a mad man. Everyone is becoming a bit more like themselves.

THE SHNOGG IN THE CITY PREAMBLE

Cruising the streets of Toronto are two of the whitest B-boys this side of unreality. *First, second, third gear. We mack every faction/ surf the hood action/ Fans all applaud in stupefaction!*

Rico bought the rhyming dictionary. It's made their rhythms extra prolix. Rico's been searching for appropriate words to go with the phonetics of *bear*, and *bite* and *your* and *ass*.

Big boy Shnogg with his Celts jersey and Adidas tearaways; sneering Rico, side-kick, incisor tooth knocked loose in fight hanging by thin twenty-carat gold chain around neck. They're cruising through Scarborough, Toronto, posing as gangsters.

"Hey, I don't fucking like the sound of this email, homes." Rico is looking at his PDA. Shnogg is driving.

"You know what I'm saying? Seems Tamponix Reforestation be hiding the goods from us. Don't like the sound of any difference, you know. I don't need *unusual*. What I really want is *predictability*, know what I'm saying? Like get in — make ten thousand — get out. Buy what you need. That Tamponix, what's their fucking game? And Bosso, he' been our crew boss for, what, four seasons now? And he didn't even email us each to each, just that group shit." Rico folds up his PDA and stuffs it violently between the seats. "And why *are* we going tree planting? Please, remind me why we're going back to the bush for our *seventh* season."

Shnogg steers smoothly through the traffic, eyes his friend over his sunglasses.

"Listen, I got to pay off the car and you need money because… well just 'cause… a homeboy needs his dough, you know."

Rico slams his hand against the dash:

"Man, I don't need no gold chains! I call it off. I can't go back. I swore by the soul of Cypress Hill that never again would I set foot in that bush no more. That last spruce, 'member that last spruce we planted? It was a ceremony, man, like a ritual of last things. That was supposed to be our last goddamn son-of-a-bitch tree ever. Ever. I swore. We swore!"

"You want back on the streets? They be even shadier."

"Shnogg, we were never on the streets to begin with!"

Shnogg accelerates angrily. Between jerks of the steering wheel he reaches over and smacks Rico on the nose. "Be strong, homes, strong... suck up the pain. Come on, homeboy, don't lose it on me now. We're bros."

Rico seems on the verge of bad-ass tears: "I'm tough and all, but guy, the bush be insanity and fear just waiting to screw me! I almost went insane last season. I lost it. I went crazé. I almost became a murderer." He pauses, breathes heavily for a second, then shoves a toothpick between his teeth. "Tree planting, my good friend Shnogg, is going downhill. *Comme ça.*" He angles his hand down. "The money ain't as good, you know, and bro, the new kids are just lamer every year."

Shnogg turns a smirk on him. "Whatever, homes, you're coming and I think you know it. All our shit be packed and sitting pretty at the digs."

Rico just stares ahead at the clock on the dash. It hasn't been reset for daylight savings. He fingers his tooth-on-a-chain.

"It's all hippies up there in Kap. Bunch of trust fund hippies be wusses. Like why aren't there more people like us, not to toot my own horn, or nutt'n."

"It's time the forest became more ghetto. That's precisely the reason for our return. To represent, my man!"

"What about Archy? Isn't he a hippie we like?"

"Except for all that crazy talk 'bout societies within societies."

"Some weird shit goes down up there. I'm…"

"Is Archy coming back this year, even?

ANARCHY

Archy (pronounced "Anarchy" minus the "An"), is standing hipshot on the dusty shoulder of an unknown highway, wearing a Grateful Dead T-shirt with Jerry bears patterned all over it, and tattered jeans with pink swirly gussets stitched onto the sides of the lower legs, giving them a bell-bottom look. His drastically long hair sways like the elephantine trunk of style. From his knapsack pokes a D-shaped shovel handle.

The ladies who dropped him off told him that their husbands always used to say that in their experience it was best to thumb in the middle of nowhere because you'd get the mercy ride. As the day lengthened into dusk, and the prospect of sleeping in some bush became reality, Archy began to question the wisdom of those chatty ladies.

He has a dog with him, that's part of the problem. The dog's name is Sphagnum. Sphag for short. Man hitching with dog is like woman hitching with man: it is smart to hide the man or dog in a bush.

He has no sign to indicate destination. Just the thumb. Sometimes replaced with the middle finger.

A semi rattles by, spinning up dust on the wind. Up goes his middle finger. The truck driver's, that is, leaning toward the passenger window to let Archy know how he feels about vagrants. Archy turns his back to shield himself and coughs a few times as the dust settles. Only a couple thousand kilometres to go... Kapuskasing, oh Kapuskasing, you are so far away, my Kapuskasing.

The badlands stretch into the distance. Hoodoos stacked against the horizon, their shadows growing longer. This prairie landscape seems long in the tooth. Archy imagines a forgotten dinosaur lumbering through the sage.

Yesterday he met a group of hitchers from Quebec heading to pick mushrooms and fruit out West. They said they were heading out early this year to escape the cold French spring. Heading to the Okanagan. Heading to the

Queen Charlottes. Heading for a working adventure. One of them yodelled off the back of a pickup as they sped off, "Hooray for the cherry pickers! And the mushroom pickers! And hooray for the tree planters!" Filled Archy with images of cargo ships loaded with morel mushrooms pushing through the pacific night towards Tokyo, caravans of macintoshes getting waxed and sent to the fruit stalls across North America. The big global network of produce. For a moment Archy wishes he'd jumped on board with that French posse.

Feels strange heading east. Yet he is convinced that the tree planter revolution will emerge in Ontario.

Right now he just wants to make a big cardboard thumb and stick it by the road while he sleeps in the ditch. And where's his whipper-snapping dog? Probably still off in the fields herding grasshoppers. The black and yellow kind that crack their wings and then flit a few metres to safety and lead you on a lark if you're trying to catch them.

As though Sphag sensed his thoughts she bounds back from her grasshopper herding.

"You're the problem, Sphag. You hippie punk rock dog. Nobody's going to pick us up with *you* around. You're a freak, Sphagnum. Not that I didn't have *something* to do with it...I'm sorry." Archy pats her on the ass. It was, after all, Archy the master who decided to apply various hair dyes to his white border collie. She's a very colourful dog these days. A tie-dye dog. He pats her on her pink-purple derriere. Piebald little thing isn't she now. "Oh Sphagnum, are we ever going to make it to Kapuskasing?"

Just then a VW van slows down and signals. It's painted in psychedelic paisley. Two baby boomers practically pull Archy inside the van with them and they blaze off down the dream-straight road. And thus begins his stint on Western Ranch with his peculiar baby boomer godparents. Kapuskasing would just have to wait.

Everybody has their heads down as we barrel along the highway. The ground looks frosted. Everybody pulls out sweaters as the blossoms disappear and the more northern trees start resembling skeletons with medusa heads. "We are going into an isolation camp of sorts," explains the lone veteran who we decided is a loser because he's on the rookie bus. "No Internet, no cell service…" For a nice guy this veteran sure is making us want to pee our pants, he paints such a bleak picture. Bosso has been quiet the whole time. He's flipped up the mirror so we can't read his expressions anymore. He's the only person we have met from the company, except one of the owners who was at the parking lot in Toronto, who'd seemed far removed from the wilderness we are driving into. The signage in this landscape has become increasingly gimpy the further we get from Pembroke. Old advertisements pegged with ancient hand-painted graphics and weird names — Bertrand the Bait Man, Gary's Guest House — or signs for strange country roads, like Rat River Road, which point down barren tracks of land, some farmland, some just murky bog that's probably impossible to develop except as, perhaps, bird sanctuaries. And speaking of birds, a bird truck passed us with beaks sticking out of cages clucking away. The clucking bird truck seemed like a peculiar reflection of us, like we're on some kind of caged migration. That's a deep thought, somebody says. We have become less private about our thoughts the longer we have been together. Cars and trucks pass us fast. It does seem to be taking forever to get where we are going and every time we ask Bosso he tells us we'll be there soon, and he always has this strange snicker going on. So we all just stare expectantly out the kid safe windows. The passing land has become less green, as if we were emerging from spring back into autumn. We are yawning and looking around the inside of the bus, silent as the dead. The smell coming in the windows seems that of factories, a deep pulpy stench, and all of us rookies use our shirts as gas masks. Bosso looks back at us in the mirror and laughs in what some of us perceive to be a condescending way. Another hour passes and people start whispering again. It's been almost eighteen hours since we left Toronto and Bosso has stopped saying anything and just stares ahead at the road. He keeps talking into his radio because the cell phone is out of range or something, mumbling numbers that, according to the veteran, sounds like UTMs, and then we turn off the main highway or something because there are fewer cars now, and no signs whatsoever except the odd kilometre marker, and then the asphalt abruptly becomes rattle gravel and we are bouncing down a logging road and the dark of the windows is descending fast and somebody cracks a weird joke about getting a hard-on with a baby in your lap. And then this guy, the one veteran who was eating the donuts, he freaks out, runs to the front of the bus, grabs Bosso by the shoulders and yanks him, yelling, "Where are you taking us, man, where the fuck are you taking us!" Bosso's face hangs back, and the mirror drops down again, his head bobbed by the shaking of his shoulders, like an autistic kid caught in conniptions of laughter. Then his face snaps back straight. He brakes and we all fly forward in our seats and the veteran at the front smacks his head on the windshield and one of his veins looks popped, like a worm that's been stepped on. "Welcome to Northern Cloners Nursery," Bosso sneers. Then the fucked-up story begins. You know, a story that starts at your ass and works its way up your spine and then drills into the back of your head.

Quick squeak of tires. Location: Canadian Tire parking lot. A mom-and-pop organization compared with the other mega stores. To purchase a Leatherman knife that Shnogg needs. Last-minute purchases. It's like preparing for a backpacking trip, or any trip for that matter. You must level-headedly deliberate over what *not* to bring, in order to keep baggage to some sort of minimum. There are fifty things you need, and fifty things you don't. Shnogg needs a butterfly-style knife that houses everything from a miniature saw to a screwdriver. It costs him $79.99.

On their way back through the parking lot Shnogg takes a few good-natured slashes at the marshmallowy Michelin Man with his new tool. He slashes it on the ankle a couple times. Just enough to create a little leak. Rico puts his hand up to the puncture hole and feels a rush of escaping air. "Oh, shit man, you fucked it up!"

They cruise by a leonine pretty woman on Eglinton, and Shnogg rolls down the window, heckles her. She gives them the finger. "Suck a lemon, you idiots," she shouts. They try to ignore her, but big egos are easily scarred.

"All right, here's a rhyme." Rico's got his thesaurus splayed on his lap, and he starts rapping while Shnogg cups a hand over his mouth and makes a big flatulent beat with his breath.

"Of bears and bitches   *bu bica buf buf*
I can't tell which is   *bica bica buf buf*
They both be hairy   *puft puft bica bica*
Little bit scary   *bica buf buf*
They be treating me like I'm just some fairy   *buf buf.*"

Now it's Shnogg's turn:

"Yeah, the bear's your bitch   *ðun ðun bica chung*
And the money be yours   *chung chung ðun ðun*
This be a soliloquy to the great outdoors   *ðun ðun*
Yeah into that bush, shake your tush   *chung ðun.*"

"Nice work, homes. I say we spend all the money we make this summer on recording equipment. We could get signed."

Silence

Pause. Hushed, idealistic reverie.

Dear Planters,

I am tied up right now working on Western Ranch. It is owing to this unplanned turn of events that I have yet to attend this year's spring plant with you all. But Archy is on his way soon, never you good folks fear. Staying out here presently with my new godparents at their way-station for the star struck in the wheat and sandstone decorated badasslands of this fair country. Some of these good folk on Western Ranch are involved in serious pharmacological research, myself included. This Albertan peyote is fantastic, what can I say! In fact, I write you with urgent news, for I have furthered some pertinent philosophical initiatives that our planting crew (Larry's, of course) was in the process of unearthing last year during our day off trip to the stars. If you recall, it was the end of contract party, and we had decided to go missioning into the forest, where we chanced upon an opening that we named "The Glades", and were all lying on our backs therein when we witnessed in the sky a satellite which we decided was in fact some sort of extraterrestrial "ship". We experienced the sensation of a deeply alien potential within the woods. It felt as though the earth was pulling us into its moist folds. We felt, as you may recall, compelled to rise... or else we'd all be absorbed into the forest floor. So we stumbled to our feet and staggered into a grove of juvenile larch trees which clung to our arms like tiny octopus tentacles... and soon found ourselves back in a clear-cut we'd planted the week before. You must remember how the recently planted saplings shone in that incredibly strong starlight. (Is it just me or do you too get the feeling the trees perform little belly dances as soon as you walk away after planting them?) Then we smelled The Skunk. The Skunk was hovering around somewhere on the perimeter. He had something to inform us, something that I had suspected all along. Out here on The Ranch I have encountered The Skunk once again, and he wised me up to some stuff. But this particular moment is inopportune for the telling. I must keep you hanging. It seems my new godparents are calling me to draw water from the well. How arid it is out here in the badasslands! I shall see you soon, though, my planting compadres! There is business to attend to in Kapuskasing!

— *Archy*

OPEN RELATIONSHIP

On St. Lucifer street, deep in the multi-lingual interior of dusty Montreal, up iron stairs that twist like antique DNA models connecting one lopsided storey to another, scurries a little lady with a blue and white checkered skirt that ends just above her knobby knees. She skips up the steps, round and around, upward toward her loft. Her straight cut bangs parted around a little dip of nose. And she is giggling in the way she tends to, at a feathery little thought which tickles her mind.

On the roof, men in stained overalls stand around puffing cigarettes that hang rakishly between their pinkish lips. Their tar job smells like a pleasant poison. She waves up at them, yelling, *"Salut, est-ce que vous travaillez fort cette semaine?"* They stare down at her mutely as she swings open her front door and stomps inside.

She lives in one of the row houses built by the rail company where the Irish track crews lived with their families in the 19th century, heating with coke stoves in wintertime and working away on the steel rails that still stretch through the area.

She has some last-minute packing to do — stuffing some final items into her Quebec Nordiques hockey bag which her brother lent her. So far she has managed to fit everything inside including her planting gear and tent.

Now she grabs the binder containing her menstruation

regularity chart, her thermometre, and her Keeper — her fertility kit. She is quite caught up in monitoring her reproductive cycle. When she heard about tree planting she was filled with thoughts of the fertility of forests and of how magical it would be to play a vital role in the procreation of trees. She is not an artist, or a musician, or an academic; as one of her girlfriends once pointed out her talent is menstruation.

Her lover Jean told her she was crazy: crazy to think that tree planting was in any way a pleasant, magical experience, and also that she was crazy to be working in Ontario, the land of uptight, chauvinistic anglophones.

Somewhere along the line, anglophones, Americans, and inhuman Corporations all got lumped into one category: English.

She does wonder what in hell she's getting herself into with this weird Ontarian planting community. Not that she hates the English, it's just that she feels more comfortable with her own. Every few weeks she receives weird emails from her anglophone crew boss.

> To: smashed@jaggermeister.com/ dogcrazy@tribal.com/ bre_ex@hotfraud.com/ tutenkamen @I'mamummy.org/canlit.sucks@ fool.don't`read `this`then`then.ca/ millenium@new.ca/ nothing_new_under_the_sun @eccleciasties.bible/ make_it_ new@EzraPound.ca/ to_who_it_may_ concern@allmyemployees.com

> What up everyone? This is your crew boss. I hired you, so I love you. Peace from BC. Greetings to believers and to those who will believe. I've been staying in Banff with my sister and all. I'm a liftee. Can't wait to get back to the Ontario bush. This season is going to be great! Last year was brutal. This year: big money and good times! Creamshow! I'm pretty baked right

now, actually. FOR ANYONE NEW BRING A SPEED SPADE TO DIG YOUR HOLES AND TRY TO BRING AS MUCH WEED AS POSSIBLE FOR CLINICALLY CERTIFIABLE MEDICINAL REASONS! I'll be seeing you in Kapuskasing, soon as I can get my ticket. Everyone who needs a ride make sure they make it to the meeting spot in T. at 8:00. Not 7:00, remember. Peace in the Middle East. <u>Eliza</u>

Medicinal, c'est quoi ça, "medicinal"? And why "brutal"? But one of the reasons she is planting in Ontario, and not Quebec, is so she can practice her English. How rusting it is. After this contract I will go to BC fully bilingual.

She hears some rustling of bed sheets in the other room. Could it be that Jean-Michel is still at home? He sleeps in late, *taberouette*. She scurries into the bedroom. Lo and behold, there lies her *chum*, nakedness half-exposed in a tangle of bedding, rubbing his eyes.

«I didn't know you were here,» she says, pouncing on the bed, and tucking herself under his arm. «Are you sad?»

He rubs his nose. He is thin-jawed and has long unwashed hair in a braid. «No, I am not sad, I am disappointed, Murielle. That you are leaving. I wanted this to be a fun summer, you know, us together having fun.»

Murielle frowns. «Jean, you are a baby. You know that leaving is part of loving. Waiting, too, is part of loving.» She pinches his cheek, and elbows him gently in the ribs, stares into his eyes.

He just lies there like an old-guard separatist. After a long pause he says, «So it's open then? We are agreed, no?»

«Everything is open, life is open!» Murielle affirms, happy that he's coming around again. «We will both have an open summer and then we will be back together. It is what you wanted, yes. That's what you said last night!» She springs from the bed and scurries out of the room. They have been together four years.

She grabs her bright red shoulder bag then runs back and looks into the bedroom again. Her scrawny lover lies there in the same twisted position. His eyes are rimmed red. Now she looks at him with just the slightest trace of annoyance. «We talked already about what it means to be faithful. Can't we just part easily this time?» She skips back down the hall and out the front door. «I must go and say goodbye to my mother!»

At the bottom of the spiral stairs she unlocks her bike. Steadying herself on the seat she tucks in her skirt and then begins peddling along the cracked streets she loves, the historic houses disappearing behind her, her eyes moist in the cool breeze. She now has a tremendous desire to leave this place, maybe forever. Jean can join her out west. When she returns to her apartment he's gone. There is a small note on the made bed, though, marked Xs and Os. It reads: *«Murielle, you are the most beautiful piglet in the world... I will be here when you get back. My love for you will bloom once again.»*

ALTERNATE WORLD

The pickup fishtails through the clay of the rutted forest service road. Larry, who is Grant's foreman, conducts the truck over this washboard.

Larry has a feather-shaped earring, and woolly mutton chop sideburns, scraggly hair. The Native side of him juts through in the long, sharp angles of his face, like a totemic heritage of crafted cedar protruding through a Caucasian face of soft wood. He is French, English and Cree, a self-described mongrel of the timberland. They cross a bridge built over a class 4 drainage.

(Historical Tree Planting Note: One of the first instances of mass organized tree planting occurred in France under Napoleon. The navy had exhausted their hardwood assembling a fleet large enough to challenge that of naval master England. The French were left with no alternative but to roll up their sleeves and start tree planting.)

"I wonder what these streams were like before all the logging... all the brown rivers around here." Grant peers out the side windows at the water which reminds him of a wormy Seine. On the west bank a couple of mule deer nibble twigs like nervous bohemians.

Larry scoffs and makes a long booing sound. "Boo. It's natural, my friend. The earth falls off the banks from erosion. Geez, Grant, you and your city points of view. The city doesn't understand what really happens here. All you see are pictures of the negative stuff, the clear-cuts and mines... they forget to show you what's left, which is a lot, man, and it's all growing back. Don't tell me you're one of those global warming alarmists or something."

"Alright, alright, Larry. Let's agree to disagree. I'm no fact pusher, man. It's not your fault you've been indoctrinated by the forestry industry." They blaze back to camp, wheels churning through the mud, mist rising from the damp cold.

The camp is still being set up when they arrive. A flatbed truck rattles in reverse with an *eep eep eep* and the warning lights flashing. A weather haven is getting erected by a bunch of planters and the massive mess tent is half assembled, the beige tarp flapping off the cylindrical structure that will funnel planters into their feeding pens. A dome. So many parts — tubes, elbows, T-joints. Always a bit of a gong show trying to figure out what pole fits where. The scene looks miniature from this distance, Lilliputian building blocks being put in place by a child.

If urban centres become uninhabitable (or even undesirable) locations because of pollution, war, or just plain ennui — if, for some reason, some day, the populace takes to the back roads like diesel-propelled nomads — it will be in camps similar to this where they will survive. A portable community.

Grant and a few other veterans were given the option of coming up early to get a head start on what is shaping up to be a particularly aggressive production schedule this season.

Some stayed behind and helped set up camp. Grant, who had chosen to plant because of his aversion to the disorganization of setup, was out on the block just long enough to get his new boots muddy. At least they aren't wet on the inside yet. All day he kept opening his ear to the land but he couldn't quite grasp what the land was saying. It remained a vague kind of metaphor. A kind of corpse of meaning. Sometimes it sounded to him as though loons were speaking in Polish to one another. At other times the creak of a swaying spruce was reminiscent of the opening of an ancient door. There is most cer_tainly a language to all this — something that always drew him deeper into the mystery of the woods.

A village sign that reads Welcome to Moon Beam, Ontario. *Smiling green creatures with big heads, and then there's a statue on somebody's lawn of a white UFO the size of a camper van. Someone says that every small town has a claim to fame. This town is called Moon Beam because the ones who came before saw lights glowing in the streams. Then the veteran says he feels kind of sick and we all agree, we feel sick too. The bluish blood leaking from the ruptured vein in his forehead makes us want to puke. He keeps pressing wads of tissue on it. Now our bus turns into a parking lot in front of several large greenhouses. Through open doors we can see people moving amid millions of tiny seedlings which stick out from black plastic trays. Bosso takes off his sunglasses and hangs them from the mirror, and leads us from the bus into the main building, underneath the sign that says* Northern Cloners. *We pass workers who are carrying buckets and garden tools, but none of them say hello. They all wear filter masks, and what look like Hazmat suits. The head grower meets us in front of his office and gives Bosso a two-handed handshake. The head grower seems very energetic for his age. He looks like a really worldly individual. He has this crazy energy as he points out the various machines. We laugh uneasily at his jokes as he shows us around the production building, where the seeds are sent* down a funnel to get carbohydrate-injected and then go into small pots which slide from another conveyer belt called the soil mixer, which is connected to the block loader and the gritter. A dibber arm comes down and punches the seeds into the little black plastic containers. But where do the seeds come from? They come from the upper floor, through the Xylophloe tunnel, but the upper floor is shut off right now. Sorry, sorry about that, says the head grower, who seems very intelligent like he's a professor or something, and he's saying something about the beauty of biotechnology. But I thought we weren't allowed to clone trees in this country, interrupts the sick veteran, holding a rag to his gaping forehead. 'Well, there's a grey area, and we are well within that grey area, believe me,' the head grower smiles like a genius. 'You tree planters are the problem,' he jokes. 'The balance must be struck between need and fulfillment. We're slumlords here at the nursery, really. It's McTree, really. Ha. Ha. It's all economics... Really... Tight means they reach for the light. This is generation Z... the ultimate generation. All green-haired... four foot tall... Ha. But never, never underestimate the strength of the human spirit... that's what I say whenever I hear any negativity regarding the future survival of the race. We can overcome, we can overcome what the slumlords have done. What I have done, and what you problematic tree planters have done. Ha.' By another conveyer belt which leads to a huge, sharp-bladed fan, the head grower says that nature works too slowly, so they had to speed her up. 'Our vision is stress-resistant trees,' he explains, 'that's why we punish them and immerse them in harsh environments when they're young. The research and development fell through, so we had to find different partners within the logging industry and beyond... beyond Clear Water mill, that is. The people who work for the logging companies are stuck in a time capsule. They're all asking me, hey, give me some advice, and I say yeah, sure, but what are you going to do for me, you going to guarantee that you're going to buy my trees? No? Well... no bargain, and they just laugh at me, and ask what planet I'm from. Ha. And I say, well, you're on your own then.' You see, there is just a complete lack of innovation. Hence Northern Cloners. The government, you see, and the public who sees through the eyes of that beast, are the major impediment to our future plans.

The cracked asphalt rises to meet the Firebird's tires as Shnogg accelerates down Highway 11. They've been driving all day and the sun is setting. The sub-woofers and tweeters blast RZA and old Snoop Dogg classics and KRS1. Hour after hour. Rico, at first silent and brooding, has finally warmed up to his inevitable tree planting destiny. Until Shnogg starts telling a story, one of those stories you hear about in the bush.

"I don't believe you for one second, Shnogg. Everything people claim in the North is either exaggerated or an outright lie. That's what I hate about tree planters. All those blanket statements."

"The mystery bus ride happened, dog. Nobody ever heard from anyone on that bus again. The whole crew disappeared into the bush. Some say they turned around and drove to Guatemala. That picking the rookies up at that parking lot in Toronto was just a false front. Their real objective was to join some religious community in a beautiful place. Lots of those International buses end up down there anyway, in Central or South America where they're reused for public transport."

"Hmmm."

1.6 more hours driving up north... then off the main road down the Swanson forest service road into the woods. The sky is cold opal above the grey spruce trees with a cranberry rosette around the sun going down.

"Hey, nigga, what the? Wrong way. We passed it! The map says kilometre 67, and we're at 80. We passed the turnoff!"

"Okay, we'll turn around at the next landing. But dog, you ain't listening. Listen, we turn around, all right, we turn around, fine. What I'm saying is the DJ, the DJ mixes it together, weaves it and mixes it. Different elements colliding, know what I'm saying? Like you're taken back and forth, homes, back and forth, til you get stupid!"

"Say what?" Rico's mind is bleary, both eyes feel like they are suffering from ptosis. Tim Horton roll-up-the-rim-to-win cups are unrolled and empty, smushed into the carpet under the seats, sunflower seed shells messing up everything.

"Like different elements coming in different directions, throwing you off, but the end, my friend, is a seamless remix of tired ways, moon rays, wild deer freaking extravagances with serious snip bop lyrics coming from us. Check it out, the snip bop diggedy!"

"Would you shut about the snip bop for a second, so we can just get there. There ain't no mics out here. You're hopped up on uppers, dog."

Shnogg turns 180° around at a landing, gets them heading back the way they came. As the Firebird makes the turn they get a view through the dusk over a field of muskeg, a swamp full of dead spruce enshrined in a ghostly mist.

"Hey, check out that tree. That's one hella phat tree. And it's green, look how fucking green it is, especially for this time of year! It's so green you can see its colours in the dark!" They both stare out the window with astonished pupils. A truly massive weed tree looms on the horizon.

As if it were as large as the Tree of Life.

THE TREE OF LIFE. The grand old tree that shows bold in the goldwork of Mexican artisans; the mythical cypress drawn on the domes of Byzantine chapels; written about by Percy Bysshe Shelley and John Milton (where each leaf is a soul); that was drawn on the first editions of the Koran in silvery calligraphy; that was figured as having ten branches which formed the ten secret paths of the Cabal; that informed the idea of the Family Tree — that holy metaphoric tree connecting all to all beneath the veinous undergarments of history; that Peace Tree of the Six Tribes after which the American constitution was originally modeled. Before the tree under which sat the first barely clothed couples in their prelapsarian love nest — upon which skinny syphilitic martyrs were crucified in the fires of the Inquisition, before the Tule Tree outside of Oaxaca more than 2000 years old, before perhaps everything that ever lived bio-style on earth, there was a sprout, a shoot that sprung, the first inkling of this tree. THE WHOLE face of this mountain-sized tree seeming to list sideways, a drunken trunk in the heavy gales that crash through those dreamy ranges, each individual tree on the mountain swaying and rushing like a leaf, so that the whole mountain looks like the crown of a massive tree. To focus in on a single leaf would reveal another family of leaves, that is the nature of this Tree of Life, that the more the hiker zooms in with his digital binoculars, the deeper the deception of depth.

And two wiggers are the first humans to have seen it in all its glory in thousands of years.

"That is one big tree, homes."

"Whatever, we're in a forest. Trees grow tall. It looks bigger because, well, come on.... Let's get out of here RIGHT NOW!"

BUSH CAMP

It's about human imagination and curiosity. What's out there? What's in the great beyond? What exists at levels we can't see with our five senses?
— James Cameron

Grant sits on the stoop of his trailer, cigarillo clamped between his teeth. Just the one a day, he reminds himself, sucking back the sinful smoke. In the time he takes to have a few smokes over the course of a day he could plant 250 trees, which equals about twenty dollars of missed profit. The passage of time literally feels like the passage of money. Everything becomes capital in these woods.

After his first few bag-ups it started puking wet snowflakes that melted into slush puddles in the mud — the North's version of May showers. Now, back at camp, his heartbeat is still accelerated. Steam rises off his wet thighs. The wind and snow whips him. It feels good to be whipped by the wind and snow.

Grant has a good view of the camp. It is some sort of abandoned quarry, the size of five hockey rinks. In the centre peaked piles of gravel or shale sit around a murky reservoir. The area looks like a section of the moon with the odd spruce stuck here and there. There are too many stones here, which seems unnatural because the land is usually soft in this area.

He stares half-interestedly at the tents dispersed around the site: blues, mauves, lots of yellows, some reds — as though the camp were an easel, and a big brush might descend from the sky, dip into those colours, and paint a synthetic rainbow through the grey. Planters scurry around to their tents, rummaging for warmer clothing, many of them shocked by the snow. The idea of snow in May just doesn't compute, even for Grant, after all these years. He recalls the time when he, too, used to sleep in a tent, back in his first years as a planter. He remembers all the unpleasant aspects — on his bum wriggling out of slimy boots, squirming out of soiled quick-dry cargo pants, sitting naked, hunched over in his damp tent, tossing through all the crap searching for clean boxers — his dick shriveled and his testicles scrunched. Then giving up the search for underwear and just wrapping himself in his sleeping bag, lying there like a soggy cocoon, munching assorted sweet and sour candy while he waited for dinner call, the honk of the company truck.

The trailer has changed all that. Ever since he invested in the old trailer, he has experienced much less dread upon waking up for another eleven-hour shift in the sticks.

Grant observes the old machinery rusted away on the other side of the reservoir: remnants of pumps, winches, a chipper, and further back, the timber edge. The rookie buses still haven't showed up yet. A good thing, because the greeners would have shit their pants seeing what he now sees: a violent mist cascading through the evergreen boughs over the strip of trees separating the clear-cut and the camp. It is a bizarre weather pattern, all rosy orange, blowing in whorls, as though the sky were imploding and twisting into a gale shroud, and Grant wonders with dry lips trembling what the hell it is. There are things you see out here, sights that seem odd in a totally impossible or exaggerated way. But you don't have time to pay attention because there is too much money to be made. Or you're too cold to stand around and watch.

Tilting his head down he observes the drop-off in front of him — jagged rocks accumulated at the bottom. He imagines throwing himself off the edge and being torn apart on the rocks. He would rather plant, for sure, than swan dive into that.

Another trailer is stationed beside his own. He can hear a radio playing inside. Few megahertz bands reach this lowland, lucky if you can even pick up fuzz sometimes. The regional manager keeps saying that he's going to get SatNet, but it never happens. Must be a short wave radio in that trailer—a show on marine biology. *Empress Fish, inhabiting huge connected lake systems in Africa. These Empress Fish have, through centuries, adapted into many subspecies, an incredible array of diversity. They lay eggs in the mouths of other species of fish. zzzzh.*

Tomorrow Grant will have tropical fish on his mind while he plants, and his head will be full of facts. He will remember this thing about eggs in mouths. And he'll be wondering about this new guy who's so interested in that weird shit.

A figure has been approaching up the path leading to the ridge. Grant steps inside his trailer and is just closing the door when an unfamiliar voice calls his name.

THE ANTHROPOLOGIST

Who the fuck could this be? The person is now standing on his stoop, apparently wanting to engage. Grant remembers the gaunt face from around camp — an older guy, who mentioned something about working on a PhD in anthropology or some shit, but Grant forgets the specifics — he shoves open the door.

"What's going on, buddy?"

"Hey, I'm Walter, the guy next to you."

"Hey, nice to meet you." Grant forces a smile. He has trouble being a dickhead to people's faces. When he's with people he realizes they are okay. When they're gone he talks and thinks shit about them. He opens the door wider and shakes the guy's hand. Walter has a bookish manner about him. The stubble on his face is evenly trimmed. The eyes exude a lucid power and vital intelligence, but the handshake doesn't feel right. A diplomat's kind of handshake, with just the fingers offered to clasp.

"Grant, a pleasure, a pleasure. I understand, yes, you are the safety officer?" Walter's face is stern. "I am curious about something, yes?... You are the safety officer? There was some confusion in the eating quarters... at the meeting, while you were gone today."

"We call it 'the mess tent'," Grant corrects him, "and no, I am not the safety officer. Who said that? Bazooka? Well, he's wrong." Grant starts to pull his door closed. But Walter steps forward.

"I see. 'Mess tent' it is, then. Also, I understand the spruce stock is treated with fungicide, this is what people tell me. I am doing some research. We *do* handle these fungicides, that is a fact, yes, and I was wondering, Grant, what are the medical effects on male reproductive organs?"

Grant has long ago ceased straining his brain over the implications of handling fungicides every day, eating food with tainted fingers. It's just another risk that you take out here, part of the job. Still, the question catches him off guard. "I really don't know the specifics, sorry," he tells the anthropologist.

Walter nods a couple of times as if this ignorance confirms something he had suspected all along. "Well, would you mind checking into it for me? You see, I am very curious to find out. To know. I like to *know* things, Grant."

Grant searches distractedly for a fresh pair of socks, remembering a "spraycation" he did a couple of years ago, one autumn after all the trees were in the ground, spraying with this stuff called Vision, and how nobody wore any masks, and how as a practical joke you would squirt your work partner once in a while. It is still *de rigeur* not to wear any gloves even when tree planting on this contract with those fungicided plugs from the Northern Cloners nursery. He remembers something about birth defects. Banana pickers rendered impotent in Haiti. A representative of Vision supposedly came to this other camp and demonstrated the innocuousness of the product by drinking back five shot glasses of the stuff.

But where are those socks? He bought a new bag of socks just yesterday at the Kap thrift store. One part cotton, two parts polyester: great fabric combination for sweat absorption and minimal inner-boot friction. Twelve damn pairs of them. All his toes would have been one happy family inside those socks. His toes could have warmed themselves by a lovely little toe jam fireside. The suspicion sneaks into his mind that perhaps he left the socks in town, on the bench by the fountains, when he'd been sitting with some locals yesterday talking logging news. He rummages around. Maybe it was that guy who had mentioned the workers' buyout of the pulp mill in Kap. Weirdly interesting info… apparently the workers joined together and bought the majority of the shares in the town mill. But the thought of somebody else taking pleasure in his socks — especially some unionized guy with his comfy hourly-wage job — is a major vexation. A state of mental self-annihilation is eclipsing the happy part of Grant's mood. Like earlier today, like every year, the tides of aggression and anger swelling. It has been a constant battle to stay calm.

He pulls open the grainy plastic drawers in his kitchenette, full of various bottled lotions, repellents, and balms to spread over areas of the body that get chafed from the rubbing of planting bags in damp weather, especially his outer thighs and waist, which get all pimply from ingrown hair. He even has baby cream to spread on his choda, that strip of flesh between his asshole and the base of his nutsac. Also called the gooch or grundle by some. He swipes the bottles to the side and reaches back into the cupboard. He notices a tube of KY jelly. What's that doing in here? It must've been sitting here since last season. Since he last saw her. Grant stares down at the tube like it might have answers for him, quickly tossing it aside as he hears the door opening behind him.

He wheels around, then laughs in surprise. "Well, hell, if it isn't my old planting buddy."

Luke steps inside the trailer with two thumps of his feet, and some younger kid follows him in. Grant takes an unimpressed glance at the kid, then turns to Luke. They stand staring at each other, the yearly reunion. Luke has a big smile as he pulls the door shut.

They bear hug each other. Then Grant reaches out to shake the new kid's hand.

"This is Ben, it's his first day. Take a look at this kid, look at the eyes. He's a small lad, but the eyes, you can see the colour of success in those eyes. Determination! I say we call him Benito because he's got a kind of Mexicano look." Grant looks into the rookie's eyes, but he is not convinced. Those eyes seem too eager, a little too confident. He and the new kid do the old low-five motion, but after the initial hand slap, the rookie extends his forearm, attempting to engage Grant in some sort of ritualistic elaboration of the motion with little thumb locks, but Grant has already dropped his arm, not knowing the rest of the low-five sequence.

The greener looks around the cabin. "This is an amazing place. How much did you pay?"

"Twelve hundred."

Luke brings in a plastic camping chair from outside.

"Ain't this beautiful, Grant, snow on the first day?"

"Yeah, it was brutal, couldn't even get my shovel in the ground by the end." Grant looks from Luke to the rookie kid. "Better get used to this. We had snow on Canada Day last year."

"Yeah, I'll handle it. I was on Outward Bound the last few years, just bought a wicked new four-season tent. I don't know about the others, though. Have you seen them out there? Some people here don't even know how to set up their tents!"

"A gong show, eh?" Grant steps up to the little window and looks out at the camp. He sees a tent flying through the air and several people chasing after it. He turns back. "Shit… Tamponix reforestation, the good old rookie treadmill."

Luke rummages through the pockets of his navy jacket, his shoulders all big and slouched, just standing there casually in his somehow elegant masculinity. "Well, you know I don't smoke much anymore, but me and Grant always do up a nice number to start off the contract. So let's twist one up. Grant, you seem stressed. What have you lost now?"

"Ah, just socks, just the most important thing in the world."

"Where's Larry at, by the way?" Luke changes the subject. "I want to use his shovel. You should see my shovel, it's got a huge crack in it."

"Hiding out somewhere with the Tomahawk, you know how he hates setup."

"What about the tree price? I heard the union was doing some negotiations or something on the tree prices. They better not screw us. I heard last year Bazooka promised the tree price was going up…" Benito is already complaining like a veteran and he hasn't even planted a tree yet.

"Yeah, union. Yeah, right." Grant snuffs.

"Yeah, promises mean nothing out here. Hey, it's a little chilly, what about your heater, is it still working or what?"

Little wood stove of old galvanized black metal in the corner beside the bed. Stove ventilation pipes connect to an ABS tube which sticks out a hole in the ceiling. Grant stuffs in some fragments of birch and two small lengths of pine that ignite with a ravenous crackle. The fire starts eating the wood and they feed it more. The thick heat pumps out into the enclosed space.

"Okay, joint's ready. Fire in the hole!"

Theraputic uses of cannabis # 1: Psychological Therapy. They smoke big cannon. Dosage: one cannon-sized joint. Effect: puts things in perspective. Result: the seriousness of socks having gone missing is lessened. Soon Grant is laughing about his missing socks. They'll turn up one way or another. And if not, hell, he can always steal Luke's. Their worries about the future dissipate in the green smoke.

Luke picks the tube of KY off the floor. "Hey Grant, you meet a new pardner, or what? She in camp?"

"There is no she. I haven't been with anyone since... well, you know what happened. I haven't been with anybody since her. Anyway, we'd better get out there and help with setup."

"Here's trouble," mocks Groucho, seeing Grant and Luke come sauntering through the mud. Groucho is standing with his crew boss, Biz. It is against Biz's crew that Grant and Luke will measure their production.

Grant keeps his head down in his hoody as he passes them. Biz and Groucho have that high-performance look about them. Like they *are* the company, or at least what the company is becoming as it expands by lowballing contracts, reaching the iron jaws of its bottom-line policy over the industry. These guys who sport all the Tamponix gear. The fleece. The visor. They even have Tamponix cigarette lighters. This is a foul trend as far as Grant is concerned: employees serving the dual function of labour as well as company promotion. Wearing this gear, smearing the Tamponix logo around the country. Getting new employees to forgo other smaller, less corporate operations, to rally under the umbrella of the big name. Remarkably clean-cut all season long, like they must have secret mirrors they refer to at night. Clandestine late-night shaving. *Tamponix, one hundred percent testosterone*, he remembers somebody saying. Not that the cock-rock listening army athlete planters aren't good at their jobs. Groucho plants more trees than anybody else — he was the camp highballer last year — and Biz's crew has the highest production out of all the crews. But many veterans in the company feel that the planting industry is being sucked dry by absorbent, exorbitant, Bad Money. Tamponix Reforestation Inc. prospered after its genesis in the late 1970s because of its rep as a group of fun-loving, nature-appreciating folk looking for kicks and sustainable profit in the great out-of-doors. The original name of the company was Nature's Treasure, run by a few medical students, their massive lines of credit and eventual salaries helping to fund the company during fiscally trying periods and providing the monetary clout necessary to beat out the other companies who couldn't afford to bid so low. But soon the more independently-minded members of the company left because planting was becoming like some twisted version of summer camp — a system for university kids to pay off their tuition. Dwindling in numbers — sort of like the Kodiak bears and redwoods — were the older adepts of the forest, the elders, who conducted work-related endeavours in a slightly looser style, but who, in the end, did the job right and cared about the community. The new breed of managers was prized for their ability to conform exactly to the whim of the superiors, to "get in line" unquestioningly. To patrol like watchdogs. The army athlete personality was coming to dominate in a big way. It was all about looking safe and saving face. These were workers who never raised a finger in criticism of anything except each other because they feared for their job security. The new management were drawn to their positions by the allure of so-called perks, free Spitz and Subway, but mostly by the legendary "management coffee" which was of a superior Brazilian quality compared to the regular planter's third-rate grind and was brewed in its own special percolator in the management trailer.

SHITTER DIGGING

The purgatory of dusk: static forms morphed into faint renditions; the mauve starless sky out of which approaches the frigid night; a rusty fender fading into a vault of foliage. Grant's vision is jarred by the big shoulders of Luke lumbering in front of him as they push through some brush. Like following his father through the forest when it was the woods where he went to play. As if his youth replicated itself endlessly in the bush. He can almost hear an image of himself laughing in the fluffless cattails.

Luke, the drywaller. The real McCoy. A "real" person, is what people always call him. Born in Texas, raised in Canada. A man's man blessed with the seeds of grace. Rockabilly and drywall, beer and pickups, manual labour. Grant knows he will never really get to the bottom of Luke because there is no bottom, he is wonderfully shallow — no big hole, no bottomlessness. He says what he means and means what he says.

Soon they approach a muddy clearing about 30 metres into the timber near the cook shack.

"Here, take a shovel." Luke hands Grant a spade from a pile.

Five planters stand around trying their best to dig pits into the moist earth. They slam pickaxes into the ground to loosen it, then somebody has to jump in and heave out the earth and pebbles with a spade. The scraping sound of metal and rock fills the air, as does the wormy odour of fresh soil. Grant and Luke introduce themselves to the group. They don't recognize anybody.

"Shit, is everybody here new? Who here is not a rookie?" Luke seems shocked at the lack of experienced supervision; he's already noticed with his keen eye that the holes are dug too close together. He peers into the hole. The diggers have been attempting to work around the roots which curl on the inside. "It's going to take some real elbow grease, ain't it? We need a pulaski. How many of you are rookies?"

Nobody answers. Seems they are all ashamed to be rookies. Ash boughs hang solemnly around the clearing, leafless arms pointing at the ground. The pine and spruce stand straight and quiet as if they were waiting for something. Bits of snow begin to fall out of the grey sky.

Before the snow makes its unwanted appearance, Murielle is busy setting up her new tent. She missed the rush for choice locations, delayed because she couldn't find her hockey bag when everyone was taking their gear off the school buses, and it turned out she was checking the wrong bus. "The buses need names," someone says.

The area nearest the main communal area is already claimed, so she has to drag her Nordiques bag up an embankment of brown grass behind it. She decides to set up next to the timber edge, between two spruce trees she can use to attach rope. She runs up to one of the spruce and hugs it, closing her eyes and pressing her cheek against the scales of bark.

She looks around the site and is struck by its beauty. The reservoir seems to her a shimmering water body. She imagines diving in naked and spearing the surface reflections. The air is so fresh it feels like she's awakened to another level of consciousness. The smell of earth and evergreen makes her heart flutter. She looks around with open eyes. And all those cool-shaped rocks like so many inuksuk just waiting to be stacked. "Your little home in the great out-of-doors," she says to herself with the joy of somebody who actually enjoys nature. After the long bus ride with all those anglophones, she's already catching herself thinking in English!

The tent setup doesn't go very well, though. She manages to piece together the sections of pole, but when she reaches the part where she has to put the poles through the loops she has difficulty distinguishing one line of loops from the other. Compounding her problems is the gusty wind that mummifies her hands in tent fabric, and blows the flaps in her face. She peers up from her confusion to note the progress of the other planters. The others appear to have finished setting up their tents and are standing around getting to know each other. She keeps thinking they are looking over her way, wondering who the loser is who can't pitch a tent. She has to catch up to save face! If only she was on that ridge in a nice, convenient trailer... but come to think of it the ground doesn't look very solid up there, and she wouldn't want to sleep so close to a cliff edge, not a good idea for a sleepwalker like herself. Distracted by these thoughts, she puts the wrong poles through the wrong loops. She tries to erect the tent, and it ends up looking like a mutant textile rack. The maniacal Mountain Equipment Co-op guy who sold her the tent is chattering away in her memory, telling her how great all this fabric is, how ultra high tech. ("The pores, miss, the pores! Like our store itself, our store has pores! Like the boots. Like the tent. The equipment breathes... The toughest multipurpose boot this side of K2. Eh, miss? Eh, miss! A true cybernetic extension of your natural skin...! Even got the corks. Did you know corks help you screef? Do you know what screefing is? These offer a seamless, high-grade leather 'body', unsurpassed in the market.")

Ostie de fatigant!

"Can't return boots, no no no, not after tree planting, no no no, warranty doesn't cover that, nothing covers that. Nothing nothing nothing!" The wheedling, simpering little clerk had accentuated the word "breathe" with a breath of his own, huffing in her face, blowing her bangs up on her forehead. She'd fled the coat section, deciding she didn't need that high tech footwear, that her plain French mountaineering boots from Village des Valeurs would do. But she needed a tent for sure, no getting around that, so she went upstairs to the tent department. Turned out the Einstein sales rep was a roving multitasker, who worked different sections of the store, seemingly all at once. Murielle crawled into a one-person tent to avoid another lecture on polymerization and forgot for a second about the external world, marveling at the safe, comfortable aura within this tent — the shades chosen by the manufacturers according to elaborate mood tests — and imagining it as her safe little haven. There was even an extra-thick inflatable sleeping mat. *"Oui, c'est comfortable, ça,"* she said, lying on her back looking at the calm colours. She'd found her tent. When the clerk, peering with beady eyes through the mesh, asked, "Miss, miss, are you impressed by this particular product?" She scuttled out the back flap and crawled into a different tent. She didn't want to ask him any questions, so she never really found out how exactly to set the thing up.

So here, two months later, she finds herself baffled in the bush.

"Crapola," she hears someone say. Murielle swivels her head around like an owl and spots another person down a slope, who seems to be having trouble as well. Murielle has an idea. She descends the slope with long-falling steps. She cannot help but glance up at the clouds as she descends, these huge chunks of somberness so vivid she feels like she should duck to avoid bashing her head.

"Je m'excuse." She begins to introduce herself in French by mistake. This girl she's speaking to has the longest blonde hair. Her blue eyes seem like big pools of concern.

"Hi, my name is Tammy, are you from Quebec?" The tent neighbour asks, her sidereal eyes surrounded by a Scandinavia of snowy skin. She is a head taller than Murielle.

"Hey, you noticed! I have so many problems with my tent!"

"Oh my god, so do I. I feel like such a moron." Tammy peers forlornly into the empty sack, then looks hopefully to Murielle. "Hey, do you have any pegs? My dad said he put some in the tent bag but they sure don't seem to be here."

The wind blows their hair around and they have to speak up to hear each other, the shrubs batted back and forth and little pebbles swept along, finding new homes in different crevices.

"Hey, sure!" Murielle yells, snapping out of the new-friend reverie, hopping back to her mutant tent. "I have so many pegs. Maybe we can give help to each other. I came to ask you for help as well!"

Right when they are triumphantly spearing in the last pegs like expert tent setter-uppers, a truck comes rolling towards them, and the driver tells them they need help with setup. "Jump in the back, I'm Ray," says the driver. Ray has a blunt jaw, and an arrogant smirk hanging below hazily mischievous eyes, and a nose with visible blackheads. The back seat is loaded with boxes and stuff, and a mean-looking dog occupies the front passenger seat. After some pulling and poking, Tammy and Murielle manage to open the tailgate and they hop into the bed of the truck. Ray begins accelerating over the bumpy ground and the tires spit out pebbles and clay. The truck rocks back and forth and they have to grip the headache rack to stay steady. It's like Ray immediately forgot they were back there once he started driving. The truck revs up a hill and along the ridge. Planters look up from their homemaking with what-the-fuck expressions, apparently not appreciating the truck ripping through camp like that.

"Rookies, all of you, eh?" Luke snorts at everybody. "Oh boy, just wait, the deflowering process is a thing to be remembered. Male or female, don't matter, blood will be drawn, mark my word —"

"But good blood —" Grant interjects.

"Yeah, it's good blood, it's the blood that wet the dehydrated sailor's throat, so he could proclaim to his mates, 'a sail, a sail!'"

Luke plunges into one of the holes, oblivious to the confused looks exchanged after his cryptic statement, and immediately starts thrusting away at a localized area with a speed that seems animal, excavating the circumference of a large stone, which he loosens and heaves out of the deepening hole. He looks up. "Tomorrow you'll be lucky if you plant a hundred trees. But don't worry, friends, you seem a good bunch, with that sort of fresh but potentially woodsy style. In a few weeks you'll be planting two thousand a day, no problem. To tell you the truth, me and Grant were looking at all the rooks and we were thinking, 'Hey, they look all right. The kids are all right.'"

Ray pulls up in the pickup.

"Hey, Grant and Luke, what's up guys? I hadn't seen you around yet. This is Tammy and Murielle, very hard workers."

"Hello," says Tammy, jumping off the back of the truck with her new friend. She looks scared. Murielle immediately spots a rock of interest and stoops to pick it up. Ray's eyes probe her from behind.

The introductions are brief.

Luke has exited his hole and is observing the progress of the others. "Five feet deep, remember! And space them wider."

Grant lights up a cheap cheroot cigar, leans on his shovel, and Ray starts lecturing the rookies while they work away on the holes:

"Basically, as I was explaining, this is where a contract's worth of your human shit goes. You'll find that you eat about a third more than in the city, and you shit way more as a consequence, maybe not more often, but definitely more fiercely and voluminously. Everything that you digest ends up right here in these pits. Like if you studied the contents of a shitter you could figure out a whole lot about the diet and health of our camp. Of course the accuracy of that sort of measurement would vary depending on how many of us pinch our loaves out on the block. I love a nice block job, at least now, before the flies start their loving."

Grant observes Tammy listening intently: her pupils are dilated beyond their normal aperture. She looks almost in shock. The assault of adjusting to something entirely new. Head cocked, starling-like, taking it all in. Murielle seems more remote, dreamy... more into the surroundings. The smell of soil ripening the air, the earth spirits rising into everyone's nostrils.

"Last year this fucking guy. Hey, Luke, what was that guy's name? That tool who got all sick, was it last season?"

"Are you not referring to Bog Breath?"

"Yeah, man, that's it, Bog Breath. That's what we called him by the end of the contract. This kid thinks he's a survivalist or something... decides, get this, to drink swamp water because he thinks it looks clean. Clean, whatever, he's a retard. Of course he gets really fucking ill, pukes in the mess tent, into his vegetable soup, into this other guy's vegetable soup. Gets driven to town, his stomach pumped, the whole deal."

Ray exits the hole, and Tammy jumps in to give it a try. They only have a few more shovel loads to go. Tammy starts giving 'er while Ray keeps lecturing. Her blonde hair gets filled with dirt. Grant is surprised to see Tammy involved in the action like that — he had her pegged as a wuss who would quit after day two. You never know, you just never know who'll make it and who'll crap out.

"... but Bog Breath comes back to camp after his stay in the Kapuskasing hospital. Two weeks later he's back like Gumby or something, trying to talk to bears, and he decides he wants to see if he's developed an immunity to the bog water. That dirty bugger! So he ladles up the ooze once again with his filthy little pesticide-covered hands. Me and

Groucho hear him crying in disgust and guttural pain. He's running toward us through our piece, clutching his stomach, his face white as lard. He trips and cuts his cheek on some slash. Me and Groucho have to carry him off the block. We lie him on the quad. We can actually hear the chemical reaction going on in his stomach, it sounds like water being drained from a sewer. Bog Breath's groaning, 'Heimlich! Heimlich!' It makes sense to pump his stomach so me and Groucho start pumping his abdomen with our fists. He's puking like a sick cow. We purged him that way. We pumped his stomach real good. And you know what, he didn't even have to get driven to the hospital that time."

All the rookies have various expressions of horror and disgust plastered on their faces. Even Grant gets a bad taste in his mouth.

"Better make the shitter holes deep enough. Don't want any nasty surprises when you sit down," shouts Ray enthusiastically.

Once the five pits have been adequately excavated everybody helps move the shitter frames from the back of a pickup. They secure the plastic flaps around the frames.

"Porta pookies erect! Good job, everyone!"

BAD ATTITUDE INFECTIOUS

Grant hates the unpaid labour. Having to help set up camp *pro bono* is bullshit in his opinion. He longs for the old days when he actually liked the job and was enthusiastic about planting trees. He has a bad feeling about this contract. The equipment buses were late getting into camp because Biz had to go back down the Swanson road to get a key from the warden, and the client representative needed to get the initial orientation done today, according to some abstract schedule. The ship's already getting a little loose, Grant notes to himself. Things are a bit loosey-goosey.

He huffs away down the sloping road toward the mess

tent. He tries to control the anger but it seizes him like a demon. Hanging with all those rookies made him annoyed. Every year, more fresh faces straight from mummy and daddy. Those fucking rookies. Take that Tammy kid trying to be tough like she knew what planting was all about. And Murielle: oh trees, oh flowers; oh farmer's field; oh some hippie dream. Tomorrow she's going to be stuck up to her knees in the mud. Benito will be balls-deep in bog. Both in a world of hurt.

CAMP MEETING IN THE FEEDING PEN

Three exposed light bulbs hang at random intervals from a scuffed aluminum support beam that runs down the middle of the mess tent. Electric white Christmas lights wrapped around aluminum crossbeams. A glow that flickers with the rise and fall of the sputtering generator.

Mittens and toques and enough fleece to cover the hide of a recycled mastodon. Everyplanter shoulder-to-shoulder at the long flimsy tables, the bench planks supported by sections of log. The crew bosses are hanging out at the front next to the coffee machines and stacks of white bread, canned hot chocolate mix (the type supplemented with thousands of tiny marshmallows), industrial-size tubs of peanut butter, and low-grade jelly. Everyplanter is waiting for Bazooka, the camp supervisor. Supervisors are always off doing their own thing. You wonder what exactly they are "working" on. Slacking? No, paperwork naturally, always the paperwork.

Grant doesn't recognize anyone at his table. He doesn't bother introducing himself. He looks around the tent, taking a quick estimate of the boy-to-girl ratio. Probably about twenty girls, thirty-five or forty guys. If he was thinking in terms of shacking up or a shag fest, he would think: not bad.

Bazooka strides through the flap. Short, massive, somewhat legendary Bazooka. He wears a dirty Jets cap and already has a healthy beard with just enough shwag to make it a proper bush style. He has a clipboard in his hands.

"All right everybody. Welcome, welcome." He positions himself off-centre, staring down the rows of faces. "As you can see, we had a few problems setting up, but thank you very much for bearing with us. And thank you for your help."

He scans the rows of planters and smiles widely. "Looks like we've got a real purdy group this year, which is good, because good-looking people have more fun."

He pauses, and glances at his clipboard. His jokes never make anybody laugh at the first meeting. He looks up with a slightly severe expression, as if this fact pissed him off a bit.

"Now, on a lighter note, I hope you guys all brought pistols with you."

"Why, to shoot the bears?" Someone chimes in.

"Actually, no, to *faire comme ça*." Bazooka pretends to hold a gun into his mouth. "You know, to blow our fucking heads off!"

He looks dead serious. It is rumoured that he has a tattoo of a tree planter on his left pectoral.

"Just joking… that's my humour for you. Takes a while to get used to."

Someone is standing up on a bench at the back. It is Shnogg.

"Hey, Bazooka — balls deep, man! Balls deep, yo! You know what we all are?" He looks around at Everyplanter. "We're balls deep in Kapuskasing! We bend over for nine cents! Up with the Tree of Life!"

"Listen to this man," says Bazooka, leafing through his papers. He then informs the camp that the contract entails 3.5 million trees, of which half will be black spruce and the other half white. Then he flips through the PMSA health and safety procedural program, Platform for Maximum Safety Assurance. Nobody really pays much attention and hardly anyone cares because they're more into ass-sniffing at this point. The numbers only mean anything when they start to dwindle, signifying that the contract is almost over.

Then it's time for the circular introductions. Everybody gets a moment in the spotlight. Beginning with the crew bosses.

Biz is all excited, saying how fantastic the season's going to be, how Tamponix deserved the reforestation award it received last year, and Grant can just tell he's putting on face. He secretly wants to run the whole show one day. If he can make it to the top he'll have power in more than mere reforestation — also nurseries, fire fighting, multiphase — the whole Tamponix shebang. Everybody knows that Biz'll challenge Bazooka for his position as supervisor.

Then Eliza, who is a short but stocky crew boss back for her fifth year. Somebody once described her smile as a Rolling Stones smile, like the lips on the T-shirt.

Eliza introduces the cooks in turn. "The most wonderful Spice!" She palm-outlines the short-haired Spice with her arty, cat's eye glasses. Spice looks around at everyone, smiling, but with the seriousness of someone who has the insanely demanding job of feeding sixty-plus hungry staff.

"I am here to cook for all you guys with loving care, but *remember*, I am *not* your mother, okay?"

Grant can only imagine how terrifying it is to be in charge of the most sought-after resource, to face that twice-a-day horde of seriously hungry individuals all wanting good food with no delays. There is much to be said for the fastidiousness and culinary courage of the bush camp cooks.

Then all the planters have to introduce themselves. Some people try to be hot shots right off the bat, though Grant knows that these tend to be the planters who are quietest once things get going. All these faces come and go like a crop.

There is one guy from Israel. Immediately after completing his military service, he came on a visa to Canada. When asked, he has nothing to say about service, about the army. He just keeps silent. Someone who pitched a tent near him says that he's been lighting joint after joint since he arrived.

As Grant's turn approaches, he thinks: "I have nothing to say for myself that won't be revealed outside my daily actions." Except Bazooka goes ahead and does the introduction for him.

"This is Grant Hackwood, our new safety officer." He pats Grant on the shoulder.

That's a shock. Safety officer. What the? Maybe the anthropologist wasn't full of shit after all. Grant's memory is jogged by the adrenaline rush of embarrassment, and he now recalls with a certain tequila-foggy vagueness something about telling Bazooka that, "Sure, maybe, yeah, I'll get back to you on that one…" Grant had been interested in the extra money. He'd never followed up with the office in North Bay though, and figured that some other vet had been awarded the position. Then he'd gone to Mexico all winter. He hadn't been in touch with Bazooka or the owners about this. Obviously he'd agreed at some point — the tequila may have distorted the deal.

Grant is about to open his mouth to say god knows what, when Bazooka pipes up. "Looks like Mick's back. We'll have to introduce him, he's our tree runner. He's brought his dogs by the sounds of it."

"I thought dogs actually attract bears," some planter comments.

"Not these dogs…"

The two mutts come sprinting through the flap into the middle of the mess tent, the big one bearing down on the smaller dog, which has its tail between its legs. The little dog turns to fight the big one and they snap at each other. The little dog has huge teeth and a jaw that looks like it's made for crushing old car parts.

Mick comes running in after them, whistling through his teeth. He's buck-toothed and wears an old leather jacket with silver stars on the shoulder and jogging pants which hang low, exposing his belly hair. To the out-loud gasps of the planters Mick grabs the big dog between its hind legs and yanks it by the testicles, which become visibly stretched in his fist. The big dog squeals apologetically and curls convulsively around to lick its master's hand.

"Oh, my god! Ow! That's horrible," some planter yells.

The spectacle causes quite a ruckus, but Mick soon has the misbehaving mutts out of there with the help of Spice, who grabs the smaller dog by the collar and leads it out the opposite end of the tent.

The planters settle down and the introductions resume.

"Ah... safety." Grant stutters, looking nervously over the swamp of new faces. He looks in Bazooka's direction for help. None is forthcoming. Grant fumbles for the right words, thinking back to what safety officers did in previous years. "I will be in charge of making sure everything is safe..." he begins, "...according to PMSA standards. There are first-aid kits around in the...ah...ah...but I'll get back to you on that one...I will be holding safety meetings..." Everyplanter stares at him with derisive smiles. They are all probably thinking: "So this is one of those legendary veterans. I've heard about these guys. He can't even explain what he's all about. A few too many good times, no doubt."

After the meeting Grant goes up to Bazooka.

"Fuck, Bazooka, I didn't even know..."

"You said so last year."

"But nobody contacted me. What the fuck!?"

"Haven't you been online at all this last month? If you don't want to be safety officer I'll have to find somebody else. You don't want the bonus?"

"Well... what do I have to do? I don't even have my first-aid certificate...."

Bazooka takes a quick look around to make sure nobody is eavesdropping. "I'll pretend I didn't hear that," he says. "You'll find the master safety manual in the cook shack under the cereals. There are a number of laminates you post around the sinks and no-smoking signs to put at the fuel cache and in the mess tent. You're also responsible for the camp safety audit. If you have questions just ask Spice. Don't get too paranoid about all that. It's all due diligence really, PMSA standards… it's bullshit, really. Stuff like this is becoming more important than planting good trees, which is fucked, but unfortunately true. How was your off-season anyway?"

"All right. Yours? Surfing?"

"Yeah, I placed fifth at the regionals in Maui."

"You really found your world out there on the surf, eh?"

"I'll tell you one thing, it was better than getting held hostage in Mexico! Nothing can tear me away from the surf. Except death. Which is a possibility come to think of it. The waves seem to get gnarlier every year. Ha ha ha."

ANONYMOUS JOURNAL ENTRY

(This is the final report from the Boreal Zone. The Industry has gone to hell. Planters have migrated to Onterrible from the West coast, a sign that things are getting really bad. It used to be that BC was the promised land, now they are returning to Onterrible. The planters are all migrants, hyenas, vagrants - quitting one company and jumping to the next, with no more loyalty than a son has to a corrupt father. Treated like animals, they snap back at their masters. Originally, tree planters were supposed to organize into unions but instead anarchy now prevails. The big companies toppled because the quality of crop was way below Ministry standards, their bottom line eventually producing bottom quality regeneration. Long bearded Boreal Bedouins, skin like rawhide, they sled on tree boxes down the ice floes in temporary mountain camps all the way to the East.)

HAPPY AND WILLING TO WORK

Wake up to a chainsaw like the sound of a massive mosquito. First breath is a misty cough. The feeling of condensation all over sleeping bag. Atmospherics of lungs in tent, breath vapour transformed to water drops on the tent roof; a microclimate. Murielle opens her eyes.

Chainsaw? *Tu rêve*, Murielle. She shakes her bangs. Her nose snuffles. With an *oh, mon dieu* she sits up halfway, her blue sleeping bag slipping down to her waist. She falls back into a lying position then reaches out and grabs her 15% cashmere sweater. She hugs the crumpled ball of fabric like a lover and smacks her lips. Soon she sits up again. She manages to assume a fully hunched sitting position, scratches her fingers through tangled hair. What day is it? How long has she been planting for?

The endorphin surge of waking to work helps indulgent dreams recede.

"Come on, you motherfuckahs, wake the fuck up, motherfuckahs!" Bazooka is shouting. "Come on, all you lazy bastards, it's time to get up and earn your bread. This is your first real wake up call, darlings! I've been going easy on you up to now. Commmmmmonnnnnn muuuuuuuthhhhhherrrrrfuuuuuckkkkers. Coffffffffeeeeee isssssssss reeaddddddyyyyy. Pull your hand out of your pants! Oh, yeah fart fart… really funny…"

Bazooka is running around with a chainsaw like a frigging maniac, revving the thing like a nightmare alarm clock.

Benito's eyes switch open. He tries to unclench his fists, but finds that his left hand has stiffened as though he's wearing a metal glove. He looks bewilderedly at his stuck fingers through eyes cracking open like ancient vaults in the archeological dawn. He has to unlock the joint of his index finger with his right hand. His finger snaps back into position. It makes his hand feel like a machine. A malfunctioning machine. The *claw*, the *claw*, he mutters to himself as he clicks and unclicks his stubborn joints. He considered ducttaping his hands to cardboard splints. Someone told him about that. He also heard of someone crapping on a Frisbee because they were scared to get out of their tent in the night.

Planters emerging out of their tents: somnambulant apparitions. The sound of rustling tarpaulin, the quick rip of zippers. Then the chainsaw again — it begins as a mechanical grunt, works up to a purr, then revs to a high-pitched, inhuman falsetto. It's cutting into a log just a few feet from his head. Laughter. Truck tires ripping into the dirt along the ridge. The anthropologist whining about something in his peculiar intellectual tone. Benito seems to remember a bad dream from the night before, perhaps even a horrible dream, but he cannot fathom what it was all about. Something about a school bus heading down a dark road at night.

Benito dresses in clothes still soiled from the day before. Using his bum as a pivot, he hoists his thighs into the cold air, squirms into muddy quick dries, then claws into an old Canadiens T-shirt, slips a yellow North Face fleece on over top. Then grabs two pairs of socks that are clean and fluffy, thankfully. The first pair are polypropylenes, doubled up with generic red-striped woollies. Now he needs boots, so he unzips his tent with a *zzzeeeett* like the sound of a mosquito whirring in the vicinity of an ear, and, with a wince and an *oh my god this is an awful job*, he slips into absolutely slimy ballistic canvas work boots that spent the night in quarantine under the vestibule.

His spinal cord pops and cracks as Benito forces his shoulders out from under his (Eureka!) tent's tiny vestibule. He stands, stretches his tendons on tiptoes, arms Jane Fonda-ed towards the sky. Feels a seismic creak through calves, in neck, at the shoulder. Buns of steel though, the hamstrings cast iron. So soon. Clavicle feels stretched on the shovel side.

Damp skyless morning, sun on the rise somewhere in the barely-above-zero dawn. Chainsaw industrial scratches have been replaced by loud music that's all bass from this distance — muffled world music coming through the trees with the mist. Camp sound system. Electronic beats through the trees. Adrenaline slowly rising through Benito's blood.

Forgot something, damn it. He breaks back into the vestibule — *zzzzeeetp* — to grab that something. Where are those somethings, *damn it*? There they are. And GoreTex shell, need shell. Benito throws heaps of gear around trying to find his shell, then remembers that shell is still in knapsack that he forgot outside the mess tent last night. *Shite. Fucking fuck.* Exits through vestibule again, this time without so much muscular twanging and popping. Heads along path up gentle declivity, and slurs good morning to a couple planters who he doesn't know the names of yet. Marches ahead of them up the path, trampling little balsams and mosses up the incline by the marvelous but unappreciated creek, over mottled grass all muddy and puddle-dotted, between clusters of drooping tents that have miniature tide pools of rain water in their rumpled tarps, then onto the hard clay and gravel of the main tent area, heading directly to coffee. Coffee will give rise to consciousness.

And self-consciousness.

He wants to pound. He wants to impress people. He doesn't know where he fits in the camp. He dreamed of his mom, she was filling up a kettle and then it was hissing and whining steam on the stove from his childhood. He swallows the sadness of that thought.

His tent suddenly starts to shake back and forth. "Coming, coming," he promises whoever it is tugging on his tent. He hears Gabby yawn really loud in a neighbouring tent. He likes Gabby, though he doesn't know her very well yet. Gabby: fourth year, tough-talking but super sociable. Nickname: Gab the Goss. He wants to know her better. He wants to know Grant better. Grant, who sips his coffee now too.

Grant who feels a pang of envy for the poplars and pine trees that loom up above him, to which the tent tarps are secured with yellow rope. The trees are dreamy and streamlined, infinitely more stable and at ease than the human operation that mulls around their trunks. Can't help but resent trees just a little; they just hang out all day while he works his ass off to plant their babies.

Heads to cook shack. Cook shack is an aluminum-sided trailer with two stoves and a fridge inside, and only enough cabin space for two people at a time. He beat the lineup, thankfully.

There are only two other planters ahead of him. He has a blue dish and an orange plastic cup. He retrieved them from the foldout shelves beside the cook shack. Everyplanter must clean their own dishes and keep them on the shelves because of the bears. Dirty dishes left out go straight to the sin bin. The only way to get them back is to do Spice a favour, wash pots or something. Last night's chicken pot pie still flecks his plate and there is dried juice at the bottom of his plastic cup. Too tired to give them a proper cleaning last night. He got away with it this time. Spice heaps piles of sizzled bacon from a big metal tray onto his plate. She dumps some eggs from a pan. He shoves a slice of grapefruit between his gums. Ducks into the mess tent.

After scarfing breakfast, Grant competes for the lunch stuff spread on a table. There is a ring of planters all reaching for pickles and grabbing at the last lettuce to garnish their hummus sandwiches, the lunch meat long gone to hungry meat eaters who get up early just to ensure they have first dibs. Refills coffee, can't forget coffee, then walkruns to bus which is already revving with crew boss impatiently honking horn because it's seven already. Runs outside to planters standing around waiting with their water jugs in hand for their turn to siphon water from the heavy blue water barrels. Somewhere in the midst of this process, Grant bumps into Murielle, who gives him a little good-natured elbow in the kidney. "*Attention, monsieur!*"

On the bus, a joint is twisted. They bump along, hooting.

Therapeutic uses of Cannabis #2: Wake up and smile. Dosage: pipe hits, two or three loads. Effect: eases muscle pain and wakens mind to general euphoria, inherent mystery and optimism of new day, feeling like Dali raising his arms each morning and saying to himself: "So, what shall Dali create on this fine morning?" A forest?

Larry takes a couple hauls from his glass pipe while he holds the steering wheel straight with the press of his thighs. He looks back at everybody in the mirror, letting the smoke snake through the gaps in his teeth.

"This is a sweet crew, guys, I'm really happy to have you guys. We're going to pound. We're going to be the production crew. Smoke production, that is." He shifts into third and the bus arcs through a clearing along the tree-line, crisp morning sun and coffees hot on laps.

"You know what today is? Day off!"

"Really?"

"Ha, ha, rookie. I'm full of shit. We have three more days. Six and ones, buddy. Sorry, that was a bad joke."

THE CLIENT

The head quality guy, named Doug Colt, jumps off the pickup with his trapper mutt Princess barking along behind him. He wears a checkered coat. A Terrorhouser technician with a blue hard hat steps out of a fancy disposable truck with some of his cohorts.

They confront the planters who stand impatiently in the vegetation. "Over here, sweeties," says the Terrorhouser tech as he hustles up the landing and into the block. The other checkers are there too, tobacco chew bulging under their lower front lips; squirt. A couple of quads are parked in the mud tracks off to the side. The usual scene.

There transpires some hand shaking. The Terrorhouser engineers are keen to leave the bush after a day of surveying timber in their cushy V-Max 8 off-road truck.

Flecks of snow begin flitting down from the cold grey sky.

The Terrorhouser guy stands on a pile of overturn and addresses the planters.

"Welcome, planters," he says, wobbling a bit on his suspect perch of twigs and moss, "and welcome to the North. This here is Doug Colt, the Clear Water mill representative." He pats him on the shoulder. "Doug Colt is a forestry engineer at the mill. After my introduction he'll tell you the specifics of what he expects. *Ahem*. And then the checkers will show you the specs for the micro sites." He puts his hands behind his back, *ahems* once again.

Doug Colt speaks the muddy franglais of the region. "'Ello planters, welcome back." He seems very different than his Terrorhouser associate.

The Terrorhouser tech continues, overshadowing Doug Colt: "Up here in the North, you see, money grows on trees. If it wasn't for us, much of New York state would have dirty assholes, as we used to say. You, Tamponix Reforestation, are a long-time beneficiary of Clear Water Pulp and Paper Inc., and its subcontractor Terrorhouser Logging. Working in harmony, we continue renewing the forests of tomorrow… *ahem, ahem*."

A pack of Export Blue is visible through the perforations of the tech's high-viz vest. It's difficult to grasp who exactly is who in the business: the government, the mill, the logging companies — the lines demarcating the separation of institutions are crisscrossed.

"Yeah, well, my sister lives in New York and she uses a bidet," some hotshot planter chimes in from the ranks. The Terrorhouser rep strains to see who made the comment, but all the planters are smiling like it was them who cracked the joke.

"Please, let's just get this over with, so we can all get out of here and have some supper."

"Sorry, dog," says the person under his breath. The Terrorhouser tech looks over the ranks again, but still can't find who the shit disturber is.

"I am proud to inform you that our first harvest of secondary human deposited growth is underway this season. Thanks to Clear Water's original initiative in the sixties, we exercise a system of renewable regrowth. Forty years ago

Clear Water first hired a crew of planters. That was long before Tamponix even existed. Now we are cutting those trees down." He pauses with a faint, proud smile, looking emphatically over the horizon of foreheads, pleased that they are pleased with that important historical tidbit of pleasing information. "And, with our new business partner, Northern Cloners, we hope to accelerate the reforestation process using state of the art techniques."

"Nobody cares," somebody whispers.

"Of course, not all trees are hand-planted... we also do extensive aerial seeding, and the residual seeds naturally — "

"Hey!" The shit disturber shouts out. "I can be a reforestation person too, ya want me to aerial tend things for y'all. I've got a big dick and I'll make big forests with my seminal devices!"

The Terrorhouser tech lights up in anger. "Jesus Christ! All right, no more jokes. No tact, absolutely no tact!" He addresses his audience as if they were not a multiplicity of personalities but rather a single moronic listener.

"Feisty bunch this year," Doug Colt says to the crews, seeing everyone as individuals. He is about to say something, but the Terrorhouser tech speaks overtop of him.

"I would like to remind everybody of the rules and regulations expounded in the PMSP documents. When the MNR guys show up all of you will be expected to know about PMSP. Your supervisor, Bazooka, will hold a meeting later, to debrief you on PMSP regulations. Very important. All right, what next?"

The meeting is adjourned. The planters march briskly under the turning sky and the twirling specks of snow.

Back in the bus, Eliza switches on the under-seat heating and the bus chugs on through the thin snow, bringing the planters back to camp.

That's when Grant comes out of the ditch and Eliza slows the bus and folds the door open and he comes in up the steps followed by Luke and sits at the front in those seats which are unofficially reserved for the camp highballers.

The top planters were working to keep production up during the meeting and fire-training of that afternoon.

Grant had been thinking something all morning in the bog and now he's inside the bus and he ceases to think about it. But then he hears somebody speaking in the seat behind him.

"Hey, you know the director of *Aliens*?"

"James Cameron?"

"Yeah. He was born in Kapuskasing. Lived here the first few years of his life."

"Cool, I didn't know that."

Grant spits on the floor, lights a cigar and rubs his now stubbly head. That fact somehow relates to a feeling, fits like an important piece to a puzzle. A puzzle that he is slowly assembling into an implausible picture. Of the way things are out here.

BEND OVER FOR NINE CENTS

Jackson Pollock. You have to move in the same rhythm with which Jackson Pollock painted — bobbing, sidling around his studio, circling these huge canvases. Stoop, splat, stoop, splat. Stoop, tree, stoop, tree.

Larry pulls the bus up on the edge of a big landing cleared by bulldozers. Planters swig from their travel mugs. Someplanter passes around a mickey of Kahlúa. Planters puff morning butts. Then Larry leads them down a trail, studying a coffee-stained block map while he trips along a spur road. He points planters to their designated sections of land.

Grant and Luke partner plant today. Their coffee steams from thermos cups set on a section of log as they sit in the clear morning light and bag up.

Eight tree tubs stacked in two piles. Hard tubs each contain a white plastic bag full of saplings, four hundred and thirty-two saplings in each. Larry is good about setting up the planters on his crew with their own personal tree caches.

Grant heaves up a tub and throws it in front of Luke. They tear open the white bags with stiff fingers, bundles of nine trees stacked neatly inside. Unwinding the plastic wrap from around the pods, they then stuff the trees into their bags. They fill both bags while standing. They stuff in the recalcitrant saplings which spring and twist out of the desired placement. Tired and semi-conscious, the only communication is the odd grunt.

Grant leads. Pulls out a length of flagging tape from a pouch on the waist of his planting bag and ties it to the branch of a fallen tree: their marker, a line of flight into the territory. It's a partial cut, large patches of poplar and willow left by the loggers for wildlife habitat. Important to throw up flags to know where they are, to counteract the psychedelic lines of convergence which constitute the spatial perspective of the land, to keep track of their boundary. The art of flagging in straight.

Grant's shovel cuts the FH layer, deep through the initial little fibrous rootlets, into the grey, greasy soil. First tree of the day. Their goal, modest because they are not yet in shape, is 2,500 trees each. He swings a sapling from his bag, bends over, tucks it in the corner of the hole that he has simultaneously pried open using the shaft of his shovel for leverage. He holds the leader of the sapling straight in the hole, and kicks down firm, closing the hole around the root collar, submerging the pod and erecting the needles which spring towards the sky. A fact flits in his memory: *Over 60 percent of the Earth's biomass exists underground.*

Luke follows him, spacing six feet off of Grant's trees. He screefs away the raw needles and twigs — duff — in order to expose the soil, spearing with his shovel. He uses a staff rather than a speed spade. Up and down, rhythmically, with good speed. They are excited to be back in this mesmerized, memorized rhythm. Stooping and stepping high over huge roots, keeping a line toward the back, the dense timber edge which is their final boundary. Hunkered over like apes. They are not ripping it up yet, not pounding.

They are just enjoying the simple practiced movement of tree to tree. Nine cents to nine cents. Stooping for dimes. Nothing too huge on the first day. The first week is all about getting in shape, not about sick numbers.

Thusly through the morning. When they finish one bag of trees, they have already planted their way to the front of their piece and they stop to eat an orange; small snacks, small sips of water. Sitting on empty overturned bins. Scribbling the numbers of trees they've planted on some dirt-streaked cardboard tab. Twelve o'clock, they have each planted 1,500 trees. On pace. It's getting warmer. The light brings out the green, the first, thin green. Trudge back into the cut with full bags slapping against their thighs.

"So, what be your dreams this year, Grant?" Luke seems to have noticed how sombre and workman-like Grant is, not saying too much, but stopping now and then while he plants and just staring off into the distant cut.

The land extends far beyond them into vanishing points of cedar copses, and ravens swoop at the point where vision fades. *Over 60 percent of the Earth's biomass exists beneath the surface.*

"I don't know," huffs Grant. "I'm not sure I really have any this year." He stops making his hole, leans on the shovel. "Actually, the same dream as last year. I didn't have a chance to fulfill that one, no. I wanted to jump a ship. Stow away in the hold with a satchel of breads and cheeses and a keg of wine, that dream. With rats and hobos, maybe heading from New York to France. A big underground feast in the hold. Singing French ballads, maybe some Brechtian ballads, and then sneak out on deck and let the sea breeze wash me sober. A new country on the horizon. You know, that old-fashioned dream."

"Oh, I remember that dream. That's an old dream, all right. Years old. I see you really got it down nice and sharp. It's almost become a story. Well, Mr. Safety Officer, sounds like you should plan a trip to Champagne. What were you doing in Mexico if you were dreaming of Frenchland?"

Grant opens a hole, cuts into the gradation of decomposing organic matter. There is something down there in the dark, there is something down in the soil. His fingers slip in, push the pod amongst the roots, feeling the underside of the earth's skin. There is something or someone down there, there is something deep underground.

He quickly stamps the hole closed. Stands straight. A noise in the distance.

The swamp machine, which looks like a bush tank with big treads, passes on the road at the front of their piece, and makes the *shlopping* sound of bins dropped into the mud by Larry, who's riding on the back. Then the big swamp machine trundles on through the bog road with Larry yelling something to Sil, the driver.

Mexico. An image of the past year squirrels around Grant's mind. He sees jungles and seas.

"So you lasted the year?" Luke has stopped, assuming the *homo sapiens*, as opposed to gorilla posture; polymorph. He peers speculatively at Grant, a vague concern shading his face. They have come to a halt in a grove of dead poplars whose tops have all fallen off. Grant shakes his head. They are just chimps in the wilderness. Was it last year, they came up with the idea: stupidity is intelligence liberated.

"You left early?" Luke delves deeper.

"I just got bored. I just left, man. Come on, let's rock. This bag's taking forever."

Grant leads down a skidder trail. He rides the rail down one edge, boots pounding on the liverwort, splits open a red rotting log from which tumbles clumps of bracket fungus. He tucks, gets the trees deep into the muck, as they follow their back boundary.

The fingers of Grant's memory reach into the jewel bag of Mexico. Memories rise and expand to fill the emptiness of the cut. He remembers the first time he went down there, before ever having planted a single tree.

South of Puerto Vallarta, this little lawless village with only paths, no roads, and no electricity. Dusty paths with horses tethered to poles sticking out between rocks. A town set on the face of a soft green mountain overlooking a lagoon where pelicans perched stoic and big breasted on the sterns and bows of anchored sloops with names painted rough on the sides, *Gringo Loco,* or *Emerald,* buoyant on the waters that over time exerted a metamorphic force, hauling the shore into the sea, creating the lagoon. He'd hiked the river a long way back from the town, trundling by pigs with huge testicles lazing beside fat eucalyptus, passing ramshackle houses with bricolage tin and wooden walls and little schools in the middle of fields where deft-footed kids played Mexican-style football with lots of showmanship and dipsy-doodle. He found a wondrous little cove with a waterfall a few kilometres along a trail that disappeared in spots or ended up at barbed wire impasses in dense thickets of tropical foliage. He'd marked the correct turns, once he discovered them, with tiny bits of red flagging tape, à la tree planting, and made trips back and forth hauling provisions and hardware to construct a tree fort, wading through the clear pools, rivulet staircases with precise eddies for steps cooling his feet. He wanted to be up in the shadows of the tree tops so he could get a view through the green canopy above the shadows of parrots cackling, of transparent shimmering webs blowing in the tropical wind strung from fungus that looked like sea anemones. Over the next few weeks he packed provisions in crates, hiked them in with a cargo scarf around his forehead like the Mayans used to carry rocks on their backs for their pyramids.

A jaguar had slunk down to town from the jungle the year before and mauled a St. Bernard and an old horse, so to be safe he slept with a machete by his pillow. Every night he heard questions whispered to him by some spectre in the great web of the gurgling jungle streams and moist foliage. "Are you alone?" asked the great angel of solitaire who flapped in the prisms of his dreams. "Are you content to sleep this eve under the stars with me brushing feathers on your oval eyelids?" To which he would murmur in the affirmative, and send little nods and blinks of permission in the direction of the ethereal voice. There was nothing more he wanted than just nothing, nothing more than the immediacy of his senses, scintillating stillness. The voice touched him wordlessly in the unknown, the outback, the perimeter. The voice he sometimes thought he heard calling his name in a crowded alley. The voice that asks him a question, presents a riddle.

The hand of modernization was sweeping into the last niches of Mexico. He left the cave to travel for a month and when he got back, the local government — which he hadn't even believed existed other than the cartoonish presence of the drunk constable — had finished installing electricity, so at night the dark hills were lit up by unnatural stars which were an assault to his precious sense of being off the grid. Increasing numbers of day hikers frequented the waterfall, and although he would try to be hospitable, offering them water from his big wooden barrel or little stories of the narrative of silence, he felt pushed away. He was left with no other option but to take his squatter's outfit further down the trail into the heart of the jungle. Or move on. He moved on. Met witches. Headed into the centre of the Mexican mirage.

He attempted to move as far away as humanly possible from everything that made him human, which meant going both outward into the world of animals and geography as well as inward beyond his social mask to the formless substrate of the unconscious. Once there, at the intersection of outward and inward limits, if such a place actually could exist in space and time, something made him switch direction. Feeling a powerful desire for human contact which rivaled a cigarette craving in intensity, he'd decided to catch a train to a coastal community where he'd heard there were dreamers and freaks and surfers and nude people and cheap accommodation and a zany nightlife — all things he hadn't found much of in his spiritualized voyages of the interior, and it turned out that on the coast his destiny as a tree planter awaited.

Grant trips on his own feet. Luke lets out a har-har laugh. From his fallen-and-unable-to-get-up position, Grant looks up at Luke with a cynic's grimace.

"Looks like we're back in the bush! To answer your question, I don't want to go to Europe, 'cause Paris is dead, just like New York, just like Athens. The old olives are rotting like a history book left in a library for too long." Grant stoops and he is not sure if Luke heard him or if his words just didn't register. Anything with a fake loftiness usually rings empty in his friend's ears.

Sitting down on the bins after bagging out, Luke looks over at Grant: "See, you always had the dream of escaping, right, roaming and shit, and I say that's because you grew up all soft and homey, but my dreams are different. I want to find a nice little homestead somewhere, meet some sweet thing, that's my dream. I wanna soften up. Look at my face. I'm only 28 and it's weathered like Clint Eastwood's."

They bag up. They enter the land.

Grant raises his chin and swivels his head while crouching, looking for the next micro site to stick a tree, and notices that Luke is still staring his way.

"See, I never really knew what you were running from," Luke says.

Larry emerges before Grant has the chance to say something stupid. Larry stands in a puddle, black-booted, a bottle of hard liquor hanging from his hand, his quality assessment book in the other. He tells Luke to come with him to help finish off a different section of the block. Grant always wonders where Larry comes from, it's like he materializes from the oddest areas of the forest, as if he transformed into an owl when nobody was looking.

"How's it going this year, guys? Want a swig?"

"Awful like usual, Larry. Awful like usual…. Sure, thanks."

"What a business, eh?"

"Somebody's got to do it, I guess."

The three of them sit on a tilted log for a few minutes, shifting leg position to stay steady, until Larry stands and Luke stands too, and they hike away, leaving Grant to finish the piece. But not before Larry manages to finish a little story. "Have you heard, heard of the spirit god of Canada, the spirit god whose mind is the Borealis?" This makes Grant and Luke laugh out loud, because Larry is getting funny on their asses. They all take a quick swig. The old lore of Larry, the mythical world that balances on a turtle carcass, the hallucinations seen through the long initiation of glue inhalation… Larry! Quiet Larry with his awesome stories. "Yeah, Larry, you told us that one… it was a good one."

Now alone, Grant plants down a windless corridor. The bulldozers have cleared this path. It is a silent tunnel with much motion in the patterns of the trees to the sides of the corridor, a tunneling inward, as in a sketch of the forest by Emily Carr. The wind picks up as he works past a finger, and in the distance, looking back, he sees two planters, just little forms who don't even appear to be moving relative to the big space, but he can faintly hear their voices, as though they were whispering. Then he high steps into the timber edge to bang in a few easy trees before he starts planting back towards the FSR. Sticking his shovel into the ground he can tell what's under there — what kind of soil, be it sand or mineral or muck — as if his nerves created a phantom extension through the steel blade and shaft.

He finds himself in a cedar swamp. The intense aroma of cedar boughs, perfumed as compared to the sharp sweetness of sharded pine or spruce. The good man who was transformed into the sweet cedar. Larry's voice echoes in his memory. Larry is always offering these little bits and pieces of lore that have, to a degree, shaped Grant's world view. He had this messed up dream a while ago in which Larry was sitting in a crow's nest, cawing out the mad ravings of the spirit god:

"'There is a unity behind the fragmentation! Caw! Craw! A green torch searing through the mist of a deranged human consciousness!' Larry was feeding worms to the little crow fledglings between sentences. 'Its presence offers more history than any of the humans with their helter-skelter documentation and bumbling ways. The most powerful part of the Canadian soul exists as a confederacy of leaves and ferns, of grasses and shoots, of everything in that unknowable, little-perceived expanse that surrounds us, into whose presence we make our way. The urban actors speak their lines against a tree-lined set. No matter how hard we try to locate our nation in a history of comfort's progress, it still remains the savage and pristine backlight of the forest, deep green, oil-based, haloed in wheat gold, which is the more substantial history. Caw, Caw... and just because I have native in my veins I have the power of story over you, white deer man! Caw, Caw.'"

Deep as permitted by the branches, Grant hears a whisper, just a faint whisper of the wind, or the gentle mew of some animal, which spooks him a bit — the dark and clammy interior and the weird animal cry combining to tingle his spine, and he turns and starts planting back quick, out of the timber. His human senses are limited in the obscuring growth. It is impossible to tell exactly what's out there further than the eye. Like a Pac-Man game in this big sylvan maze.

Grant peers up to see what bird might be in the branches of a lone tree. He thinks it might be a raptor. Then he is surprised by a big spruce that looks shockingly like a gnarled old woman with these big knots that flop downward like sagging breasts, a cracked bole and grey, dead branches like the craw of a derelict tropical bird. Just from this angle, yes, just from this angle the tree evokes an old plumed spinster, anthropomorphic. Bird woman.

The clouds have started to streak in cirrus overhead, signifying a change in temperature, and Grant's shovel hand shrivels in the cold wet. When he opens up his holes he keeps thinking he's sticking his shovel into some sort of flesh. The wind kicks up some topsoil and a speck of twig blows into his eye, blurring his vision. His fingers are too dirty to remove the bothersome particle, so he keeps planting — one eye watering, the other one squinting. Plant through the pain.

Every time he thrusts the pointed blade into the low areas, it makes the succulent sound of opening meat. He has difficulty levering up the weight of rocks and root, and once he does, there's a white/grey fungal powder on the root systems. He wrenches his speed spade in a circular motion to open the hole up bigger. He recoils in shock. There is an eye staring up at him from the hole in the earth — a bloodshot eye with a bruise around it.

The eye of his dreams.

Empress fish. Lava stacks. Chemosynthesis.

James Cameron. The eye of the other world.

Moon Beam. Moon Beam.

Over 60 percent of the Earth's biomass exists underground.

Mercy! On the road Grant grabs his water jug, pulls out the retractable tap and pours a stream of icy water onto his eyeball, purging it, blinking rapidly to expel the liquid along with whatever was stuck under his eyelid. It clears out his eye just fine. *The things one imagines one sees with sweat, DEET, and dirt granules in one's eye!* he thinks to himself, fumbling for an orange in his daybag. His thoughts were getting a little out of control there — all the facts were lining up in a weird series, seeming to indicate... something. Something he can almost make sense of. He focuses on the orange, the orange which glows like an orb. One of those perfect oranges that have a precisely perfect colouration and peel clean every time. He pops the neat sections into his mouth. Then takes out a hardboiled egg, removes the shell. He rests the naked egg on a plastic bag on his lap while he rips out and pours a little packet of salt onto it; then he pops the egg down his hatch in two bites. After the egg has dissolved pasty down his throat, he peers back into the density of his land and wishes that Luke were still around to plant it out with him. He grabs his shovel from where he wedged it in a stump and slogs back into the piece.

I am your stork, with my satchel of babies around my hips...You start thinking nonsense out here, and it feels great... Humans take themselves so seriously... *We're just storks with bags full of tree babies.*

Soon he's digging again. Diving deep into the waves of the lagoon. Finning down and opening his eyes in the stinging salt water — flowing sashes of oceanic bronze shifting through the aquamarine like starfish curtains. Swaying thighs of light: the veil of the Virgin of Guadalupe — her dress swaying down into the depths where the dolphins circle, chuckling in the cool currents. He would have finned deeper, as if he had something to say to the bottom of the ocean. Except his lungs are bursting. He has to fin his way back to the surface where his head breaks out into the rough waves and the sun laughs down on him.

"*Merde!*" The limbs are grabbing at Murielle's planting bags, clutching her thighs, and there is something about them, like they are a bad-breathed crone clawing, whispering something, saying come in and have some juicy fruit, it's going to move you.

"*Shit*, this is tough," says Tammy, rebounding a translation back at Murielle. Tammy's red hardhat keeps falling off whenever she bends over. Planting for three hours and they haven't yet finished a bin. Their hopes of immediate profits have waned significantly. Murielle had to show Tammy how to squat to piss. After that, Tammy started pissing every fifteen minutes.

"Hey, Murielle, that's some nice blush you got on there." Tammy tries to joke, but she's spoken too quickly, and Murielle doesn't understand that she is referring to the mud streak along her cheek, and the difficulty in communicating makes Tammy feel even more isolated. She is consumed by a feeling she can only rationalize as that affliction called Homesickness. It rises, tangible, in her chest, from some deep well of childhood.

"My *bêche* will not go in the ground. Everywhere there are roots."

"I think the trail leads this way."

They dead walk away to some softer ground.

"Where are we?"

"Let's go back to the road."

"Follow the trees back to the road, that sounds like a good —" (ears attentive to a noise in the willows.)

"We will look like idiots. It's been hours and we haven't even planted one hundred trees each!"

A crashing noise.

"Ahhh, taberwhett! Ours, ours!"

A shadowy form passes through a willow swale. It's Eliza. Stands with her high-viz vest bright orange and her big smile white as can be. "Hey, girls," says the crew boss, forcing her way through some willow. People have different styles of navigating the bush: there's the stealthy Hobbit method where you slip around obstacles; then there's the crash-through-shit, hard-nosed style. Eliza's smile gleams in relief to her ruddy tan. She's a crash-through-shit kind of gal.

"I was watching you girls from back there. You're *way* lost." She horks, spits, then slaps Tammy on the shoulder.

"My pants are soaked from stepping in all these puddles," Tammy complains.

Eliza chortles. "The fastest way to dry your pants, honey, is to keep wearing them. Your body heat will do wonders."

She gives them a crash course in clear-cut geometry. How to establish a grid, imposing the idea of order onto the formless void of bush. "It's all about developing your spidey sense. Intuit where your next tree should go. Lean into your C-cut. Warp time."

"I can't wait to take a shower later..." Tammy confides in Eliza after the lesson.

"Fucking Bazooka. I told him the rookies would wanna shower this week...." Eliza seems distracted by a string of annoyed recollections and grievances for a second, then her mood, or possibly attitude, changes slightly. "This is tree planting. It's extreme. Most people only shower on days off."

"Six days!"

"Don't tell me you already have the ring of fire!"

"*C'est quoi, ça*? Ring of fire?"

Later, in the secrecy of his deluxe RV, Biz does numbers with Eliza. Groucho is hanging out in there too, leafing through an auto magazine. He made five hundred dollars today. He looks up from the images and gives Biz a crass smirk.

"Yeah, buddy, we'll turn 'em into veterans on day off. Do them missionary, then flip a leg over, then finish them doggie style, then whoops, wouldn't you know it, you're a veteran now!" They clink their beers together.

Eliza, who has been quietly filling out her tally book, looks up with an unimpressed expression. "You guys are fucked, you know that. No wonder you never get any, you're all perverts."

"Whatever, 'Iza. In my second year I learned probably my most important life lesson. Girls like to be treated like shit."

The morning. The light is orange. They march single file along the slash at the sides of the road. The road is nothing but thick, rich muck, huge puddles verging on ponds. It smells like shit. Literally, like feces. The earth is digesting itself — the moose carcasses, the flowers, the stalks, the twigs, the moss, the ferns — decomposing and becoming this greasy, fart-smelling muck.

Murielle is trying to get around a grey snag that sticks out of the bog. She feels the water already soaking through her Village des Valeurs boots. Her left foot gets stuck on a log which throws off her walking rhythm and she kicks out her right leg desperately to avoid falling face first and finds herself up to her hips in the muck with the skanky water collecting around her groin.

"Balls deep!" shouts Groucho, who sees the slip from across the road.

"We all have balls in Kapuskasing!" Somebody else shouts. "We're balls deep in Kapusmotherfuckingkasing."

"This walk-in is cunting me!"

"Fuck it, I'm taking the shortcut." Some kid starts running through the fields of moss as if there was a way out. The only refuges are the days off... one of which is, mercifully, one day away.

Shnogg and Rico are getting the party started with their annual "tree planting rap school". Bazooka's gone to town to buy 50 cases of 50. Everyone's got baseball caps on backwards, or sideways, eating creamy pie off of Frisbees to top off the special steak barbeque that Spice surprised them with. Typical Spice humour that on the white board it said in red marker: *Today's Meal: Meat Curtains.*

Someone comes running by with a Ziploc bag full of urine, and empties it into the shrubbery. "I dreamed of golden oceans last night, dudes!"

Shnogg and Rico are snip-bopping in the DJ booth of a rotted stump, rapping along to beats from the camp sound system.

"Yo, da world's on drugs, you bet   *chica yo yo ya*
thank god there's no bugs yet   *chica yo yo ya ya*

it's a global gong show, it blows   *chica yo yo ya ya ya*
we're on death row, I know   *chica yo yo ba sta cla*
planting a forest worth of trees,   *chia ya ya bo sto clo*
only way for me to save me…   *chica yo yo ya*
the human race has a disease venereal
of the mind's cock, like surreal cereal!
Yo! Yo! Uh! Uh!"

And all the tree planters stomping around on the gravel, the sky all flexed and hardcore and the trees too, spruce gangstas backdropped, criminals chained together by the sky, which is their paddy-wagon.

In the middle of the rapping, Rico suddenly goes all pale and his eyes cross.

"Whud up, Rico?"

"Wow, his eyes are all messed up. Rico, Rico, you need spectacles, bro."

They gather around Rico, who has hopped off the stump, a three-foot drop, falling forward onto his knees, still cross-eyed, staring at something on his nose, and that something is growing, pumped full of blood.

"Ahhhh… mosquito number one! This ain't no fun!"

And as though to embellish that feeling of anticlimax and the coming storm of the reality-out-here, the sound system cuts out and silence descends over the camp.

The next morning, they're informed that day off has been delayed another day.

WILD LIFE ATTACK

Larry guns it on the way back to camp at the end of day seven. The road is wet on some of the turns and he pulls the shifter down to second gear for extra traction and the bus motors on through the wavy tracks of clay, hitting a raised culvert at one point, sending everybody seated at the back two feet off their seats and the piss packs and fire equipment crashing to the floor. "Yeah, Larry — you're turning us into flying yogis, whoopee." Larry tilts his eyes up in the mirror and they jiggle from the motion; he isn't about to apologize, because he made it clear already that his driving policy has always been slow on the way to the block then fast back to camp at the end of the day to narrow the time lag between their growling stomachs and the steaming hot meal awaiting them in camp.

They might have to call in a grader if the ruts get any deeper on this section of the road. Stuck vehicles fuck production.

"Hey, man, isn't Rico like having a rap festival tonight? It's day off. It's going to be awesome," says some idiot, some complete moron.

"You fucking idiot... that was last day off... what happened to your memory?"

"I had a cyst on my brain when I was child... it's not my fault."

Production is already well underway; the camp had a great day seven. Eliza's crew put in approximately 23,000 trees, Biz's crew pounded about 21,000, and Larry's lowballed at 19,000. Larry doesn't seem too concerned about being at the bottom, because it's still early in the contract and he has on his crew many solid, trustworthy veterans.

He keeps gunning it. Grant reflects that driving fast around blind turns isn't altogether safe, but whatever, these roads are built for speed, after all, these crossed roads of the North. The laying of roads has been a lucrative business. It's another government boom time bursary for northern workers, just like the pine beetle program. Tons of road contracts. Roads reaching out on strange tangents, imbecile and illogical roads serving no function except as convenient access for hunters. Roads that disappear in bogs and start up again on the other side. Some strange roads. Roads not worth following.

"My god, I'm starving. My stomach is literally eating itself," Larry bellows out, looking back at everybody in the mirror. Dirty faces with white eyes staring out like those of coal miners.

"Hey, check out the swamp donkey!" Benito spots the thing, and points it out to Gabby. She shouts out, "Swamp donkey! Swamp donkey!"

The moose looks kind of stupid, galloping awkwardly in front of the bus. Larry has to decelerate a notch, lay into the horn with his elbow. The shocked creature doesn't know from engine sounds, keeps galloping along like the steed that could, like Quixote's Rozinante. Then it veers awkwardly off the road and shoulders its way into the brush. It's a tough life for those beautiful but clumsy moose, the crusty winter snows cutting into their shins each year, living off of bark and bitter bud, and then prey to the ticks come spring and summer. Grant knows swamp donkeys. Luke knows swamp donkeys. Gabby knows swamp donkeys. One summer, the three of them encountered a bull moose in the headlights of their little coupe at two in the morning in a sea of darkness near Wawa, and it was like seeing a god's face in all that hairy flesh taking up the whole windshield.

After the moose, Larry accelerates to at least seventy kilometres an hour, careening around the rather tight and blind corners. Not safe, thinks Grant, definitely not safe. He doesn't mention it, though. Nobody else seems concerned. This is the bush after all, he tells himself, rules have no backbone. Not like he's in charge or anything. He's just the safety officer. The position is a joke.

Five minutes later there is more excitement.

"Check it out guys, a black bear." Everyone seated on the right side of the bus stands and leans to the left, slapping their dirty hands on their friends' shoulders. All anyone can make out through the mud-splotched windows is a furry ass receding into the brush. The bear fades back into its wooded world. Even staring at that exact second at that exact spot you can't see it. As if it had dissolved.

They sight three more on their way back to camp. Scrawny bears, confused and constipated after another long winter, chewing grass to cleanse their colons.

"Are there usually this many?" asks an inquisitive rookie.

"Usually they cull a bunch of them, but the Ministry banned the bear hunt last year."

"They look like orangutans."

Not like storybook bears, for sure. The coats on these bears are a rusty light brown, and they don't possess the paunch of storybook bears. These ones are branchier, wiry. Larry looks back at Everyplanter in the mirror. "You know, if you've ever seen a skinned bear, they look like humans. They have the same upright appearance. Really spooky. Like a skinned human. We found one last year, we found a bunch of skeletons all in one spot."

Back at camp everybody is buzzing about all the wildlife and there is mention of getting the safety alert whistles distributed in case some of those bears make an appearance on the block searching for protein. Distributing the whistles is Grant's job.

A pack of planters scramble out the back of the bus and nobody remembers to shut the door. The emergency door-open-alert whines annoyingly. Luke grabs a fire shovel and whacks the cable that connects the circuit to the alarm, severing it.

"Sorry, safety officer!" Luke jokes when he sees Grant giving him the evil eye.

Grant can sense his new duties beginning to divide him from even his closest friends; he must enforce rules they have always found joy in breaking.

Grant tells himself that he'll fill the piss packs after dinner and hand out the whistles. But Bazooka gets him hauling garbage. It puts him into a fucking awful mood again — all this garbage, all the human refuse. He forgets to distribute the whistles.

The whole camp is pretty much asleep by the time he finishes tossing all the garbage bags full of leftover camp meals (All that mashed potato! All those pork chops, meat still clinging to the bones!), but Bazooka's light is still on so he decides to drop in and shoot the shit with the boss man. Cut-up knuckles poised to knock on Bazooka's trailer door, he hears the supervisor's voice, stressed-sounding, presumably on the satellite phone.

"What do you mean? Our ladies need pruning! No alternative?! No, listen... hold on for a second and hear me out... No! That's way too much of a heat score... this is fucking... fucked! We're screwed!"

Grant decides to retreat back to his trailer, not wanting to intrude on Bazooka's problems. He thrusts a log into his stove, grabs a tin of balm from his cabinet and greases up his knuckles. He gouges his mosquito bites with his fingernails, making Xs on the inflammation. Fucking Bazooka, he mutters to himself, the supervisor extraordinaire, and all his pot plants growing out west, his "ladies". The guy's spread a little thin.

Finally resting his head on his memory foam pillow, his thoughts get dreamy, migrating to Mexico like neurochemical bird formations, coming back resuscitated, tropicalized on waves of sleep. Remembering how he met Bazooka and Eliza and Archy down there. It was in Chiapas that he'd discovered his destiny as a tree planter, of all places. The jungle, the beaches... it all seems so far flung, like a massive emotional painting, recollected in tranquility, in Mexico, yes, in Mexico! How far away, but now dreamingly close. Not long ago he'd been laying low on the coast, recharging for another trip into the jungle where he was helping build a school for a supposedly desperate community who it turned out never really wanted the help anyway. The waves.. hmmm, the waves... the waves on the resuscitating beach breaking in deathful laps, the waterfowl swooping over the chaotic riptides, stem of the margarita glass twirling icily between Grant's fingers, books in his daybag about Mayan ruins, Popul Vu. And beach people, some nude, strutting lazily about through the snow-like sand, a Mexican man squatting with very large dick hanging from hairy coconuts — a nude beach where only the well-endowed seemed to take it all off. Grant goes back to the kayaks riding those deadly waves. Who were they? One of them had walked by Grant and he saw the tattoo of what looked like a person with a small tree in their hand. His first glimpse of planter art on Bazooka's shoulder.

Later at the beach-side bar. "Looks like fun out there on the surf... deadly as fuck though."

"It's fun indeed," the tattooed guy was saying. "It's our way of saving the fucking world. Though we wouldn't have come all this way for wave kayaking necessarily. We had other plans. Which were fucked in the ass by the politics of this place... people call me Bazooka by the way. "

"I'm referred to as Grant. How did you end up here anyways? It's the most dangerous surf around."

"Expedience, my friend, pure and simple expedience. It all went wrong, let me tell you about it." Bazooka took a sip of what looked to Grant like a Tequila Sunrise, which, when held aloft to the pearly sunset behind the wicker-style bar, made for a curious asymmetrical parallel. Archy and Eliza, among other planters, were sitting at the back of the bar with tropical drinks, healthily tanned, chillaxing after a day of cresting waves, shooting the shit. Replenished, Bazooka commenced relating to Grant what had happened on the kayaking expedition gone haywire. They'd paddled about 40 kilometres down the river, Bazooka said, when they'd become entangled in some sort of net laid across as a trap. Masked people with retro rifles emerged on both banks and demanded that the planting kayak team come ashore, where their wrists and ankles got trussed with leather rope and they were driven in rusted pickups to a shack in the middle of a farmer's field. There were more Zapatistas in the cabin, angered farmers staring them down with eyes which were serious as only desperate people's eyes can be, and, at a table in the middle of the room sat some scary-as-fuck judge kind of figure, easily recognizable as the revolutionary poster boy that he was, none other than subcommandante Marcos! Chestyle cigar in mouth, jungle-patterned camo pants. Archy felt like a normal Canadian kid would, were they kidnapped by Mario Lemieux. Extreme Stockholm syndrome. They waited for hours while the Zapatistas discussed the fate of the Canadian gringos. They were made to sit on these creaky wobbly chairs in a side room with vegetation growing through the floor boards, and they'd amused themselves throughout the long feudal trial by poking these leaves that curled up biomechanically when they were touched, sticking up from the floorboards.

They didn't know what was going to happen, but the Zapatistas seemed like kind folks to be held hostage by, offering guava juice and smoking them joints, but the little southern mosquitoes ruined everything, behaving differently than their northern blood relatives, a different toxic saliva against which the usual immunity gained from a season in the bush was totally impotent. The mosquitoes were brutal in there! It was Archy, with his passable Spanish, who'd relayed the information to the room where the other planters were forced to sit cuffed, getting chewed alive in their short sleeves, Archy saying that Marcos wanted what amounted to one thousand dollars a head for trespassing on private land, a fee unaffordable because the planting season had been short and the extra luggage fees for all the kayaks and the rentals had already sent them into line of credit issues and at the depressing thought of what might happen if they didn't pay, one of the planter hostages had taken out a little tarnished flute he kept in his pocket and began playing "Dueling Banjos" with a mopeful expression while they scratched their itches and gave each other exasperated eye rolls and headshakes. After a long, body-odour-triggering wait, involving a sardonic flute hoedown with one of the farmers who took out his own flute and played along, the situation bettered somewhat because it became apparent that Archy was almost sweet-talking subcommandante Marcos, as they could see in the middle room a smirk under the hero's mouth-cloaking kerchief, and at another point in the negotiation Archy actually put his hand on the revolutionary's shoulder and came back to the prisoner's room, telling his fellow imprisoned tree planters about the deal they could accept or not, depending on whether they wished to get out of there unscathed, that instead of paying the bail money, Marcos was prepared to let them free in exchange for some help instituting an action plan to reforest a few hectares of marginal ranchland that the Zapatistas wished to convert back into forest. So they spent a week teaching planting techniques to Zapatista farmers, ordering planting ribbon and shovels from Canadian and Finnish and Chilean companies, organizing the importation of pine saplings from a nursery in northern Mexico. Archy had seemed caught up in a sort of fervor ever since, and had offered to make a special trip to San Cristobal to get some pamphlets for Marcos and distribute them on the coast.

Bazooka, smoking some Mexican grass during his storytelling while he slurped his Sunrise between tokes, the flow of his story at some point dividing like a river hitting a delta into tangential topics, segueing into some other story about his cannabis endeavours in western BC, which may or may not have been related to the Marcos story. Archy came over looking interested, like he had lip-read something, talking about how, "Tree planting should be about knowledge and partnership and sharing and all that fun but difficult woodsy stuff… little communes in the woods… beautiful." To which Eliza, who was also up at the bar, rolled her eyes and said, "Don't listen to him… last year Archy was all about pop singers." All this chit-chatting culminated, as the various divergent rivers of the conversations and stories merged again, with the final assertion of, "Grant, you should plant with us next year!" And the margaritas, tequila-charged, made it all seem so easy… a wonderful idea, and the truth is that it was… it was just the kind of seasonal job that Grant needed to keep doing the things in life he still wanted to do.

"What's the name of the company?"

"Tamponix."

"Uhhhh-huh."

"Yeah… it's a fucked-up name. Ownership change last year. The new owner is getting sponsorship from feminine product companies."

"Okay then. I don't know how I feel about planting for a company called Tamponix."

"It's just a name. Don't read into it too much."

Later that night, the planter posse, with Grant the new inductee, de-normalized, smoking a Nicaraguan cigar offered by Bazooka, discovering the taste of leaf tobacco for the first time, checked out the black thrashing ocean, whitecaps like creamy mounds. So disturbed, green and dark in the night, so fundamental, the ocean and the forest.

"Well, looks like the kayaking's going to be an adventure again tomorrow!" Grant remembers Eliza saying with her Rolling Stones lips, horking into the surf.

Just as Grant enters full-throttle sleep in the Meso Ontario night.

"If this ocean takes me tomorrow," Bazooka had shouted over the water, "then, provided you find my corpse, cremate me in a camp fire, and scatter my ashes in a regenerating cut block…"

And Grant dreams, dreams, and what he accomplishes in his dreams is somehow responsible for the creamy block his crew gets dealt that day. As if through not prayer but a calm wishful openness that wishes good upon the giver too… there was the gift of cream bestowed. Partner planting and it's like your mind merges with your planting partner's, like you'd been tree twins from the beginning, ever the more conjoined as the contract progressed, and the first mosquitoes come out, almost like tentative lovers… you develop these "connections" with people, maybe through the mosquito-exchange of sweat and blood particles. Luke cur-plashes hunting boots through water-soaked vegetation. The higher land is tough and unforgiving, and must be taken with everyday acceptance and respect. And that's how she goes, you take the cream and the black bile in the same smoothie. Things are what they are, is what they is, and just sometimes the cream works its way through.

Plant another tree, Luke, more trees, another bag, one more tree. One more tree, one more bag up. One more day, one more shift. One more season. A patch of life awaits you under the sky, in the future, in the breezy future, saving for that future. A week of cream would be nice. The cream they were promised. The past seems like it was creamy and the future's cream too, and the moment is a fresh cherry, picked by a woman on a ladder with a basket under her arm.

To think all imagination. Dancing queen, money making, disco breaking, totally video game zen, no, just move, healthy tree, sharpen blade, this night, this night sharpen blade. So sharp blade cut earth bag up. One more tree, one more bag… pounding, pounding, real good now. Hump day tomorrow. Moving keep planting keep loving keep dreaming moonshine gorgeousness creamshow morning, creamshow dreamer, radiant, keep mind on quality trees no weak duff shots and keep 'em straight, the philosophers all have crappy quality, all airy brain, Grant planting down a corridor of golden sand, the chaos alleviated for a moment and it's like the future of his life is on his tongue but he feels so solid in his motion like Luke, assured, where is Luke? And the sun and the tree limbs and the insane sensory rush of life, is all reassuring for the future of the world and cosmos in general. Luke is over in the far shnarb — the slashy steep side of the block — while Grant is in the cream, just a cream day joyride on his own. This moment of planting appreciation. Luke will get his own. He feels connected through the invisible limbs of the tree, he can inhabit the past, it's marvelous, all that soil and growing, not mechanical, not computerized, but soily, slimy, skiing, skiing gold sand big days planting, golden sand which compliments Murielle as she works with sleeves rolled in adjacent block.

DAY OFF IN KAPUSKASING

Kapuskasing is built around a circular town square, where there's the confectionery, the coffee shop, the furniture store, the sex shop, the greasy spoon, and, just down Cain Ave, the bike repair shop with flames on the sign that all but screams Biker Gang. This historical logging town has a population of 9,500ish, and seems, maybe more than anywhere else, the embodiment of the Canadian spirit. In other words, you might say, "It doesn't get any more Canadian than Kapuskasing." At least that's what Queen Elizabeth said, on her famous visit to Kap in 1951.

The town motto, in Latin, is *Oppidum Ex Silvis*; in English, Town Out of The Forest. Kapuskasing is the Cree word for "bend in the river." At the time Liz was a princess, and Prince Philip was along for the ride. They repeated these town mottos to themselves like aristocratic sages learning a new dialect of the divine, with amused smiles, after the mayor tentatively spoke to the royal couple in an attempt to convey the soul of his most promising town. Liz replied, "Such a fitting motto, for a fine Canadian town with a wealth of future. I understand that you have forged quite an alliance with the New York Times. I hope that your prosperity continues!" The people of Kapuskasing were pleased as punch with the Queen's much-lauded visitation. It was boom time, as not only newspapers, but also the tissue paper industry, namely the ass-wipe giant Kimberly Clark, was fueled by massive truckloads of Kap pulp and print. The original Clear Water logging crew, and the Clear Water Mill, were growing, Terrorhouser not yet on the scene. The now multinational company had yet to buy out Clear Water.

Indeed, Kapuskasing is a town of royal heritage, and of ostentatious mystique. On the outskirts of the town are many fields, and in these fields are many claw-footed bath tubs. True to the region's francophone roots, poutine is the side of choice — and with a nod to the anglophone tradition, you get the choice between Quebec style made with cheese curds, or the Canadian style heaped with grated cheese.

Various shops and bars have hanging, pasted-on old saloon fronts, and odd hotel restaurants, and all sorts of people whizzing back and forth from Hearst or Val d'Or (Las Vegas of the North), folks driven by dreams of agrarian or mineral conquest, or busted dreams of industry with the eventual hope of sending kids down south (south referring to Ottawa or Toronto) — population drain. But then again, what of the mountainous area with huge waterfalls to the north-east, along Moose River and up the Abitibi way, as if transplanted from the rocky mountain west? Or the soothing family vibe, buying coffee from a 13-year-old working the cash for mom at Back to the Grind, the wooden-shingled siding of derelict houses with that particular shade of pine plank, the sense that the sky veers into the brine of refreshing green waters? This all invokes a maritime feel, as if Kap were a small Halifax without the sea. In fact, certain elements of the entire country hang together in this region.

On days off, the tree planters make ostentatious appearances in small towns. The muddy buses appear on the town's uncluttered roads, dirty post-pubescent faces staring out the kidsafe windows; drivers accustomed to logging roads suddenly contending with stop signs, blinking lights and bovine pedestrians. There is a bit of an attitude associated with this foray from the bush. Like the planters own the town. There are towns where tree planters have been banned from the motels. To the proprietor of these motels the visitation of the planting brigade is like having a whole crew of the living dead show up asking to try out the fresh linen. Corpse-like they often appear — after a few weeks they have burned so many calories their skin is so tight against their ribs and skulls they practically look like zombies. It's the ghouls' night out. Day off.

In Kap, the planters stay in a huge loggers' mansion. In big orange on white letters, it states itself: *The Kap Inn*. The upper quarters and conference rooms are barricaded off, leaving only the long single-storey motel extension out the back and the big cathedral-like front lobby in regular use. The lobby itself hints at the Inn's glory days, with marble-ish floors and big white pillars, and the walls lined with many black and white photographs of the Queen in a convertible Cadillac on her famous visit in 1951. A crumbling emblem of the old days of optimistic prosperity, the Kap Inn has now become a refuge for bush workers and highway transients.

"It's fun poking around upstairs. I went up there last year." Winger puts a guiding hand on Benito's shoulder and they sneak from behind a pillar over to the stairwell, and then slide over the table-barricade. Winger's expression seems more serious now, staring ahead into that dark tunnel. Benito is surprised that she's interested in hanging out with him like this, because she has that untouchable aura of a pounder. "That a-boy, Benito, you're a real prince. Just be quiet now. We aren't really allowed up here. Quick, while her back's turned."

The lady working at the front desk spins with surprising athleticism when she hears the first creaks on the termite-weakened stairs, and catches Winger and Benito tiptoeing up the ancient stairwell.

To their surprise, she doesn't seem to care. Instead she tells them, "If you two see that kid, then do call him by name, and tell him his mother is looking for him. Please and thank you." Then she turns around again and appears to be examining something on the wall. "His name's Joey," she continues, speaking to the wall. "He's always up there, and up there is the terrible asbestos problem. He's a disturbed and lonely child, we worry about him and the odd games he devises out of that imagination of his." Benito and Winger are disappearing up the stairs as she speaks, and they cannot hear her because of the poor acoustics.

A while later, once they've descended back down to the

front lobby, they feel strange; as though upstairs they'd entered an emptiness which was illicit to disturb, as if upstairs was no place for a human. They hadn't seen any kid, they hadn't seen much of anything. Just empty conference rooms and boxes of old memorabilia. And then there was the Queen's room, cordoned off with velour rope that had polished brass snap ends. There was nothing much inside except for a fancy quilted bed and more photos from the time of the Queen's visit. On the locked door beside the preserved Queen's room some weird word was written in graffiti.

"It felt kind of wrong being up there, don't you think?"

"Yeah, I know. It was different last year. What did it say on that door?

Xyloph — "

"Xylophloe."

They hook up with some other planters, drive a company truck to the grocery store to buy snacks. It turns out that both Benito and Winger get rung through at the same time and the cash registers ping in unison. "Oh my! oh my! – look at that, both their totals came to exactly the same number," one of the cashiers squeaks. Four dollars and twenty cents.

"Fuck: Four twenty."

"That's the same number…"

"As the room with *Xylophloe* sprayed on the door."

Grant shares a room with Gabby, Luke, and this guy named Styler, who highballed Kap last year. He put 6,000 into a moss field one day. He's a tough one to budge when he passes out.

Their belongings are strewn around the yellow shag carpet, their bodies all molasses over beds which sag in the middle from years of overload (paunchy men in pairs, three girls per bed, pillow fights and long-jumping bed to bed). The last time an interior decorator came in here was obviously some time in the seventies. Something to do with the plasticized patterns of the wood paneling on the desk and the old-fashioned tan brown Gideon in the desk drawer. As in most of the rooms, a faded print of the Queen hangs on the wall. In towns like this, material culture is reused and recycled out of necessity and habit rather than big-city eco logic; as long as an object is still in okay condition, someone or some place will find a use for it. Tomorrow they will hit what the planters refer to as Ten Cent Annie's, where there are piles of clothes for pocket change, like great old cardigans with owls knit into them. All the habiliments for the aspiring small-town hipster.

The planters have one night and one day to recuperate. First things first: showers. Gabby says, what the fuck, I'm the girl, let me go first, and Luke says, fuck off, there is no such thing as pussy power in the North. It's this ongoing joke they have, neither holds back — like if Luke is complaining about something, like having to hump bins for himself then Gabby will be like, "That's *weak* Grant, really *weak*, what are you, a *girl*?!" As if both man and woman are striving for a certain masculine ideal, sensing that this is a man's land and it doesn't matter who you are, you aren't man enough.

Luke hops in the shower, having called it on the drive from camp. Whoever's last in line for the shower has to cope with a dirt-spattered tub, the drain tangled with hair, all the white hospitality towels used up and sopping in the corner, and all the complimentary shampoo reduced to a pile of spent, scrunched packets on the edge of the tub. The old pipe system of the Inn creaks and groans behind the walls as thirty or more showers stress the boilers, the central pipes. The water changes temperature without warning, from pleasantly warm to arctic cold, then scalding. The curses come right through the walls.

They scrub. Scum and dirt funnels down the drain. But the hands never come clean in one washing, as the pores and palm lines have assimilated the dirt. Cuts have opened, then closed over, and the mud shines through from underneath the skin.

Hands feel like they have a hundred paper cuts. Grease them up with bag balm. Udder cream. Tit cream. The stuff Shania Twain uses under her eyes to prevent bags. The most famous tree planter ever, aside from Peter Bond of Ontario and Otto Frank from out West. Strikes deep into inflamed udders.

Styler has a bag of frozen peas on his swollen shin. The ice machine's now empty. Grant is complaining about numbness in his forearm. Repetitive stress from the sheer number of times they bend over (fifteen thousand times a shift sometimes), twist knees between slippery logs, hit rocks with the shovels that clang and rattle their skeletons.

They take turns showering, the lead circulatory system of the Kap Inn rattling and squeaking into the basement passageways and underground parking lot long out of use.

Walking in the basement corridors of some of these old motels, you catch glimpses of women in bright white skirts and button-up short sleeves with hairdos that look like boat wakes or beehives, standing statuesque in industrial boiler rooms full of tanks and pipes, folding the sheets and towels. Thoughtful planters leave some money on a pillow for these chambermaids, a little extra because they work extra hard cleaning the planter's filth.

Luke yodels away in the shower, and Gabby starts getting pissed off about all the dirty socks left negligently in the middle of the room. Grant tells her to not even talk about socks. Gabby spits back, "Listen, I have at one time or another sucked both your guys' cocks, and neither of you reciprocated with anything close to cunnilingus so please, just pick up the socks." Her hands on her hips glaring at them. They can do nothing but oblige her for the sound basis of her reasoning, so they collect the socks off the carpet, open the back door, which looks out onto a disintegrating asphalt alley, and lay them on the curb to detoxify, or perhaps decompose. The exposed oral truth leaves things a little socially awkward for a few moments; to Grant, it seems kind of unfair to have two discrete acts of pleasure conflated into one, as if Gabby had pleased them on the same night, which makes it sound more perverse than it actually is. Truth be told, a solid year separated those oral acts, so.

The door swings open and people come in without asking.

"Party at the Chateau tonight! Hey, Groucho is running naked around the parking lot! Look!" Luke, out from the shower, exposing his big brawn, wrapped in a white towel around his waist, hair slicked back behind ears all fresh, he runs straight out the door to check it out and Gabby jumps up and runs from the room to catch a view as well, and Grant and Styler are left in the room all silent.

They both stay where they are, lying on the sagging queen-sized beds, bodies not responding to stimulus, watching some news about war, oil prices on the rise, consumer confidence up. The images flicker distantly.

Luke tumbles back into the room. "I didn't see any nakedness out there, hell, I don't want to see nakedness out there. Hey, you know, Groucho was screaming that he wants to fight you, Grant, he was saying, 'Bring Grant here, I want a rematch from last year, I was too drunk last year.'" Luke plops down on the corner of Grant's bed, making Grant jiggle. Grant's not interested in a scrap at the present moment. He's leafing through some safety forms, stuff about emergency procedures. Skyler is still staring at the TV.

Then Gabby returns, with Winger, who is probably the most highly-respected planter in camp. She's short, with blond hair and a small head, and is seemingly as unaware of her beauty as of her planting reputation.

"So, this Winger girl is a bit psycho, I must inform you," Gabby slaps Winger on the back. "Like all of us."

Winger retreats into her quietness, bending her thin, muscular neck towards the task at hand, which is rolling a fatty. She cracks out a bag of weed and cuts up some white-haired buds with scissors. She proceeds to twist up a perfect fatty, calm and workwomanlike. She seems very grounded, with a curious smile.

Gabby continues. "Anyway, Winger, so what's that French girl like? You were planting with her yesterday, I saw you. Give Gab some goss."

"Yeah, she's really nice. There's something special about her. She's like a little nymph. I was teaching her—"

"Who?" Luke is all ears, swilling his beer. His hair is drying and starting to puff up at the back.

"That girl, what's her name, Murielle, she's so funny. I was giving her some pointers on how to plant and she was listening to everything I said, all the little tricks. She's cute. I wonder who she's going to shack up with. Wild in the sack, I bet." Winger cackles softly.

"Probably Ray. He's moving in already."

"Damn that Casanova, if only these girls knew his bush history. I think Murielle would appreciate a good guy like me. I'll treat her like a little missy, you know." Luke looks like a polished coin after that shower. Radiant.

"All Ray does is mack on chicks. His dad is V.P. of Calvin Klein and shit."

"My dad's V.P. of welfare," chimes in Luke, "not to knock the old man."

"What about you, Granters? You think that French girl's cute?"

"Nopers, not really. Too cutesy." Grant is lying — he has exchanged a few words with Murielle and she seems very interesting. In fact more than interesting. He pulls at the corner of his beer's label.

Looking up from his beer, Grant realizes everyone in the room is staring at him with mildly amused expressions, as though they could see right through his lie. Damn. Grant grabs wildly at anything else to talk about. "Hey, Gab, what do you know about that Walter guy? I went to piss last night and his trailer light was still on and it was probably three in the morning. He listens to totally fucked-up radio stations."

Gabby's eyes flicker in recognition and she takes a swill

of wine, looks over the top of the tilted bottle and holds up a wait-a-moment finger. Then she lowers the bottle, revealing mauve lips. "That guy is a freak! He stayed in camp for day off, to 'study'. I don't know what he's up to, but Spice told me that he's really weird when he comes into the cook shack, he's always sort of grim, and analytical about his food, always taking her to task about what's in it, what vitamins. The other day he was reprimanding her for never putting any citrus in the salad. Haven't you guys seen him with that little workbook of his, scribbling away, or *reading*? I mean, who reads up here? He was late getting up the other day and Eliza went to get him but he wasn't in his trailer and she looked inside and she said there were these huge stacks of papers, and shit written on the walls. Crazy, eh? We have a real psycho with us this year. I want to get to the bottom of that guy, Grant. I say we pay him a little visit."

Gabby the Gossip. Grant knows her well, has done some canoeing with her in Algonquin. He has theories about the source of her gossipy tendencies. He thinks it's an incredible drive to master the circuitry of a group, and then manipulate the strings which control the dynamics; pluck these social strings, affect the whole scene through the sheer power of conversation. From what she's told Grant of her life story, Gabby's mother's social life was for the most part insulated, with a book club on Mondays, and a knitting circle on Saturdays, both events being held once a week in their large, mostly empty house. Well, Gabby, being the precocious little lady she was (and remains, as far as Grant knows), absorbed the various gossip tactics used by this older circle of women, learned how to collect and deflect information, from whom to withhold and with whom to barter whatever juicy information the week may offer — in short, little Gabby picked up the entire underlying power politics of the community, the behind-the-scenes sort of stuff that ousts mayors, sends drug-dealing sons fleeing town, and captures infidel husbands red-handed in affairs. Just the sort of stuff that comes in handy in any tight-knit community, transient or otherwise. Grant is semi-curious to talk to Gabby about how they might come to learn some of the darker secrets of this Walter guy, because when Gabby detects a suspect aroma, something invariably turns out to be rotting at the back of the fridge.

At the mention of the weird anthropologist, Winger gets up and leaves the room saying she wants to check on something upstairs. She'd been examining the print of the Queen, running her fingers along the coarse canvas, and Grant noticed that she almost resembles someone from the royal family, with her classical and somewhat mannered attitude, but then reminds himself she's just small town Ontario. After she leaves, Gabby lets them know that Winger is cute, but trouble. It's incredible that she plants so many trees, for someone so slight, someone so seemingly shy and reticent.

Over dinner, Grant pursues the idea of snooping on the anthropologist. The Bloody Caesars bring out the Sherlock in him.

When Grant asks Gabby on what pretext they might snoop into Walter's trailer, her scheming rationale says immediately: joint. "We ask him to burn one down with us, and if he denies, then we force him through planter pressure."

Psychological Benefit of Marijuana #3: The bringing of people together. As a professional gossip, Gabby has replaced her mom's knitting circle with the joint-smoking circle. Weed gets people's tongues wagging.

Grant's first question is, "All fine and well, Gabby, but does he smoke herb?"

"Don't take me to be foolish, Grant. I wouldn't have suggested this if I hadn't noticed that he has a marijuana emblem sewn onto his weird briefcase-knapsack." Typical that a medical anthropologist would be a stoner.

Back at the Kap Inn Gab picks her nose and Luke interrupts, saying: "Is that a good pick? Looks like a great pick, I think I got something going on too, let me check..." He starts digging in his own nostril with a forefinger. Grant has his clippers out and is working away at the corner of his big toe where the flesh meets the nail, pruning the inside to avoid getting an ingrown nail like he did last season.

Everyplanter is going out to party. Everyplanter has on their snazzy day off shirts. Gabby's wearing a big turquoise belt buckle with a loon engraved on it. "Let's rock!" she hollers, raising her arms over her head. "Balls deep in Kap! Wooeee!"

Before they leave, Grant goes to the bathroom to take a shit. He sits on the toilet flipping through the Safety Manual. His eyes focus on something; they widen. Studies. Guinea pig studies. Guinea pig sperm.

Someone bangs at the bathroom door, so he slams the binder shut, wipes his ass, and heads out to party.

It is no way to treat a town, but the rudeness comes with the territory, the need to wreak havoc upon an unsuspecting village. The whole group of sixty-some planters heads out like a living dead army of partiers, eventually splitting into small phalanxes or guerilla units with individual mayhem tactics. The rookies have no respect whatsoever, running down the dark streets screaming like they were still wanking in the forests, sliding on the dewy cars at a dealership, jumping onto the hoods and slicking over them headfirst off the other side, the odd foot tearing loose a wiper. Then to the all-night coffee shop lighting cigarettes inside with no respect for the no smoking signs, getting in arguments and fisticuffs with townies who don't like being conquered by a bunch of spaced-out dirty people, buying bad drugs from locals in shady interactions, taking dumps down by the river, making out on the lawns, groping each other at four in the morning on park benches, and then somehow all coming together again back at the Kap Inn, generally not arrested, not dead, just way too poisoned by alcohol, not a good thing for bodies in such critical need of healing, collapsing in the sagging beds, hotboxing the bathrooms Jamaican shower style, having group sex (rumoured). Basically a parent's nightmare...

and then in the morning finding sobriety with muff-divers and milkshakes at Wendy's Extra Crispy Waffle House.

The next day while their laundry is cycling, Gabby and Grant go strolling by the old railway and see the crows with ragged feathers and twisted feet on slag heaps and on top of graffiti-bombed grainer cars. They stand in the wind, Gabby's hair flying off her shoulders like restless raptor wings and Grant's coat flapping against his chest as they attempt to light tobacco down their shirts. Standing like jaded characters in some old photo of the North, standing by a plaque set into a block of concrete outside the town's museum, which is pretty much just a shack by the railroad. In the window are pictures of the internment camp they had here during WWI — Turks, Ukrainians, and Germans — nearly 1,200 POWs (political aliens) were sent up to Kapuskasing. Living in a makeshift shanty town. The photos look a lot like a tree planting camp. Skinny European immigrants squatting in front of huts in the mud in the days before DEET. Forced to help work building the illustrious railway, to dig out an area in the bush for an arboretum in which to test crops that might grow in the difficult northern soil.

Grant and Gabby smoke and stare at the photos while the wind blows. The sky is moving tectonic plates of the darker spectrum. Then they head back for their laundry. Grant stuffs his load into a black garbage bag, throws it over his shoulder, and wanders off in the general direction of the beer store.

BACK INTO THE BUSH

Everyone meets in the parking lot at seven, having spent the day hanging around the traffic circle, running little errands like buying duct tape or pornography, hanging out at the laundromat. Some guys found this particularly raunchy porn mag, some independent with one section depicting an Asian girl pleasuring herself with avocados and a big carrot. Some rookies have ripped pages out and duct taped them to the side of the bus.

"This bus is now officially the tree slut bus," some planter says.

Planters try to remember the forgotten shenanigans of the night before. At The Chateau Bar, all the rookies had been driven crazy by the mad desire to shack up.

An instinct thing: when living in a harsh environment, the need to find a mate increases, a subconscious method for securing body warmth and carnal insulation against the desolation.

The knowing veterans hang back for a bit; they wait for the initial keener to boast and brag and to move too quickly in the game, their tactics too showy and put-on. After the first botched shack-up attempts, the field opens and the women take more interest in the solid veterans.

The bus now turns, describing a barge-like arc. Rain plays like finger drums on the roof. Down Highway 11 for about ten minutes, then the Swanson road disappears into the horizon of conifers. Everyplanter huddles into their jackets, fleeces, lights smokes. Take-out Chinese lifted to hungry maws with plastic forks. Beer caps popped with cigarette lighters.

Grant remembers the regional manager: "No drinking, absolutely no drinking on the buses… blah blah blah…"

Grant downs a couple, then picks up the guitar and strums from D to G, singing.

"Fill me with junk
'cause I'm a skinny junky
pack the surplus in the trunk
we're heading out of Kapuskasing
heading into the all-embracing
wonderland of the backwoods
where the lumberjacks once stood...."

The great yellow-green bus chugs through the rain. Chocolate milk mud washing up the front window and then the rain swims in diminutive tributaries and the wipers slap the mud off and it washes off the cheeks of the window, the wipers squeaking and skipping.

A caravan headed out of space and time: summer camp, this childhood glee mixed with the harsh adult world of horrendous suffering. Grant continues his crooning.

"I'm jonesing in the gloaming
give me all the calories
24 hours to recharge the batteries.
Buddha of these Canada roads
instead of lotus leaves
so many forests of waving spruce trees
growing in my footsteps...."

When the bus pulls into camp it seems eerily still, and the smell of northern grass comes through the window with the wet dew of evening, and mosquitoes hover through the open window too.

They plug the grinding wheel into the camp generator behind the cook shack. Grant and Luke sharpen the blunt shovels for anyplanter. Sparks scream into the night as they grind the edge sharp on one side, but leave the other as is.

OF WIFE BEATERS AND BLACKFLIES: DISPATCHES FROM THE BUG WAR

"They're like an army," says the anthropologist, wiping the side of his jaw. The bugs have chafed and blistered the back of his shoulder, making it look like pulverized salami. He was planting beside Murielle and Tammy, trying to impress them with his pounding ability, and it was one of those low pressure awful bug days, the days when most planters have wrapped themselves in whatever they can, and are experimenting with all the home remedies because the quantity of DEET it would take to repel the onslaught would practically melt away the skin. Someplanter's got a sheet of Bounce hanging off the back of their hard hat, and another genius idiot has a bottle of Tabasco sauce to dabble behind his ears, there's even planters smearing themselves with vegetable oil. All in vain! Eyes flick around at invisible assailants, the quantity of weed consumption getting higher and higher and higher. The pastoral scene is rendered menacing, a horror show.

"The blackflies are the infantry," the anthropologist says as he smushes the little bugs against the window with his fist while they sit in the truck waiting for Bazooka to get back from town with their care packages. "It's an army, an army trying to defeat us. They want to devour us alive. The blackflies are armoured, it's like they have flak jackets. Random yet precise. They aren't even at their worst yet. Manipulating the randomness of the wind to orchestrate their attack, following the wispy currents of carbon dioxide emitted from our lungs and veins. At first they appear harmless. Just bumbling along the hairs of your arms like toy soldiers trying their best to impersonate a ladybug: 'la-de-da, just visiting your arm-hair garden'." The anthropologist is starting to scare Benito. He seems, despite his academic credentials, to be some whack scientist who's watched lots of television science shows and read lots of sci-fi.

"Forget them for one split second and suddenly you find that they're all business, those little cunts, up on their hind feelers like murder, masticating into and through the skin."

Benito pulls his hoody over his forehead and looks out into the grey mass of bugs and confusion outside the truck window.

"T'is an orchestra, is it not! Conducted by the mosquitoes — those mozzies, to put an Australian slant, they're the cavalry, coming in a-charging and courageous as they do, their lances out and ready. Unlike the blackfly, the mozzie must have blood for the propagation of the race. The blackfly on, the other hand, just indulges in flesh when it can, as a sort of treat. The female mosquito in particular, those freaking unicorn vampires, those blood derricks… are the most Stoic, kamikaze-style of all, even-keeled no matter how extreme the environment. They perform their crimes out in the open, you see. The more obvious, the less obvious, is the mosquito's philosophy."

"I wouldn't give them so much credit, you know," says Benito like a know-it-all. "When will those damn bugs learn… they are so stupid, they walk right under our palms. They don't care if they die."

"These creatures live very close to death, indeed," Walter looks around him with the wide eyes of a hunter, scanning more bugs to slap out of existence. "They have death programmed into their operating systems. All it takes is one of the cunts to get some of your blood, you may kill a hundred others but that one that got away will breed a thousand more. Death is a diversionary tactic of this bug warfare. I studied that once… the anthropology of man-eating bugs."

"Yeah, I picked the head off of a horse fly and it was still alive. Is that kind of what you mean?" Benito is starting to come around to the metaphoric train of thought. "What would this horse fly have been? A tank?"

"Sure, they could be tanks. To be certain, this is where it gets how shall we say heavy, Benito, for we are entering the domain of double metaphors, where the vehicle becomes tenor for another vehicle simultaneously, and there is a layering of abstraction. But to the point, we are not really interested in similarities, we are interested instead in relations. Not that the deer flies are *like* tanks, but they *are to* our flesh as the tank *is to* an obstacle. Or shall we say the tank is to the horse as the a priori fly is to the smaller flies… They have adapted to the point where they are able to squirm through the fur of the black bear, the down of the owl. It's a sad day when one of those gets into your pubic hairs, let me tell you. They crawl in and clink on. They have mutated though billions of generations. The saving grace is that our technology evolves faster than biological evolution."

"What about the no-see-ums?"

"I almost forgot, the most mythical and mystical of all the man-eating bugs out here. The no-see-ums… the no-see-ums… yes, ah yes… many a night my scalp has been squirming with itches from those micro cocks. Shrouded in mystery, like what by Job kind of name is a no-see-um? Straight from the redneck encyclopedia, I tell you. But they're really like spirits, you see. They are like spirits because you cannot record them, because you will not see them right away, but you will know they are there because they kiss away at you. You know… there are bugs out here I've seen which I'd wager are in no book… oh, shit, here comes Biz. He looks mad… he's going to make us plant. Look at him. He's going to rip our assholes off. Look how the bugs stay away from him. Because the blood running through his veins is cold, cold like a witch's I say, a mage!"

BOREALITUDE

Grant's sandwiches taste real good today. He'd sat up late the night before with Murielle and she infected his heart with some sort of sprightly electricity, like her personality was a cultural defibrillator. He is still unsure if it's correct cultural grammar to call somebody from Quebec exotic. She seems more open to touch, to massage, she's always putting her arm around someone or working a knot. He'd been wearing a Canadian flag bandanna and Murielle hugged him and pulled it off sneakily behind his back. It felt good to have the flag pulled off his head like that.

Better to think about Murielle than imagining songs which drown and gurgle and turn to curds in his mind anyway; better to dream of traveling with her down some golden path out of the clear-cuts than reproducing fragments of songs that haunt him on the block; better to look forward to seeing her little duff-dusted cheeks than playing those nightmarish cerebral renditions in his mental jukebox.

But still, he cannot fully reach outside of himself — he feels as if he's got one foot in the forest, while the other foot is toeing around tentatively in this new potential relationship territory. He remembers the night before, and winces.

"Come on, come and play some cards in the mess tent!" she'd said.

"What are they playing in there, poker?"

"Oh, I don't know. I just thought it would be a fun way to get to know each other."

"Look, the mess tent is the last place for getting to know someone. The light in there is too bright."

"Oh, then there's something you don't want me to see, is there?" Murielle put a hand on his shoulder and gave it a little shake. "I can see through you, Grant."

"No... it's just that I hate poker. It's all about deception and profiting off other's losses. I don't like those things."

She looked at him quizzically. "You are cynical, you know?"

"Oh, fuck off, Murielle. You're a freak, you should know that. Look, I have to fill out some safety forms and stuff. Have fun playing poker."

Grant winces again while he leans into his c-cut and opens his hole, then sticks a tree in. You blew it, buddy, he says to himself, as he heel-closes. The thoughts soon pass though. Like weather patterns, these moods float by, temporarily complicating the perfection of the pure sky. If only they could have mood meteorologists. But it's always an unforeseen occurrence which triggers...

Unlike some planters, he finds it is easier to block unpleasant thoughts when he's planting. He prefers the exterior mysteries of animal behavior and plant life to the internal riddles of selfhood. He kicks the hole shut and stands, looking for a good place to stick his next tree. He spots it, a promising area beside a stump, where there's often good soil.

No, there's no way he's ready to hook up with Murielle, because that would mean looking inward, and also looking into the past, and those are not places he wants to go. No way. It could lead to… He plants the thought out of his mind. He keeps planting along into a new moodscape.

It's beautiful, despite the first blackflies swirling in a disorganized group around his knees, transparent, and not really biting, but still awakened and interested. Grant looks up as a plane zooms through the fat sky from the southwest, cutting a diagonal across the radiance of the big blue, this micro-dot plane tracing a corpulent contrail, and Grant imagines all the people in their padded seats with their cabin service orange juice, going to the other side of the globe, or merely flying home, and he's hit by the sense of a great slab of sheer distance, so much sky out here, especially on this open hill, and the small twigs secured to the earth around his boots, shrine of fallen trees silvered on one side and shadowed on the other, how those precise formations of wind-thatched twigs are anchored in this unwitnessed location while everything rotates and streams overhead, how this little place is somehow beyond experience — at least beyond mass experience — this scree, this moraine — soon to be lost once again to the swarm of regrowth.

Grant's fondest memories are filled with trees.

Sitting on a random stoop in the shady part of the city when they had a day off in Montreal, that summer when they planted in Quebec, that summer when they were drinking *Le Cochon Rouge*. Trees are the staple of that memory; there was the crown of a huge sycamore hanging over the houses outside their friend Patrick's apartment building, where they were conversing about vagaries in the warm night. One of those trees which is like a permanent exploded firework over a good portion of the street. It would flare up through spring, summer, autumn. Then in winter, the bare branches would resemble an ash aftereffect. Huge tendril flowers plummeted everywhere on the ground, thudding gently on car roofs. The sheaths looked like the shells of grasshoppers, long resinous buds hanging out of them. There were miniature yellow flowers clustered on the dense catkins hanging out of the insectile shells. They laughed at this obvious display of fecundity, and swilled their wine all the more vigorously, cheering on nature. They tied the catkins into chains and wrapped them around their heads and ears like they were the anointed ones. That was a good night. The environment made sense, things were speaking the same language. For some reason he really wants to describe that night to Murielle.

Somehow if you thought your way into the city deep enough you'd come back to the bush, as if it all led back here so naturally.

Those trees that sway against the bright lights of the city. The city that is high on lights and tracers.

A mouse darts out from underneath the fall of his shovel.

One tree at a time. Careful not to decapitate mice.

RIP OFF

The regional manager visits camp that night. A weaseling small man who has spent a long time in the company and it shows. You can tell he has ideas. At least he makes an attempt to relate to the planters and management in buddy-buddy mode, but he still comes off invariably sounding fake and untrustworthy.

After dinner Bazooka introduces this man as "my boss", and then the regional manager starts talking to the camp with a dour, apologetic countenance. He starts off by informing everyone that he is happy with how the contract is going so far. He says that Terrorhouser and Clear Water are really solid, loyal clients and he wants to keep it that way. But that the tree price for the second half of the contract has been lowered as a consequence of certain changes in the payment regime. The rumours are true. He raises his hands the same way insurance brokers do to fend off hostility. His small lips move quickly as he explains that the change in tree price will not make a huge difference in planters' pay — it's only one cent after all, eight cents down from nine, and after all, the tree price on the Kap contract was historically Tamponix's highest, so that in effect this change will make wages fair and equal throughout the company. They're downsizing everything, including the budget for reforestation initiatives, because of the softwood lumber dispute and a downturn in the housing market.

At the mention of the lowered tree price the whole mess tent erupts into angry murmurs. The regional manager is drowned out (by such shouts as, "Hey, that's 30 bucks a day, for 40 days. I'm going to lose like 1,000 bucks. I have to pay my frigging school loans, fuck!") and he leaves the tent, letting Bazooka take over. Bazooka addresses the bear issue. This gets everyone interested. The bear threats are always a good diversionary tactic.

"There are many of them," explains Bazooka, raising his hands to hush the worried masses. He looks faint and doesn't even comment on the lowered tree price. The regional manager has come back in and is looking on approvingly.

"There is one bear in particular. Spice hid in the cook shack most of the day because of it. It wasn't listening to reason. It is a serious alpha bear and we don't want any trouble with it. We are looking into getting it relocated, and for the remainder of this contract there is to be absolutely no food in the tents. I mean, these bears aren't dangerous, you hear of the odd incident, but most are funny stories like someone waking up and finding a bear curled up outside their tent."

The regional manager opens his eyes wide and steps forward woodenly, raising a palm. "Bazooka is absolutely right, like I'm not saying go up and pet these bears, but in reality they are about as dangerous as stuffed animals."

"We want cream!"

"Did I hear cream?" The regional manager cups his hand to his ear. "I say… Bazooka would know better than I would about your cream… there's some cream in these kid's future, isn't there?" He puts the spotlight on Bazooka.

Bazooka looks at the ground. "Like usual. We have some creamy blocks for you guys." You can tell he wants to say something else too, but the regional manager takes over again.

The MNR guys come in with a green metal bear trap and back it up behind the mess tent, and Bazooka baits it up with molasses and bread.

Then Bazooka and the regional manager take off into town.

"He looks pissed," comments Gabby. She squints her eyes a bit. There is something up with Bazooka, besides bears.

Some planters stand around, others sit on an open tailgate, discussing the lowered tree price after the meeting.

"We gotta do something about this. I thought they were supposed to raise the tree price, not lower it."

"Talk to the union."

"Pass me the joint."

"Here. The union can't do shit. We're only part of it in theory, see, to get the full benefit you have to be a member for three months. It's there to benefit the loggers and mill workers, not the tree planters."

DAY 2, SHIFT 5

Luke is partner planting with Grant again. Larry comes into their piece to have a word with them.

Larry informs them in hushed, serious tones, that he'd gone to check up on Benito the Rookie, and discovered him just standing in the middle of a clearing, staring at the ground. It looked like he was bawling. Larry had run up beside him and Benito had started sobbing and sunk down into his equipment, explaining between paroxysms that he just couldn't take being so alone out here in the clear-cut. His mother had passed away from lung cancer two months ago. "He kept repeating, 'I can't. I can't. I just don't think I can do this. I knew I wouldn't be able to do this.'"

"But I told him, like I tell everyone, that if you stick with planting you'll be better off for it. I recommended he stick it out at least one more week. One day at a time."

Luke scrambles onto his feet and says. "Shit, I'd better get over to Benito's piece and plant the rest of the day with him. Sounds like the kid needs some company."

Day 3 the shitty weather picks up where it left off. Grant gets a knock on his trailer door and it's Murielle with water dripping from her nose. "My tent is leaking," she says. "Tammy is sleeping in Spice's tent, can I sleep here?"

She drags her sleeping mat into his trailer and they lie quietly staring into the darkness.

"How's Benito?"

"He put in 3,000 today. His personal best. He must have been planting to honour his mother, or something. Or planting to forget."

They wake up.

Pounding trees in the rain, working in tough unscarified crap land. The crotches of stumps fill up with water. The green becomes greener. Mushrooms smile. The kaka dumps from previous days shine again like they were freshly pinched. The trucks get auto-washed by acid rain. Boots slip on naked logs. Bag out fast. Ache in the joints. Premature arthritis.

The day ends as quickly as it began.

The bus is the hottest thing going. The bus is the *hot set up*. Always the delay before venturing off the bus into the cold camp.

Everyplanter just sits and groans, not wanting to leave the warm bus. Then the dash towards tents to make sure they survived the heavy downpour. Everyplanter is anxious to observe the damage. Winds have really picked up.

Pond-sized puddles have risen anywhere the ground is low, and at the base of the shale piles where the packed clay is too dense to absorb any water. Anyone who pitched their tent on the hard clay is fucked — their half-collapsed lodgings sag into the puddles, and planters just stare in disbelief, unsure how to cope with the muddy puddles that have devoured their meager shelters. The diagonal rain plasters their faces. The trees, the lines of things — crooked, warped.

Grant, too, has looked out the bus window and seen something very disturbing. Where his trailer had been it is no longer. His trailer, it seems, took a nasty spill. There are planters standing near the base of the ridge where his trailer used to be. Luke is there, squatting solemnly, huffing and aheming, and looking from the pebbles at his feet and then down the escarpment. He looks up and makes eye contact with Grant, then looks back down.

Grant observes, serenely, sniffing a couple times out of his snuffly nose. He looks at the indent his trailer made as it careened nastily down the rock-studded hill. It must have been a thunderous sight. His eyes follow that wake down to a clump of rocks in the middle of the slope which are stained with white paint chips, and covered in broken glass and part of his window frame. There are more planters standing around down at the bottom of the hill. There is the trailer on its side, windows shattered, door hanging open, turned to garbage by the storm.

He stumbles down the track that his trailer made. There are many objects strewn around that appear to be made of cloth. Socks. Loose socks, scattered around the rocks in the mud. He jumps and slides to the bottom of the escarpment. Lasers of rain zap through that open door. His bed hangs into the mud. He hears somebody consoling him.

He looks back up the hill. The anthropologist's trailer sits up there, undisturbed, and there is Walter himself staring down at him, his eyes wide, hollow, shadowed from this perspective like black holes.

SLEEPING IN THE FOOD CACHE

"So, was there much of it broken? I mean, will you be able to fix it?"

Tammy and Murielle are huddled in the same sleeping bag, peering over at Grant who's nestled in a damp down bag that Larry lent him, staring comatosely at the ceiling. A kerosene lamp sits on the floor between them, lighting up the damp interior with its warm light. The generators have long since gassed out. In response to the question, Grant turns his back to them and curls up in a fetal position. He mutters something. He has had it. He's through; he is imagining a different life, a new life. He wants to tell them that they should quit while they're still ahead, it ain't too late to find a different summer job. Save your souls, save your souls now!

It smells like vegetables in here. Shadows of food crates, the apples stacked over the brim shadowed on the wall like a heap of stones. Smells like celery, beets, moldering prunes. A bag of rice serves as his pillow, redolent of the produce section of a grocery store. He hears Tammy and Murielle whispering, and he turns over and says to them, "This is brutal!"

Tammy and Murielle had tried to set up a 40 by 30 tarp spanning both their tents after their leakage issues, but the edge of the tarp was insufficiently extended, so when it began raining the tarp turned into a gutter, channeling the rainwater, forming a substantial puddle which quickly permeated their tents. Murielle had forgotten to zip one of her windows, and the rain had done its damage through there as well.

So they made trips transporting all the wet stuff to the dry tent. But the jet heater is busted. Bazooka was out there for a while with Sil, trying to get it firing again, but no word yet about success.

Grant doesn't say anything, he shows no pity, he just lies there, back turned.

"Grant, have a little cup of our tea."

He turns around and Murielle says *"voila"* and hands him a mug of something steamy. Grant raises himself on one elbow, and takes a little sniff, and his nostrils open up to an overwhelming lemon scent. He takes it from her. Their fingers meet on the enamel handle. Her fingers are warm from the hot mug. The tea tastes great. One sip can't help but lead to another.

Murielle's complexion exudes a rosy excitement, like she was having an awesome adventure, like this mishap was part of a big string of unforeseen occurrences of some cinematic adventure. Grant smiles as he blows on his tea.

The drink has a soporific quality. As he floats into sleepy blankness he turns on his side and observes Tammy and Murielle and again smiles a little. They're whispering to each other in the little blanket folds of this off-and-away adventure. "I'm the one who should be in a position to cope with this situation," he thinks, "accustomed to punishment as I am." He knows there is an end — how great it feels to saunter into the horizon at the end of a contract. But Tammy and Murielle, perhaps most of all Tammy, are like kids watching their mom disappear down the hall at playschool for what seems like forever, the mother being their final sight before they get swallowed up by the forest. They have no intimation of an end. They think they will always feel the way they feel this very moment — excited in the thick of the new challenge of experience. How wrong they are. The contract has only just begun. Soon they will want to escape, but they will be unable to escape. Part of them will forever be a prisoner of the land. Grant observes them drifting off to sleep. "Hey," he whispers. Murielle opens her eyes and raises her head. "Thanks again for the tea," Grant smiles for the first time in awhile. She looks at him groggily, and then her head slumps down on her pillow which is simply a pillowcase stuffed with her soft hoody and sweat pants, her only vestments still dry enough to use as cushioning.

Grant dreams that night. Grant dreams deeply of making a fist and driving it forward. He dreams that his father and mother are bathing in a bottle of purified water. He dreams of his fist, of his fist clenched, striking out at somebody or somewhere. *Fuck this world of endless loops and holes. Of the guilt you feel just from breathing...* He hits someone he loves. She screams. Sirens. An open road.

Morning. Murielle beside him again. "*Tiens,*" she says, "I can't believe you slept on that, you silly." Grant lies on a food skid. His neck is killing him. He sits up. "It's late, the buses are leaving in ten minutes, we wondered where you were. Let me see your neck." Grant lowers his head and Murielle places her boney fingers onto the rigid brontosaurus bones there. She keeps one hand on the back of his neck and places her palm against his forehead and applies the most amazing pressure. She hands him his jacket; he is too tired to figure out where she retrieved it from. "It's going to be wet and cold. He sits up and hears the rain rapping furtively on the roof of the cook shack.

Soon he is stumbling from the food trailer over to the mess tent, slipping on the clay, the clay piling up on his boots.

All these hands and mouths, all these motions of me, me, me. The table is surrounded by grumpy, half-asleep planters grabbing selfishly at sandwich toppings, the last little shavings of smoked meat and pastrami filched by cranky early morning planters. The peanut butter knife has been lazily tossed into the jelly tub, leaving unsightly clots of peanut residue in the fruit. Grant barges into the melee. He just forces his way to the front, brutally pushing Benito the Rookie aside with a forearm, grabbing big chunks of lunch treat — crusty chocolate chip cookie cake cemented in a baking tray — dumping it all into a plastic milk bag while Benito looks on bewildered and upset, but Grant doesn't give a fuck. He slathers some crappy tofu spread onto white bread. He glares at someone who is taking their sweet time with the hardboiled eggs.

Maybe time to slurp down a sausage.

These people are all merely obstacles to him. All these *tools* — these rookies and lowballers — he knows they enjoy seeing this fallen Goliath with his busted trailer.

He exits the mess tent chewing on eggs, spitting shells and slurping the coffee. He deserves it; he is entitled to a bigger piece of the pie. That is, after all, the way things work out here, the segmentation of piece work. One's pay should, in his opinion, be directly proportionate with the number of trees he plants — the better you plant, the more money you earn, the more sex you get, and the more lunch treats you are allowed to pack away each morning — this is how it ought to work, and this is how it usually does work, like even the coolest guy from the city, somebody who is used to being Mister Popular, well he isn't necessarily going to be the shit out here. He might also be a tool.

Grant goes to fill up his water bottle, but there are too many planters crowding around the big blue jugs. The pump appears to be broken. Luke is dealing with the situation, orally siphoning the water through a black plastic tube. He's got the tube in his mouth and he's sucking. The pressure bursts and the end of the hose pops from Luke's mouth and water spills around. He grabs the end and directs it into someone's jug. Grant decides to just steal water from other people today, fuck it. The warm Murielle moment passes like a quickly dissolving Life Saver on the tongue. Gone.

As he strides towards the bus he remembers he forgot to audit for first aid kits, but who cares about that now that the trailer thing happened. There's his trailer, off to the side — all lonesome, muddy and bashed in — where they dragged it with a tow rope. And there is Murielle in the window of the bus looking down at him all singsong. He feels a deep annoyance with her chipperness, giggling in the way she does, and he regrets that tea she gave him, he regrets having believed for a moment in that tea when in the end it did nothing for him. When she beckons him to sit next to her, he ignores her and proceeds to the back of the bus.

Even with the heaters cranked it's shiveringly cold. Nobody wants to go back into the bush. They have the heightened sense of immediacy akin to that experienced by a group being led to the executioner.

Tomorrow will arrive, one way or another. The humiliation of staying at camp, sick, is the undesirable alternative. So you hold on to those last moments, the bus ride to the block.

THE WOMAN OF THE WOODS

And some god heard
the girl confess her guilt: her final plea
was answered. As she spoke, the earth enclosed
her legs; roots slanted outward from her toes;
supported by those roots, a tall trunk rose.
Her bones became tough wood...
Her blood was turned to sap;
her arms became long boughs; her fingers, twigs;
her skin was now dark bark. And as it grew,
the tree had soon enveloped her full womb;
then it submerged her breasts...
— Ovid, *Metamorphoses*, Book 10: Myrrh

Later that day, Grant is alone, standing at her green toes, the long rustling grass: this part of the piece is called "the foot". Down the hill, past the foot, a residual group of poplar reaches to the ozone heavens at the "midriff", and Grant can make out from this distance a skin-toned grass mat forming a belt like a soft belly. Then, at the back, through alleyways of scarified land, the kind cedar with matted perfumed hair, and these watery "arms" stretch to staggered "fingers", "fists", drawn by the skidders that gnash through the brush. This is the etymology of the cut; the loggers have created the negative of a woman. There she lies sprawled over a series of hills and gullies. He must fill her in. He has already planted a line of trees from her toe to her breast, to her clenched fists.

Mosquitoes hum around his ears and shoulders, and he can practically hear them multiplying in the wet fronds and boughs and droopy grasses.

It is imperative that they close their pieces in Block C today. To avoid massive clusterfucks which suck sweaty balls because too many planters on one piece makes for a sloppy, poorly executed job. Too much dead walking.

As he works quickly, too quickly, through some particularly tall ferns, he slips on a concealed log and bails through more brush, thrusting his legs to right himself, but falling anyway headlong into moss and more soft stumps. He lies in the ferns, listening to mosquitoes hover in the green. He wipes cobwebs from his face, and thinks: *I am performing a function about as dignified as plunging a toilet.*

Yet peace, levity. There is a strange lightness to his being. Over the days of wetness and sunniness the land greens around him. Like staring at the minute hand until you can see it moving slowly between the big numbers on the clock face, the green will rise toward the sky and subsume the land's contours, her hips, her face, her neck.

Rain is coming down hard and warm on his face. He plants back to the breast, where there is a creek. He pauses there, and looks at the bank, and gasps. There is what appears to be a woman's face imprinted where the bank has sloughed off.

He remembers striking out, lashing out and then bashing open the screen door, running out into wet streets of black concrete. He remembers the feeling of striking something so beautiful, something that he loved. And the repercussions.

And then one day (as if time could shuttlecock in fisher rackets — as if somehow he skipped days or seasons) on dry, high land with the strong wind and sun at the end of a sweaty day down the dusty road, walking down this path using his speed spade like a walking stick, he's struck by that peculiar feeling of being unable to pinpoint exactly what season it is, as though he'd always been out here. He passes Biz and Groucho and Bazooka who are working in a ditch, trying to make a corduroy bridge so they can get the quads across a stream that courses through, but they don't have enough cable to lash the logs together into the desired pattern so they have decided to fuck it, environmental standards be damned, and Grant curses them and himself under his breath and passes on down the road, uncertain as to his direction. The yarrow and dry grasses wrap his boots in their fibres, flowers awaken and the sun turns and he is a shadow around a bend, and he keeps walking around those bends, dusty sand cascading behind the scuffing of his boots, and all these abstract aromas awaken under some imperceptible veil of climate, cast away by the warm spring winds. Walking around more bends and empty bins wondering where Everyplanter has disappeared to, the scenery seeming to repeat itself, that same mossy moose skull and the brittle skeleton of that tree with those stencil leaves clinging tenuously to their stalks in the breeze, emerald distances of leaves, leaves deep and aflutter. If he continued stumbling along he would reach some water rushing through a deactivation and he would keep coming back to that petite river — this stone, this rock, this sky, this skull: beautiful repetition.

The next few days go by in a whirlwind of trees. Putting saplings into the ground and sleeping in the food trailer, and eating, and slamming more trees in the ground. Planting through the disaster.

The circumstances surrounding the demise of his trailer remain ghostly. But he has no obvious enemies; his life is not so black and white. Unless luck is his enemy. His past creeps back through the fissures in this new landscape.

He disappears into the gloomy cold night, leaving the late-night crowd tossing their cards around in the mess tent. Laughter and rye. Stanchion light glares through points of rain that are lit up like snow in a flash, and under his skin he gets the feeling of liquid daggers seeping to the bone, his toes squelching inside wet boots that he hasn't bothered removing — slouching through the dark wet centre of camp. He ruffles the collar of the lumber jacket he borrowed from Luke, part of the gracious pity offerings that his co-workers have donated. He walks up the escarpment, panting like he could perspire through his tongue like a dog, wishing he had a flashlight because his tired steps seem to be hitting all the stones. Walter the anthropologist's light is on. Grant walks quietly by the trailer, the shortwave radio tuned to that nature channel. Grant pauses for a trifle to listen, and, yes, now he can hear it: something about a species of bird in Africa. *These birds, once the symbiotic friend of the wildebeest, entrusted to eat parasites off its back, have here turned on their friend in his time of weakness during the drought, and are pecking away at his flesh.*

What sort of disgusting shit is that? Grant wonders, as he stands in the dark beside the trailer. What the fuck is that freak doing in there anyway, with his notes? The thought of actually going in there all sleuth-like with Gabby as they planned is not so appealing. What does Gabby have up her snoopy little sleeve? He walks to the edge of the ravine and looks down at the place where his trailer fell. He can just barely make out where his trailer used to be, like a vestige of his former self. He compares the distance to the slope edge with that of the anthropologist's trailer, wondering why the anthropologist's stayed where it was when Grant's crashed downward? Luck of the draw, he supposes — that certain fault line.

The door of Walter's trailer is open, and there is Walter, in the shadow, his light now dim, nothing fully visible. He observes Grant.

"Out for a late night stroll, are we?" inquires the anthropologist.

"Just up here checking things out."

"Well, all right, then. Oh, Grant. I am so sorry about your trailer. I was in here when it happened. Such a sickening crash. What a mess. What a shame."

Grant stares back at him incredulously. The anthropologist is growing out his beard. He looks more ragged and much skinnier than he did in their first fresh encounter.

"Listen, Grant, it says on the information board that the pods are treated with the least harmful of the fungicides and pesticides, yet... what should we make of that? That is what I am asking you, Grant. As safety officer. I know you had that personal mishap and for that I offer you my far-reaching apologies, but really, what about those chemicals? You know you are legally bound, Grant. You are implicated in the ethical conduct of Tamponix Reforestation. And what is Tamponix reforestation if not a breeding ground for ghosts and ghouls. Ha!"

THAT NIGHT GRANT DREAMS OF THE NEMATODE WORM

Murielle asked him if he wanted to sleep in her finally dried-out tent but he just grunted no. Instead, Grant heads back to the food cache to sleep, setting his head on a sack of rice and dreaming of the world of fungus. There is a constant battle underground. The core of these fungi is for the most part subterranean, a large area of filaments that soak nutrients. Little filament lassoes snare the nematode worms that wriggle by. He imagines little worms swimming by but they look more like sperm and then these little micronooses are lowered around their heads and then all the sperm are hanging from the gallows.

The next morning, there is a commotion around the bear trap. A bear fell for the lure of molasses and bread. The green metal cage rocks back and forth from the brute force being exercised inside. Claws click like forks in a pan. Larry, up close and peering at the bear's silhouette in the iron grille, estimates that it is a four-hundred plus. It swipes at the metal cage with its claws, leaving four dented lines. The whole cage bucks around, as if it could burst at any moment. Planters want pictures and they move in really close.

Grant tries to yell up the hill, to order them stand back, but nobody hears him, so he just ducks into the cook shack to grab some grub, not wanting to deal with the situation. The further civilization pushes into the wild, the more humans must accommodate the presence of wild things. Some people will learn the hard way.

That night, the new food load is trucked in so Grant is kicked out of the food trailer. It's like he is a hermit crab who has lost his shell and is searching for another. His arm is tingling all over. He squishes his toes around, slinks over to Murielle's tent.

She kisses him once on each cheek as if they were in Quebec. She has her halogen head lamp on, helps him tear off his wet clothes so he can crawl in with her. Her hands on his bare back make him yelp and smile a bit, and she calls him silly.

He opens the binder and shows her the guinea pig studies. After talking to Walter last night he had finally gotten around to reading the studies in the safety manuals, an found some startling facts about the emasculating effects of certain chemicals used on the trees. How, in some lab trials the sperm count was lowered, and led to a decrease in male zygote production. The edges of the papers are soggy. *"C'est sérieux, ça."* She leafs through the sheets. She takes a quick look at the studies. Then she steers his gaze with uneasy eyes.

"What is really the problem, *monsieur* Grant? Don't be so silly. Every time I see you, your eyes are full of questions."

He lies in the ethereal blue of her tent. The air thick with the fumes of a forest's worth of plants. He wants to tell her how he has been seeing paths that were not paths, evidence of previous passage. How women's hands hung from the natural images of the bush and that bush chickens hopped through the underbrush with their keen orange eyes, and how he saw a swamp donkey move like an oak snag through the back brush, and the bugs were starting to fucker him, and he wanted to go home but his mom and dad were hung up in the bottled water business and they flipped along the shores of primordial oceans like half-fishes in the slime of beaches, and the sun smudged up dense ferns and such, and he had fucked-up dreams of bus rides from hell, boy is the bush getting to me, Murielle, that's what he wants to say. He looks at her and opens his mouth, except nothing comes out.

There is a chart open on her sleeping bag, which distracts him. "What is this, Murielle?"

"It is to record my womb. To record my love temperature. Tomorrow I will no longer be ovulating. We can be lovers tomorrow night."

Tears ball up, then spill from Grant's face. They splash onto Murielle's little arms.

"I hit her. I hit the only girl I ever loved. I punched her out. I hated her. I hated how happy she made me. I fucking smacked her and I left and I haven't gone back."

The bus grinds to a halt, heater cranked. There were leaves and fronds batting the windows and everybody had to duck but that's over now. Bosso clicks the gears around and they screech like coyotes. Then you can tell he is standing, don't ask how you can tell his darkness from the rest, it's just obvious that he's looming up at the end of the aisle surveying us. This whole time the feeling that you wanted to get up and do something about this, but it was like one of those waking dreams where you have no control over your body, you just can't quite crawl out of your rib cage, your brain sending useless signals and your body not the least bit responsive. This one guy who is sick to his stomach whispers that when he was a kid there was someone who used to stand by his bed staring at him and he thinks it was Bosso. Bosso's voice sounds distant like it were issuing from a far-away room but you know it is right there. I have a great surprise for you, I have a surprise that will blow your minds. We are finally here. He pulls the long metal handle, swings open the side door and we hear him step out. We can see this big ripe moon hanging and the rest is darkness, except for a tree batting around in that moon. And now we can hear him talking to somebody outside, but the words are just dead and meaningless. One of us is sniveling and there is the sound of puking, someone is vomiting, maybe from fear, and it seems it is the kid who was sitting all alone during the hacky sack game. Then Bosso is back at the end of the aisle and we cannot help but stare at him now in a new vague light. He has an Aphex Twin smile on his lips, lit by radioactive orange moonlight, and he's holding a shotgun, moving the gaping hole from one planter to another. All right you pathetic fucks, it's confession time, he snarls. A red light blasts up his cheeks and he begins walking up the aisle looking at us one by one, holding the shotgun to our faces, looking for the right one to kick off the confessional. He stops about halfway down the aisle and stares at the floor and says whose puke is that? And then he repeats it a second time, low volume, and then again and again, louder, he is saying whoever's puke that is get up to the front of the bus and it is obvious he knows exactly whose puke it is because he's staring right at the kid who has his head down and is just sniveling away.

FILL PLANT

When conditions are extreme, plant neutral. When conditions are neutral, plant extreme.
— Sir Winston Churchill on tree planting

Larry's crew is gang planting this big block with large stock, filling in the spots where the previous crops failed, spacing off of pre-existing trees. The planters, moving in a disorganized line, look like grazing cattle, and Larry is like the cowboy, jumping up on stumps and herding them along. It's getting to that point of the contract when things are dirty, difficult, less about the good times, and more about the race for the money. For some reason this year the good times never really happened.

They're doing their thing when a Terrorhouser truck pulls up and some of the techs get out and come into their land with poles and various electronic devices to examine what's going on.

"What are you doing?" asks Benito, annoyed because he's just starting to find some rhythm, and these officials are now directly in his way.

"We're checking on the work of Doug Colt. We do have reason, based on previous assessment. Even the checkers must be checked."

"Well, I'd love to stop and chat, but…"

"We understand, you must continue to fulfill the silviculture prescription obligations of the Ministry. We are from the tree improvement board. We are interested in the failure of the last crop of scions. While cross-pollinating certain genotypes we discovered that the progenies went into dormancy. Our express purpose today is research relating to selection, hybridization, and vegetative propagation leading to healthier form and vigour for generation Z."

But Benito has just kept planting along, away, away…. He's getting better and better at this. He's thinking about how great it will to get home and pig out on food and play vids for a month straight.

He set his alarm ten minutes early so he'd have some time to prepare for what he hopes will be his first big day. Some creamy land, finally. He's gunning for 3,000, the rookie milestone that nobody else has hit so far this season.

Benito pokes his head out of his tent, his morning-fat eyes scanning the camp. He startles a raven or crow or whatever the hell it is and it spasms off a spruce bough into the sky, flapping madly. The trickster, Benito yawns. The old trickster, just like Larry taught him. Not going to trick me today. He yawns again and watches the gentle pit-pat of rain on the surface of mud puddles and surmises that today will be warmer than yesterday, when the vile conditions had forced the camp to quit early because of symptoms of hypothermia. *All I'm going to need today is a fleece*, Benito the Rookie tells himself. After all, he's heard from the hardcore veterans that the only article of outdoor wear you really need for cold 'n shitty days is the plastic fluff because it's a wicked water repellent. That no matter how ballshrinkingly frigid the rain gets, the fleece will buffer the vital areas. That when the rain passes, fleece dries quick. Benito decides to leave his warmer gear such as his jacket, his toque, his gloves, his rain pants, his sweater, even his gaiters, where they are — stuffed in the corner of the tent with the sunscreen and the wet empty packs of smokes and condom wrappers beside his therma rest. His focus brings out every little detail... the blood stains of the mosquitoes squished on the tent's transparent yellow walls, dirty wet socks that are still moist from day one and here he is at day seven of a marathon shift... it all seems so familiar now. He pulls his navy blue fleece over top of his ratty T-shirt, and he figures, yup, I'm ready to pound.

But before exiting his tent, he takes a puff off his glass one-hitter that he bought on his "high" school graduation trip to Puerto Rico a year ago — he'd lent the pipe to his foreman and finally got it back last night. It's clogged with resin, so he has to puff hard to get the smoke through. Then he jumps out of his tent into the easy rain and heads to the mess tent with his head down and coffee mug in hand. Nothing quite like a little wake 'n bake to start the planting day right.

He's eager to get out to the block and start slamming. His planting bags are already stuffed with trees from the day before, tucked neatly under the Silvicool tarp; his boundaries are flagged impeccably, and he's already planted a couple lines. He's set up. Plenty of exposed mineral soil. The veterans who walked by his piece yesterday told him that it was creamy. There is a lot expected of him because he has "showed promise".

The rain splatters the mud-greased front windows, slopped away with a slaphappy squeak of wipers. The soggy clear-cuts roll by like empty Tim Horton's cups. Benito looks up every once in a while from duct-taping his tree hand and watches the rain and landscape through the side windows. The bus is silent inside except for the muffled engine noise. Everyplanter's boots are still soaked from the day before. Benito visualizes the day that lies before him in all its glory. Ah, the rain: turning the hard land soft and the soft land downright creamy. The Cinderella story of duff transformed to soil for a day.

By the end of the day the wretched face of it will be begging for mercy, and he'll give it one more jab with his two-piece shovel and then swagger away with his first 240-dollar day and the number 3,000 on the tip of his tongue.

He saddles up and waddles into that land with full bags slapping his ass. He starts whaling away at seven-foot intervals before anyone else has even entered their land. He warms up fast and is on record pace, glory flashing through his mind. He is possessed by fantasies of record rookie numbers. He has three bins planted by eleven o'clock! He's producing far beyond his wildest dreams. He actually feels like a pounder. He will be able to rub shoulders with Winger and Groucho and Grant, and they will pat him on the back and accept him as hardcore.

He doesn't have time to even check his stopwatch what with all the pounding he's doing, and he doesn't notice much except that the wind is picking up and the rain has lapsed. Snot pours down his chin as he pounds. He just keeps pounding away, stopping once to piss, but it doesn't come out fast enough, so he holds it in and keeps planting.

He tries the little bodily manoeuvres he learned from the veterans, such as the farmer's blow — blocking one nostril and blowing the snot out through the other. He wants to try the flying dump, where you pull your pants down and support yourself with your shovel and let loose the shit and then pull up your drawers and keep pounding, maybe wiping with a little sphagnum moss. But he doesn't have to shit.

All morning long his hummus sandwich doesn't even tempt him, because he's so horny for the big money. He's running on adrenaline. He's going to highball, he can feel it. Bragging rights, one hundred percent. Every once in a while he looks over toward the road to see if any passing planter is admiring his speed. But all he sees are another couple ravens or crows or whatever they are, circling around above the slash piles by his cache. *Fucking birds*, he thinks.

Around eleven-thirty the winds grow feistier, become chaotically powerful. He feels the chill cut through his fleece. The temperature must have dropped since the rain stopped. He works all that much harder to warm up. Sweat forms on the tip of his nose, plunks. His nose starts leaking like a faucet. He gets warm again.

After bagging out the first half of his fourth bin, he decides it's time for a little fuel; he will take the time for a hummus sandwich. He stomps out to the road and removes his bags. He grabs his knapsack and notices that it is open, and one of his lunch containers is sitting beside it. He picks it up and is surprised to see a hole in it. He looks around the trees. Fucking crows or ravens or whatever they are. Undid the snaps of his bag, poked holes in his sandwich container. All he has left is his hummus sandwich. He takes it and sits down on an overturned bin. He unwraps and bites into his sandwich. The sandwich is soggy and tastes like raven or crow piss.

Eating the piss-soggy sandwich, that's when his body temperature plummets. He notices steam wafting off his wet pants. He touches his shovel hand and is unable to feel it. He bites his two duct-taped fingers; he even licks his knuckles to see if he can feel that. He licks his knuckles some more, but cannot feel them at all. Suddenly his body is wracked with a horrible, crippling chill. He pulls up a flap of the Silvicool which covers the bins at his cache, thinking he can get away from the wind, but the tarp is too skimpy and ripped to provide any warmth.

His whole body and mind have slowed right down. His fleece feels like a soggy skin. He starts limping up the road, looking for the bus, and walks under his raven/crow friends. A piece of crust falls from the sky and bounces off his head. He doesn't even look up. His whole body feels strange and numb. He slips all over the place with clunky clay boots. The sky looks like a slab of ice. He hasn't seen Larry all day. He saw Tammy earlier, but way earlier and way in the distance like she was finishing off her piece and was going to move to the next block. Benito has the bone-chilling thought that perhaps Larry took off on him. What if they all high-tailed it back to camp without him? It wouldn't be the first time his foreman had forgotten somebody on the block.

The timber edge in the fog spooks him, the cold mist and the root systems swarming hysterically.

He hears muffled voices coming from inside a cache concealed behind a partial log deck. He addresses the white tarp, and his voice feels weak. Voices are returned, muffled, from under the wigwam of Silvicool. Benito lifts up one of the corners to see who is underneath.

It is Shnogg and Rico, and Tammy. They yell for him to hurry up and come inside. "The temperature fucking dropped," Benito squeaks, as he crawls into the shelter. "No shit, Mulder!" responds Shnogg. They are squatted around on two empty bins. The space is cramped elbow to elbow. Benito tries to look brave. "It isn't *that* cold. Come… on…. keep planting. I'm on my fourth bin already. We'll warm up if we keep planting. Look at you guys. I thought tree planting was supposed to be extreme. I thought this was *fucking* tree planting. We're wasting all that cream! I thought you guys were *pounders*! This is *not* cold, this is *not* cold. Winter camping up at Herring Lake, now *that* was cccc-ccc-ooold." Rico speaks up: "He-he-he's all, like, chattering, that s-s-sucker be cold." Rico coughs, "that sucker, he… kid, your lips are *blue*." Shnogg bends in real close to Benito, inspecting his face, straining to see in the dim light. "My-my-my h-h-hands are numbered." Benito stares back at Shnogg, his pupils wide and curls of his hair plastered onto his pale forehead. "Let's see this," Rico takes one of Benito's hands and examines it, hunched down beside Shnogg, like the two of them were paramedics. Tammy looks on. "Man, your hands are blue, too. We must start a little fire, warm the kid's hands up, warm *us* up. Do we have any hot shots?" "Kid, is that all you have to wear? A fleece, are you that stupid?" "Ye-ahhh, yea-hhh." Benito is still mumbling away about how he wants to get back out there into his land, plant some more. Shnogg holds up the lighter to Benito's face. "Ah, that sucks, look, his lips are turning purple, I swear, ah, geez, just look at that now. Purple. Have you ever seen that?" Shnogg is slapping his knee and he's all like *har har*. Then he gets serious. "Okay, here's what we're going to do." He turns to Tammy. The whole time Tammy has been looking rather smug in her two-piece, fully rubberized and hooded rain suit with her warm orange cork boots. "Actually I don't find it that cold," she'd been saying all complacently before Benito had come along. Now Shnogg turns on her, putting an arm around her shoulder. "All right, open up your rain coat, sweetheart." Tammy stares at Shnogg quizzically like he's just joking. When he reaches out to unzip her coat, Tammy yells out, "No way!" She recoils, pushing back on the Silvicool teepee and dislodging the hem of it so a particularly icy curl of wind sneaks in and shakes the whole thing from the inside. "Listen, this is an emergency, we need to heat up Benito's hands with your body warmth! Do you want him to lose his hands!? Look at your huge coat: you harbour the most heat!" Shnogg grabs at her zipper again and implores her, manic-eyed, "Come on now, just do it! He's freezing, okay!" Tammy knocks Shnogg's hand away and unzips her jacket a few inches, and then Shnogg grabs Benito's arms by the elbows and forces his hands and wrists underneath Tammy's coat and pushes them up towards her armpit region and they look all tangled up together, Rico bending in to look and letting out gasps of disbelief, and then Tammy lets out a huge cry from the frigid fists that are now entering her shaved armpits. Shnogg hushes her. "Okay, now, let's just get those hands in the armpits now, let's just get them in there, now!" Shnogg forces Benito's hands into Tammy's armpits. In a moment, the two unwilling participants relax, Tammy putting her head back a fraction to let Benito really get in there, and Benito groping in there without the forceful aid of Shnogg. After two minutes, a look of discovery dawn's on Tammy's face. "I've never had somebody's hands in my armpits before! It's really cold, but... are you warming up?" "I'm warming up," Benito affirms, licking his lips. And Shnogg says, "Exactly, y'all, we are doing precisely that, warming up — the armpit, centre of the universe's warmth! Right on, once Benito gets his hands back on their feet he can go back out there and plant some more trees — right, Benito? — cause this be fucking self-imposed slave labour and Tamponix Reforestation be stopping the production machine for nobody, don't matter how motherfucking hypothermic they be, just like you said there." "Gotta piss, gotta piss." Benito has removed one of his hands from Tammy's coat and is clutching his crotch. Tammy almost looks upset at this withdrawal, like she'd been enjoying him copping a feel. Shnogg smiles wryly. "Now don't worry, this is natural. It's the old fingers in the warm water diuretic prank... now wait... okay, I gotta piss too, let's get out of here." Shnogg rips open the Silvicool and they step out into the frigid air.

"Shnogg, what are you doing?"

"I'm going to piss on your hands.'"

"No, you aren't, you fucking psycho."

"Oh, yes I am, just watch me." Shnogg grabs one of Benito's hands and unzips his fly with the other and then proceeds to urinate on his hands. "Now let's see the other hand."

Benito, still benumbed just goes through with the process.

"Now, is that not *way* warmer, or what?"

Benito blinks and says, "Yeah, it is warm, but it's kind of sick, don't you think?"

"Nah, pee is clean."

SPHAGNUM MOSS

"Hey, Murielle, nice hair!"

Early morning, day five. Shift seven. Murielle's hair sprouts around her muddy bandana.

They plant.

"I have to pee." Tammy stands on a hummock. There is a pond in their land filled with floating, soggy, yellow flowers.

"*Alors, vas-y.*"

"Actually... I think it was the sausages, or something, but I was clogged up yesterday... oh, geez, I have to go really bad. *Je doit aller dans la forêt pour une minute.*" Tammy finds that her high school French is slowly coming back to her, still full of errors.

"I don't want to end up like Benito did yesterday... I'm so glad the sun came out for a bit today." She scratches her hands.

Murielle pulls her bandana tighter around her temples. "*Je vais être ici, ma chère — vas-y, vite!*"

Halfway towards the intended bush toilet Tammy stops

and whirls around, with an expression of extreme distress. "But, Murielle, you tossed our shit tickets. I told you we would need that roll even if it was wet…."

Murielle sticks her shovel in some duff and plants a tree. Tammy watches her, annoyed that she isn't paying attention.

"Look at all those leaners! You're turning into such a tree slut, Murielle. When the checkers made us replant the other day it was because of your bad quality. No wonder you always bag me out."

Murielle grabs a handful of something from the edge of the pond. She holds whatever it is up in offering. It looks to Tammy like a mass of tendrils. She stares at it with a tense expression.

"Here, wipe with this," Murielle passes her the handful of wet colours. Tammy pulls away in the same way a dog might from an oily toad.

"This sphagnum moss is good to wipe with," Murielle assures her friend, taking a step forward and holding it out.

"Sphagnum is the dog who is coming with that Archy guy."

"No, Tammy, it is in fact a moss."

"Moss? You are *fou*, you are absolutely *loca*, Murielle. I am going to shit my pants right here and it's going to be your fault."

"Listen, sphagnum moss is in no way *fou*, it contains the essence of life. It is multi-purpose. Isn't that what the anglophones would say? It is multi-purpose, like all your products?"

"Let me look at that." Tammy takes a hold of the segmented, spongy moss: lime greens and strawberry pinks, and vibrant yellow nodes all clumped together. Like something from a reef. Then she looks up from the moss at Murielle. She winces. "This will have to do!" Running toward a willow bush.

"It feels like getting licked by a cow tongue!" Murielle yells after her.

Tammy quickly pulls down her rad pants. Then she

yells back to Murielle: "How the hell do you know what it feels like to be licked on the ass by a cow!?"

"Hey, didn't I tell you I grew up on a farm?!"

After a moment: "Hey, it *does* feel like a cow is licking my bum. But it's so cold, and cows have warm pink tongues, don't they? This feels more like the tongue of a giant lizard."

"Teehee. Tammy, 'ow do you know what this feels like, this tongue of a lizard, you silly!"

"Didn't I tell you I had a perverted reptilian boyfriend? And what about you and Grant? That must be kind of slimy!"

"Grant... don't tell anybody, but he has trouble with another girl. He punched out a girl... and I feel bad for him."

"You shouldn't feel bad that he punched out a girl, Murielle!"

"Well, I do! I am a healer. So there."

In the bus they ask Larry, the knowledgeable one, about this miraculous moss, and he informs them that the sphagnum mosses, of which there are several varieties, are the ultimate primary growth. He explains that sphagnum holds water like nothing else, that sometimes later in the season, the land becomes incredibly dry but the sphagnum remain these buoyant bastions of H_2O and nitrogen — the perfect spot to plant spruce. Always keep an eye out for it, because you hardly even need a shovel, you just slip the pod right in, easy as pie. This serves the useful purpose of incubating would-be spruce trees, and projects coolness up into the planter's person, unlike the dry heat that emanates from the sun-blazoned slash or exposed sandy areas. On a hot day it's nice to have lots of sphag in your piece. He believes that it is a close relative of the sea sponge, that sphagnum laid roots in the bog land as the North Sea receded. That sphagnum evolved from some aquatic species left behind by the deluge that shrunk away into what is now James Bay. The early inhabitants used to use the stuff as a sort of natural tampon, to stem the monthly tide. When the moss is dried out, it can be used as tinder to start a fire. It even has preservative properties — bog dudes found in the archaic mires of Ireland owe their intact condition to the sphagnum that served as their impromptu embalming material.

After the solemn sharing of wisdom Larry resumes his downcast demeanor and lopes away to his fishing hut.

"Ah, I couldn't put something like that inside me. I just don't think it would feel right," says Tammy.

The rest of the day Tammy works on some planting lyrics she's been thinking about, inspired by Shnogg and Rico.

She impresses Murielle with her hip-hop prowess.

"I'm going to sing it to Benito," Tammy muses at the end of the day, after she's finished committing her lyrics to memory. "He's cute... hey, what's bugging you now?" Murielle seems kind of down in the dumps. She walks away towards their tent and Tammy looks after her and can see Grant stooped over by the tent, pulling off his gaiters. Murielle says something to Grant, and they walk over to one of the shale piles, and scramble to the top, away from the bugs.

"Tell me of this girl you smacked — tell me all." Murielle's in a grey mood wearing a hoody with confused gecko designs on it, sitting with Grant while he smokes his cigar to keep the bugs away, puffing in her face at her request, the situation made manic by the constant bugs... shifting, scratching... "You seem better... but anyway, you don't have to tell me right now." She looks at him for a single beautiful moment, and he's smiling, which has become a rare breed of expression in his facial wilderness.

"I have to grab a sweatshirt," she says. Grant needs to get something warmer from his borrowed tent as well, so they separate... he looks over at her and she has her head down while she walks back to the tent, her arms swinging at her sides. When they meet again on the way over to the fire pit, she has something to tell him.

"You remember this game," she says.

"What are you doing there…"

Murielle has pulled her arm through her sleeve and is sticking her fist out her stomach. "Press my fist."

Grant remembers the game. He grips her fist and pushes her arm in toward her stomach.

"It's like an alien," he says. "Oh, but now it popped out in a different spot." Her spring-loaded arm is sticking out again and Grant tries to push it back but she pokes it up in another spot.

"Are you trying to tell me something, Murielle?"

"Grant… I know you have changed for the better. But be careful, because the more you press them down, the more they multiply."

The fires get going again that night, that hot night — the mosquitoes make an appearance on the backs of sweatshirts, and planters scratch their ankles and move in close to the fire in an attempt to fumigate the buggers. For a couple minutes a light rain falls, but the hot smoke burns it away from the dome of warmth. Planters warm stones then wrap them in towels and bring them back to their tents.

The sunset goes down full of art. Perhaps as only a sunset particular to the gaseous quality of the Meso Ontarian sky, blooming with these deep AY Jackson colours of northern purples and blues. Up here there is a purity to the atmosphere — smog-free distances of sky except in the valleys where the industrial pollution pools. The same as on a clear lake you can see the pebbled bottom, up here you see the highest, sharpest clouds. The red pine that Larry hauled in from down the Swanson road is full of blebs pressurized within the hardened sap. The heat expands the air so occasionally the logs pop — actually, they blast open, sending mushroom clouds of ember tumbling and bouncing like red-hot potatoes into planters' laps and the smoke drives people back with arms over eyes for protection. Nothing out here is ever quite comfortable enough, not even this fire.

Just sitting in a camping chair by the popping fire like melting mudmen letting all the pain dissipate, and beyond the fire the mosquito-filled reaches and glens, and valleys full of shadows that could be bears but you won't know until you step into them. Drinking electrolyte dehydration mixes. Smoking and spitting or doing nothing at all like Zim who just sits there in his lotus with the features of a dragon resting upon his face. His after-work-yoga sessions have dwindled until nobody is showing up anymore.

The talk meanders tiredly like a drunken stroll along uneven streets — someone mentions how dirty the three buses have become. They are in horrendous shape: strewn with beer bottles, empty cigarette packs, crushed thermoses, scrunched newspapers, apple cores, orange peels, pages of porn, dirty strips of used duct tape, and, the greatest faux pas of all, dried saplings that were never planted, full bundles even, all falling apart. It's all over if the checkers discover that!

As planters leave the fire and fade toward their tents, the atmosphere becomes a little more intimate and the embers begin crackling all devilish. There are a few methods for avoiding the 'morrow — like staying up late burning cardboard boxes, telling dirty stories. A piece of sociality is sometimes more salubrious than a slice of sleep. Tammy, after a couple beers, busts out her rhymes for Benito:

"hitting perfect 7s
no less, no more

my spruce they stand so straight and tall,
it's a wonder they don't beg me to plant them all

fuck u checkers, check this out,
I'm the best rook' 'round, without a doubt

in perfect shape, don't need no flagging tape,
I'm so super, they're gonna give me a cape

I don't get distracted by nuthin,
as I bag up, I eat a muffin

and all day I rake in the dough,
wowing those loggers with my perfect ratio.

I'm not bothered by sticks or rock,
making perfect holes all over the block.

cuts on my hand, bruises on my knee,
thank goodness I made my camp fee

later at night we relax at camp,
when it gets dark I pull out my head lamp

when the time comes, how could I say no
all you who love planting, holler at me, yo."

Benito, who'd been all quiet and depressed that he wasn't a better planter and a better person cheers up after Tammy does her rap routine. Someone hands him a beer and it's all good. He feels like he's learning so much about how to cope.

Larry's all tangled up in the brush. "Ahhh!" He swears. "These damn Wait-A-Secs! The most cursed plant in the kingdom. Wait-A-Secs and Devil's Club! Bane of my fathers and my father's fathers!"

The miracle of spring has come to the clear-cuts, new botanical life popping out of the soil everywhere, the planters up to their hips in greenery. Some of the land is occupied by running pools of water, by bunched calyxes of bullhead flowers, by daffodils breaking forth in the Kap hospital parking lot. Rough grouse squatting, strutting along. Everyone beginning to roll with the punches and it is true, the land is getting more beautiful.

On the walk out, Benito trips up on some low-growing vine things. He curses, and Larry, who is ahead on the path, turns. "You have fallen victim to the legendary plant, Wait-A-Sec. Step high, and you will find freedom from its grip."

THE STUDY TRAILER

It wasn't easy for Gabby to secure this date in the first place. She'd approached Walter the anthropologist on the block, and asked him if he wanted to smoke a joint with her that night, and he'd frowned, and told her that, as an academic on site, it was of paramount necessity that he remain as clear-headed as possible. But then Gabby was like, yeah? What do you have behind your back then? She ran around to see what he was hiding, and he twirled to conceal from her whatever it was, but she caught up after about five hundred and eighty degrees. There, in his skinny academic hand, he clutched a Tupperware full of chronic.

"Don't be intimidated by us, we're actually kind of smart, too, once you get to know us a bit better." She came on smooth like butter, and Walter, haggard and weak, reluctantly obliged to the rendezvous that evening.

Gabby confirms the date with Grant. She yells over to Luke who is by his tent sharpening his shovel, to see if he wants to come, but he isn't interested. "Who cares about someone else's deep dark secrets? You guys are barking up some sort of twisted tree, I can tell you that much."

"Forget about Luke," says Grant. They haven't been talking to each other for some time; they are sick of each other in a man sort of way.

Instead of Luke, they bring along another head instead, this five-year veteran named Carlos. His nickname is Hippie But Not Hippie, in other words he's a hippie redneck. He's a chill, talkative planter who floats from group to group all contract long, smoking with anyone who is game. He is a competent social pot smoker, and Gabby believes he will help create a calm ambiance for their meeting with the volatile anthropologist.

It all begins like a joke: knock knock.

"Who's there?"

"Gabby and friends."

A thin hand pushes open the trailer door, and Gabby pulls it the rest of the way. It's large inside Walter's trailer, as if the interior was of a greater volume than the exterior suggested, and the place has all the accoutrements of an office away from home.

Walter has a steaming metal cup of hot liquid placed on a professional desk, with a brass table lamp illuminating the aluminum top, casting a chalky blue glow onto his stubbly face. He looks almost sexy in a sultry sort of way; this smoldering virility revealed for the first time.

"Hello," he greets them in a raspy voice, "have a seat." Gabby seats herself on the cushioned chair beside him at the desk, and Carlos and Grant sit on two milk crates. There's a little kitchenette in the back, like in Grant's trailer, except this one seems operational.

"So you guys want to get high?" Walter leers maniacally, with this eerie Dostoevskian sweat beading his brow. His three guests exchange uneasy glances. "Well," he continues, swiveling his chair fully around, looking each in turn, "who's going to roll it up, then?"

That would be Hippie But Not Hippie's job. He knows the art of rolling dubes by the book. He is a master roller. Off his magic hands come rose-shaped spliffs, multi-crackers, conaires, circular joints, lizard joints, and all sorts of other smokable longies. He places a glass bubbler on the table. It has a Sherlock-style mouth piece.

Carlos switches seats with Gabby so that he can roll on the table. He brings out a weed bag and removes one of the biggest, reddest-haired buds. The anthropologist looks from the dope to Carlos, then back to the dope, and seems to be satisfied by the competence of the designated roller and the quality of his product.

Then the anthropologist and the Hippie But Not Hippie start discussing fishing.

"Yeah, I caught a ten-pound bass up around here," says Carlos.

"You know, we take the bass for granted, we really do. Look at us, always yearning for salmon and cod when we're blessed with some of the best smallmouth fishing around."

"Exactly, same with hunting, like up here they take the moose for granted."

"You hunt? By Oxford, you must be kidding me. I had you pegged as a nature-loving pacifist. A Buddhist type, who strives to bring about freedom for all sentient beings!" Walter seems dumbfounded by the many personality paradoxes that are Carlos.

"They don't call me Hippie But Not Hippie for nothing."

Presently, the dube is complete. Carlos fires it up and it does the rounds, making everyone conscious and eager and a little bit shy. Carlos has on his salamander grin. He and Walter continue their genial conversation.

Then, for a second, Walter peers up at Grant and Gabby as if he were passing evil tidings their way.

"Funny, some things were misplaced from my hut, you know. Must have blown out the window," he mutters.

Worried that things are not going as planned, Gabby asks the long-anticipated question as innocently as possible: "So, tell us about your new studies. How are they coming along, and what exactly are they?"

Carlos reaches out for the stack of papers on the desk beside Walter's elbow. The anthropologist's eyes flash lightning. Carlos puts on his guilty dog look, removes his hand quickly. "Wow, sorry, man."

"Oh please, excuse my effusion! I do get so very anxious whenever people look at unrevised work, you see, some of my findings are not entirely substantiated, not as of yet, that is...." He takes a couple big hits off the glass bubbler. He is getting really high, taking really big hits. He starts coughing. He is coughing and laughing at the same time. He hands Grant the bubbler, and motions with his other hand in this *save me, save me*, gesture. Grant takes the bubbler away from him. Walter recovers and spits out the words, "my study!" and starts laughing, and repeats "my studies" over again. He is beside himself coughing and laughing, as if the notion of a study were the funniest thing in the world. Carlos leans back in his seat, and moves a dread away from his eyes.

"What am I studying?" Walter laughs again. "Well, well... *cough... cough*, my research involves..." He takes a sip of water.

"Tell us," spears Gabby. "We want to know." Gabby has the chong sticking out the corner of her mouth. Then she has an idea. "Hey, Mr. Anthropologist, have you ever had a shotgun up your nose before?"

Gabby blows a shotgun up the anthropologist's nose. He is more than willing: the smoke shoots like a lithe white worm up his hairy left nostril.

"Why, my studies are simple," the anthropologist resumes, the stream of greenybrown smoke to his brain seeming to have jogged his memory. "I am studying murder."

They gawk.

Walter continues, having achieved a calm. "Well, shall I say, the environment that creates murderers, and the murder frame as a methodological paradigm within which to analyze this generational case study, simply."

They all freeze up even tighter.

Walter continues some more. "What kind of murder, you might ask? Quite simply, mass murder... and punishment, and termination, and sadism. A whole slew of equally cheery topics." He uncrosses his legs, and reaches for his papers. He leafs through them.

"Why, yes, there has occurred an interesting turn in my studies, and I am working on a governmental bursary, you see, so my thesis is a bit controversial in certain circles, you see. What began as comparative study of remote transient communities quickly took a strange twist."

Gabby interrupts: "Now wait, wait. Who exactly is going to kill who? Cut to the chase."

He looks at her with daggers.

"It has indeed struck me that at the heart of the murdering pathology lies a complete lack of respect for one's fellow man. That is, in a camp such as this 'Kap' contract, where everybody fights for the bigger piece of the money pie, there will eventually be created the odd individual who will, as you say here, 'totally lose it'. Firstly, his or her pathology will begin on a rational creative level, in fantasizing about him or herself as a killer, and in the privacy of his or her own mind devising plots to murder his or her brethren, justified under the aegis of a desperate, sort of schizo-spiritual attempt at carnal transcendence. You see, we are much like chicken which, in overcrowded cages, turn on each other and start eating each other's feet, if you follow."

"What exactly are you getting at?" asks Carlos, snuffing out the bowl with the roach of the joint.

"My thesis is that in a modern world, many individuals are seeking to partake in certain regressive acts of self liberation. My test group consists of a predominantly urban group of individuals, taken out of their normalized social context. Politics of mind and morality have been superseded by the politics of the act, you see. My test group is comprised of, well, you. My idea is to become one of you! My aim is to apply the theories of Dr. T. Sycophant, Emeritus Professor of New Mexico College, in his study: "The Theoretic Made Flesh: A Guide To Concurrent Field Researching" to our little camp. In a tightly-knit group, certain social acts will become coterminous with those of the group, and this can be seen as pertaining to a neotribal paradigm shift, wherein the researcher too is transmuted as an agent into the gestalt as a whole. Behaviour specific to an urban setting will be superseded by regressive tendencies, learned behaviour such as etiquette, manner, politeness, cleanliness, will be lost in the primeval social structure... a diminishment of modern consciousness. The fart as fertility rite. Social implosion along patrilineal lines as a result of certain corporate pressures. The urban mind devastated, if you will, by the lack of visual and auditory stimuli. The acting out of what was hitherto latent, namely brutality, but also a complete instinctual liberation."

"Oh, so the old Lord of the Flies hypothesis. That small, wild communities will eventually go to shit?"

"Oh, not exactly. I have watched your struggles, indeed I have, and what I am implying in these papers is that all of you are going to die. There is no room for all of you, you know, don't you see? This whole enterprise will lead to death, nothing but death, death and more death. Oh, I am quite sorry, quite. This pot is absolutely killer, ha ha!"

Gabby has grabbed a piece of paper that is pinned up to a piece of bark which hangs on the wall.

In big letters it says on it: *YOU GO INTO THE WOODS AT NIGHT.*

"What the hell is this?" She says, and Walter seems excited that she noticed.

"Ah, yes, that. It's part of a riddle that I am most fond of. It was at the Kap Inn that I was first introduced to its most eloquent and existential contours. I challenge you to try to guess the answer to this most challenging riddle. It goes, in its totality, *YOU GO INTO THE WOODS AT NIGHT AND YOU GET ONE. YOU LOOK FOR IT BUT YOU CAN'T FIND IT SO YOU LEAVE. WHAT IS IT?*

They all look confused.

"It is my belief that the answer to this riddle is of great importance to some future event. It could be the key to a new civility. Like many riddles, it is at least a key to meaning. Try to guess what it is. It is a challenge for you."

They all think for awhile, and then Carlos raises his hand. "Haunted, right? You go into the woods and you get haunted, so you leave."

"I love it. A superb deduction but unfortunately a flawed one. You see, a haunting is something abstract and the object we are searching for here is very concrete."

Walter jovially cracks out some wine. "You may find the taste evocative of brambles, peat, and moss with a hint of blue sky and eagle. A true northern rosé, my fine planting friends! Now let us forget about the riddle of the future for a moment and drink a little joy."

They down their wine-filled Dixie cups quick and everybody gets drowsy. They leave his hut, all the more baffled. They walk down the carapace where Grant's trailer fell.

FUCK-AROUND DAY

"This planting thing is a crock."

"Whatever, man. Nothing's all milk and honey. Like I was coming out here to find some sweetness, but of course it's going to suck just like that other stuff in my life."

"Yeah, but it sucks even worse out here. These bugs are brutal!"

"These bugs are heinous!"

"These bugs are egregious!"

"Hey, look who it is. Come on, Benito, why don't you stop making money and take a break with us. Here, take some DEET spray, dude."

"Still no trees?" Benito is covered in grime… focused on pounding… unwrapping tree bundles as he stands.

"No trees. Sil is off screwing a bear carcass again. Looks like you have to make puppies with us now, sucker," Planter Without a Name says.

"Gabby said there were trees coming. I saw her back there." Benito sticks his shovel into the ground.

"The truck with the trees is stuck."

"Fuck, really?"

"Come on… sit the fuck down Benito. Have a smoke. And dude, we have a riddle for you. "

"You know they named the town down the highway

from Kap 'Moon Beam' because the natives saw lights shining from the streams. There's a fact for you."

"I saw some weird little creature shoot across a puddle."

"Oh, this sucks *so* bad."

"Okay dude... so, here's the anthropologist's riddle. You go into the woods at night and you get one. You look for it but you can't find it. So you leave. What is it?"

"Why is life always so tough? Biz keeps telling us it's going to get better. Where is the cream we were promised? I want cream."

"Yeah, I had one nice piece last week. In block K. Now that was sexy land. Wow. But it was only a half day."

"It hurts."

"Actually, I think what you guys need is a little physical suffering," Benito says, sucking on his smoke.

"Benito! That, my friend, is masochism. You think if you went to a psychiatrist and told them you were fucked in the head they would prescribe physical suffering?"

"It's working for me."

"Pleasure is the remedy, Benito. You got everything backwards. Didn't you know that in Norway a psychologist is allowed to prescribe a trip to the tropics for depression. Better than pills, yeah. And definitely better than physical suffering. You can't cure one kind of suffering with another! You hang out with those weird older planters. Maybe you've been listening to Larry too much."

"You guys are like the biggest bitches around here. Quit bitching about the suffering. I'm telling you, you need it," Benito grinds his butt into the soil and spits on it.

"All I'm asking is where the fuck's the cream we were promised?" says Planter Without a Name.

"You have to learn how to make money in the bad land too..."

"Money... what is money again?"

"You know what? I had a dream the other night that I was on this crazy bus, the apocalypse bus."

"That sounds a lot like my dream."

"Mine too."

"It's a bad sign when you start dreaming about planting."

"Hey, what's that noise, is that the swamp machine?"

"There is no swamp machine today."

"Well, I believe there is, to the contrary."

"The crank shaft busted."

"Oh, suffer, suffer, suffer."

"Pass me a dart. Any of those candies left? What? Only two darts!"

"I hate how you call cigarettes 'darts'."

"You go into the woods and you get crazy."

"You go into the woods and you get sane."

"So you leave."

"Because you can't be crazy and sane at the same time."

"No... ahhh... you go into the woods and you get lost, so you have to leave."

"You can't leave if you're lost. You can only leave if you're found."

"Listen, fuck all y'all. I cannot believe I have to sit out here with y'all. You're harassing me."

"What is that supposed to mean, Benito? Mr. Friends-With-All-The-Cool-Veterans."

"Tamponix sucks. They make us hurry up and wait."

"They're better than the smaller companies."

"Fuck that. Small companies rule!"

"Yeah, tune out and drop in."

"Hear ye."

"Hey, who's that?"

Bazooka comes around a corner in a cloud of various bugs, looking confused.

"Cops are after me," Bazooka says in a cop voice, then makes his way into the bush for no apparent reason. Weird-ass supervisor. A fierce f-bomb resonates from that bush and Bazooka comes out onto the road again seeming really pissed about something now, scraping the sole of his boot on a log.

"Fuck! Whose caca is that right in the middle of the quad trail back there!?"

Noplanter'll fess up, and Bazooka glares at them, then begins quoting Deuteronomy: "With your utensils you shall have a trowel; when you relieve yourself outside, you shall dig a hole with it and then cover up your excrement. Because the LORD your God travels along with your camp, to save you and to hand over your enemies to you, therefore your camp must be holy, so that he may not see anything indecent among you and turn away from you."

"Wow, dude, he got, like, Biblical on our asses."

"You have your trowels, now use them!" Bazooka screams. "And by the way, you idiots, there are eight tubs of trees fifty metres down the road from here. Plant more trees!"

"Ha ha... I love that guy."

Bazooka goes into town twice that week and he leaves Biz in charge. Biz holds a meeting saying that Bazooka is being questioned by "officials" in town. In his absence Biz wants things run tight.

Groucho picks up the mail on a water run to town. He chucks the box full of brown packages and white letters on a table. "Bazooka never picked this up for you guys. Regular letter-runs will be part of the new order once he gets fired."

Everyplanter leafs through the box to see if they got any love. Grant hears his name called. Another letter from Archy addressed to Grant. The first one had been amusing, but another one seems a bit over the top.

As Grant reads the letter the lines seem to waver slightly as if the words were not firmly attached to the page. Why would Archy be sending me a letter? They are friends, but not in the pen-pal kind of way.

Grant, I am on my way.

I feel that, of the camp, you are the most mature and able to deal with the information I am about to divulge. I have heard that you are Safety Officer. This is another reason why I confide in you, my friend. My godparents and I believe that the saplings are not saplings at all, but rather dimension-warping growth agents. Remember the strange celebration Terrorhouser held deep in the woods to celebrate the 250,000,000th planted tree? Remember the secrecy of the event, how the planters weren't invited even though our camp was just down the road? Remember that ceremony we witnessed as we watched from the top of that hill? Tamponix and their client are involved with another race, it is apparent to me now. We have been hired to plant their offspring. Northern Cloners, Xylophloes, Tamponix. These are the agents. The upper chamber of the Kapuskasing Inn is the fulcrum… of something… it was the site of first contact, we believe through the royal line…. Please be careful, Grant. I might not be able to make it to Kap for another week or so, as I finish off my initiation into the cosmic Leninist society. To tell you the truth, the whole scene on this ranch in Alberta is beginning to freak me out a bit. My godparents seemed like normal young Baby Boomers, but they have changed over the course of our being together. They have become far more materialistic in this eerily spiritual way and they dress really weird… anyhoo, enough with my personal qualms. They might be able to give me a ride to Kap…. I am sick of hitchhiking. Too many snags along the river highways.

Things are under way already on my side of organizing the *coup de plante* which we discussed last season. Please do not let our plans for revolution fade away as yet another think-big drunk plan. They say socialism can't work on a large scale. That's why we're going small. Getting out from behind the screen, I began to see things happening in reality that really shocked and frightened me. Imagine a creature sneaking through the darkness on the perimeter of the monitor glow, on the edge of the cell phone, as if all these media technologies added up to a massive distraction. But more, more, when I see you. Please, keep an eye out for mysterious activity involving the Northern Cloners tree nursery. They are readying a new batch of experimental saplings.

Adieu, Archy

PS: This message will self-destruct with your help. Please burn or rip to tiny shreds ASAP.

MUD FEST (NO SHIRTS ALLOWED) AND MARIJUANA CONSPIRACY

Trying times often end up in major mud fests, like this day, after the grueling walk-out, Everyplanter attacked by deerflies, horseflies, stableflies, wending flesh-lusty swarms, hordes, legions, sneaking to the very follicles of their hair, crawling towards the core blood heat, oh, indomitable insect! Those evolutionary years, the mutation of mandibles over time to incise the perfect bite. Planters and management alike (except for Larry, who's immune because of his natural Métis DEET blood) letting out the shrieks of the bitten, running along the deer ruts on the edge of the mud-fucked roads and the big smudged sun sending rivulets of salty sweat pouring into eyes.

Une aprés l'autre, a line of planters exiting Block X, sprint jumping off a springy log that sticks from a slash pile. Diving and somersaulting into the mire to avoid the storm of bugs. They rip down to bras and underwear, up to waists in the muddy water. Mud-splattered planters whipping stringy primary growth into each other's faces, the mud pit warm on the top like a stew, coldish in the oozy bottom like refrigerated pudding. Everyplanter gives in to the wonderful muck. Then back on the bus like wet dirty dogs and a pit stop at the weedy lake to clean off.

There is kinetic potential energy in the air as the heart pumps and the adrenal glands squeeze out their fluid after a big production day. On the flattest ground between shale piles two bins are positioned as nets, and a game of bush hockey gets underway.

Someplanter bikes around camp waving a jolly roger flag, to remind everyone of their mortality as terrestrial creatures. A potato gun, fired from an ABS pipe using ignited hairspray, bangs with a hollow echo, sending spuds off into the air.

The ground in camp has some integrity, unlike the office bogs. They bought hockey sticks from Canadian Tire on day off. Crew against crew against crew.

Biz's crew against Larry's crew. Slam into each other. Dirt spits up and it's lean mean planter against lean mean planter. Zim referees the match, and he arbitrarily intervenes on the action, jumping Ray's back, kicking the ball away from Gabby. No penalty calls, no off-sides, no boundaries — a free-for-all.

The orange ball skips over uneven ground.

Players waiting to sub in sit on plastic chairs; this guy Josh does a somersault over Luke and his jaw gets ground into the dirt, bashing into the "bench", flipping planters right over in their chairs. But planter bodies are like superhuman bodies grown invincible through the grind. You could throw a planter against a wall and they'd get up and walk away as if it were a funhouse balloon wall.

In the collision Luke managed to chip the plastic ball ahead. And who picks it up on her blade but Gabby, and she's got a clean break for the net. She's a bit slow on the move, failing to keep her head up, and Groucho is soon running her down like a lanky bull. Everyplanter yells:

"Shoot!" and she takes a quick and haphazard snapshot which glances off of Biz's freshly shaved cheek, skips into the air and flies between...

They quickly lose count of the score. Afterwards they will all sit on pine benches and crack bottled beer like a commercial set in the wilderness.

Everyplanter wants to know what the deal is with Bazooka, and they figure that veterans like Grant will know.

"I don't know, he just took off," Grant says, out of breath after the game.

"What the hell, you don't just take off out here. Like, where do you go?"

"I don't know, weddings, funerals, those important things."

"I think he's in trouble. He seemed all withdrawn on day off. Gab said she went to see if he was coming out to party, but he was just sitting on his bed waiting by the phone. What's happening with our supervisor? I'm guessing it's something about his grow operation."

"Don't ever fucking talk about that," Groucho intervenes.

"Not to intrude, but, like, that shit really isn't so secret. I think we all know — you worked for him out there, didn't you?"

"Shut the fuck up, Grant. There are some things you shouldn't say. Some things are just better left unsaid."

"Come on," says Gabby, puffing on a dart, "let's just hear it."

Groucho looks nastily around. "Well, okay. What the fuck, maybe you guys should know. This is some serious shit. That whole grow operation stuff isn't as cushy as it's made out to be. Most people imagine a bunch of friends living on the land. You think it's super chill. Well, it isn't. You get an in, or whatever. They transport you in a van with black windows way into the mountains. You have no way of really knowing where you are. Once you get to the plantation you are forbidden to leave the premise unaccompanied. Everybody stays in a group at all times. It depends on the operation. If it's a big one, and say the proprietors are involved in more than weed — sometimes there is an intermingling of industries where the family also runs meth labs, so they mix and —"

"So Bazooka fell in with the wrong partners?"

"Fucking bad-ass trailer mafia guys. You know, Bazooka always worked this certain valley for the last few years. He said it was the most beautiful valley, his dream of Shangri-La with hammocks on a hill overlooking some eight thousand plants budding in the sunshine. But then he starts getting visits from these Japanese entrepreneurs who were driving in limos in the Kootenays searching for land. The Japs are into luscious Canadian bud. They found Bazooka's land and they wanted it and suggested introducing a new system of hybrid seeds, or whatever, promising they could quadruple his yield. Something about slicing killer tomatoes and codfish fertilizer and shit. So last year Bazooka and his growing crew decided to try a co-op. I think it was crazy stupid in the first place, and yeah, he's in trouble now. I'm pretty sure they got busted. I don't know how they really would have tracked him down in Ontario so fast. An investigator was in town the other day when I went on the water run. Maybe Bazooka's partners aren't too happy either. I think it's kind of good that he's gone. That guy was way too laid back to be a supervisor. Biz will perform better. I think if Bazooka does come back we should all have a vote, see if he shouldn't step down. Fact is, the man ran a loose ship."

Grant speaks up in Bazooka's defense. "Biz'll turn this company into more of a slave-trade business than it is already. I'm pretty sure everybody here knows your agenda. You and Biz want to own this company. Your own porta-potties, your own reefer. I bet you ratted Bazooka out."

"Grant, why don't you shut the fuck up? I think everyone here is sick of your whining. Speaking of stepping down, of retirement. You're losing it, dude, things aren't the same. You have to work harder in this world, be more efficient, and man, the big money, five hundred dollars a day, was a fantasy that you were lucky to be a part of, but the economy has changed. It's a competitive market. To succeed you gotta be really tight. If we ever do run this, or any company, we're going to weed out the old drunks."

Grant tightens his grip on his hockey stick.

"Yeah," continues Groucho, "you're not really putting in the numbers like you used to, are you, Grant? You're turning into a slow, weird lifer. This is your prison, man. You know there's more to life than fucking planting trees, but you waited too long. You're here to stay. People know you abused that woman, Grant. But don't worry, there will always be room for a slut. A quality slut like yourself."

Grant's eyes shine. He remembers what someone said about his country once: *Nice people, but they let everyone walk all over them.*

"You fucking faggot!" he fires back at Groucho. The words hangs heavy in the air. They were the wrong words.

Groucho is immediately at him. He gets Grant by both wrists, pushing his arms back against his chest. "You know what they'll do if you call someone a faggot in jail?"

"All the tough talk coming from the business major!"

Blam. Sock. Thud. Then someone jumps on Groucho's back and tangles him up and Gabby grabs Grant by a nipple and twists him away and he shrieks out like he'd been pussy whipped.

The conflict creates fracture lines in the power structure of the camp. Some planters become supporters of Bazooka, others of Biz. There are debates over who is better. Bazooka, the laid back, ad hoc planting supervisor, who likes a healthy social scene in camp, or Biz, the money and production man.

Planter Without A Name asks Benito what he thinks, as

a rookie.

"I dunno," says Benito. "Either way, this is a crap job. But Biz has always given me pointers about how to up my numbers."

"Yeah, well Biz can be a cruel son-of-a-bitch. Did you hear what happened to Tammy. Poor Tammy, he left her on the block…."

Benito, wrapped in a plaid blanket and shivering every now and then, is munching on a wiener while he listens to Planter Without A Name.

"I'll tell you one thing… there's nothing more a girl hates than being made to feel like she's a girl… Tammy's a fucking awesome rookie now, but man, she was with Biz's crew at the beginning and was having a really tough go of it… and then came the worst storm of the season. And she was all alone finishing her huge piece. A wide open piece, way too big for someone of her skill. I think Biz wanted to put her in her place. And in comes the rain. In comes the lightning. A complete clear-cut, not a frigging tree in sight. You know how the storms come out here. That first storm that destroyed Grant's trailer. You know the storm is coming cause it will be galloping over the clear-cut on sixty click winds. Just like it happened to Tammy. She was slow and ornery. Spoiled. Biz was fed up with her. That's why he left her alone in the big piece she'd been working on for days. The rest of the crew moved to another block up the road. Biz checked on her maybe once during the day. He would have sent some other planters in with Tammy but her land management skills sucked and her piece was planted randomly. She was the only one who knew where she had planted, so she was the only one who could finish the piece. Anyway, here comes the storm like storms do, and this stupid rookie wants to run to the bus, but she can see the bus way the fuck up a hill and she'd walk up there but she's scared shitless of Biz because the day before he had caught her hanging out in the bus and had threatened to fire her and people around camp were starting to call her the gardener because she planted so few trees. Biz had really scared the shit out of her, threatening her with a shovel and everything, and she really didn't want to get fired. Finishing this contract is like her rite of passage, do or die. So just imagine, the lightning is blazing up trees right and left, the storm is closing in. And I mean a real storm, like even me, I was scared of the storm. It was raining and hailing so hard that I could see my frigging silhouette where the water ripped around my figure. It must have felt like the storm was actually hunting her, like a massive black monster in the sky. She's thinking in her weakened lucidity, thinking of what to do, think, think, think — does she bolt for the timber edge, or lie down and wait out the storm? She's thinking back. The past is the only place she could go for advice. She's trying to remember what to do, racking her brain for an answer. Her instincts are failing her. The flight doesn't know itself from the fight. She's trying to rationalize the shit, which doesn't work, right? Then it happens. Some words from the past pop into her head: "Head down, bum in the air, head down, bum in the air, head down, bum in the air." One of her summer camp counselors had told her to do this. Summer camp, right. Bum in the air, bum in the air: it's all she can frigging think. She remembers her favorite counselor demonstrating, tucking his hands around his ankles and sticking his bum up. The explanation being if you're going to conduct one-hundred million volts, better through your ass than your head. So she hunches up, sticks her ass toward the sky, and, well, just stays that way with big drops of icy rain splattering her ass and the backs of her arms. For hours. The storm was so fierce, rocking trees down, rocking the bus. Biz'd forgotten she was even still out there. Or he thought Larry had picked her up. There was confusion, let's put it that way. It took us all over an hour to realize that she was still out there. Biz is, like, 'Shit,' really loud and he runs out the bus to her piece and starts yelling her name but the storm just soaks up his words, and he runs around frantic, thinking the kid is dead and imagining what it will be like with a death under his belt and everything, how that would sure put a dent in his Tamponix glory. But then he sees this thing sticking up and he exclaims, 'Well, if it isn't Tammy's cute ass!' And it was. It was Tammy's ass capacitor."

"I just had the worst day of my life today." Benito moans when the story is done. "Just like her."

"It is important that you have the worst day of your life. A lot of people miss out on that definitive worst day of life. It is very important that we have these days. For perspective, you understand."

Benito nods off with white rabbits puffing on his closed lids; Larry and Planter Without a Name help him through the dark to his tent.

Shnogg's Shift:
Day 1: 4,800 trees
Day 2: 5,200 trees
Day 3: 4,500
Day 4: 6,000
Day 5: 4,800
Day 6: 3,500
Average Trees Per Day: 4,800

Rico's Shift:
Day 1: 4,800 trees
Day 2: 5,200 trees
Day 3: 4,500
Day 4: 6,000
Day 5: 4,800
Day 6: 0
Average TPD: 4,216

On day six, Rico sits on a log, eating an apple in quick, nervous bites and twitching his foot. His eyes are beady and dart about, following the flies.

"Come on, we're going for the record, brother! Seeing you sitting there like that every time I come out of the land is slowing me down."

Rico's all jittery. He stands and starts pacing.

"Ya want another pill?"

"Those pills are giving me chest pains. Not good."

On day off they can hardly move. Gabby goes to wake them up to see if they want to go to Dutchy's for some extra-crispy waffles and finds Rico sitting on the cabriole chair with his feet up and two pea bags on his shins. His eyes have thick purple sags under them. He groans and rolls his head around in an inflatable neck support.

Shnogg lies bedded on his stomach with bare legs spread wide, and the skin of one of his testes is hanging out from the rumpled crotch of his striped boxers. He pulls the pillow away from his face and speaks through parched lips. "We aren't going anywhere, Gab. We ordered a day room... we're fucked after last week."

They can't put together the numbers next shift.

Shnogg's Shift:
Day 1: 4,800 trees
Day 2: 2,500 trees
Day 3: 2,000
Day 4: 2,300
Day 5: 1,500
Day 6: 2,500
Average TPD: 2,600

Rico's Shift:
Day 1: 1,020 trees
Day 2: 2,100 trees
Day 3: 1,500
Day 4: 2,000
Day 5: 3,000
Day 6: 100
Average TPD: 1,600

"What happened, homeboys?" Winger asks them. She averaged 4,300. Word's gotten around that Shnogg and Rico are hopped up on uppers. They fried their nervous systems, blew their gaskets. Winger moves into the highballer position.

DAY OFF # WHAT? # 6?

Grant and Luke are all changed and spiffed up in their best day-off attire, flashy button-up shirts. Luke even has some ice cream scented gel in his curled hair.

They are about to strut off to the party at the Château Bar when one of the ladies from the front desk knocks on the open front door of their room. She is the one with the hair that looks like a boat wake. She walks right in and presses a folded piece of paper into Luke's palm.

"Doug from the mill was here earlier, and wanted you to have this."

Grant watches Luke's expression as he scans the little missive.

"Oh, no, no siree, I ain't getting involved in this now." Luke throws Grant the note. It hits the shag carpet and Grant picks it up.

Hey Grant and Gabby,

This is Doug Colt, the Clear Water Future Vision administrator, and, as you know, also head quality checker on your contract. I am hoping that you, and whoever else you think will fit, will be able to make it for some coffee tomorrow at 4:00 PM at The Chateau. We must discuss the future of forestry. My wife would be delighted as well. Look for the motorcycles parked out front.

THE HAPPY FIGHTS THAT HAPPEN AT NIGHT

A strange character makes an appearance that night — a lanky, mule-faced guy wearing a trench coat and stirring shit up, making the night stupid in its disguise. From what Luke heard, the guy just pulled up on his motorcycle, and came on in with a couple of his friends. Larry has seen the guy before. Says he's seen him riding with Doug Colt. He's a regular on the small town scene. According to Larry, he's an unpublished poet with an unquenchable thirst for attention.

"Yeah," says Larry, leaning back on the stool at the bar, downing a kamikaze. "I heard the guy's riding across the continent reading poetry at every bar that'll let him. Something about a long poem, like an epic. He used to work for a steel distributor up in Hamilton, now he's written this really long poem about the history of Ontario. But he never got past Kap. He's been here the better part of a decade. People say the poem sank him."

The guy calls himself Old Malonie. He wears a trench coat, a fedora, and goes around to every planting girl in the bar, introducing himself, and telling them he can out-plant anyone in the camp.

Old Malonie and his two friends, they look like toughies. A crew of swaggering, liquored townies, with music cases possibly packing weapons. Looks like it's the 57th parallel crew. In no time, one of them is twinkle-toe two-stepping around holding Eliza's hand. Eliza is laughing at his jokes.

They sit at a round polished table by the dance area and the jukebox. Luke comes over with a tray of tequila shots. "Two each," he says.

The night proceeds.

Soon Styler, who's playing billiards, calls the eleven, and Winger has to inform him, "Ah, Styler, that's the *one*, actually, not the eleven."

Styler raises his wobbly eyes and looks cockily at Winger at the same time as he pulls back for the shot —

Styler's patented no-looker, a particularly disrespectful way of finishing an opponent. But he misses the cue ball completely, contacting way low so it hops off the table, then someone tries to catch it but succeeds merely in fumbling it up, and it splashes into Ray's pitcher as he squeezes between shoulders, John Deere cap poking through like a platypus' bill. Ray looks into his pitcher, shrugs, then takes a big gulp, drains the brewsky until he's left with the cue ball balancing on his lips.

Wrapped together in flagging tape, Murielle and Tammy are dancing around drunkenly, grinding, kissing each other on the lips! The jukebox belts out *Iron Man*, Molson signs shimmer woozily. There is somebody pissing on the dance floor.

Then, the jazzy blowing forth of a sax. One of the salty dogs who came in with Old Malonie stands on a bar stool, reed and mouthpiece clamped between his uneven teeth, his stumpy mechanic's fingers tapping a dented, unpolished old sax. He is playing in a hipiddy bloop style, the tone now full bodied, then squeaky, as if the reed were split, body bending around and eyes creased, swaying above everyone else at the bar, who sway around him and yell and raise their dirty hands in appreciation.

Old Malonie jumps up on top of the bar, hunched over, yelling, "Hear ye, hear ye, the Canadian Poet in the barn!" He pulls out a mickey of bottled-in-Canada liquor from the folds of his overcoat, swills it three times, then stands up straight as he can, his head slightly bent to accommodate the presence of the ceiling. With the sax now squeaking at a hyperkinetic bebop pace, Old Malonie rips open his beige overcoat, and puffs his stomach out the bottom of a faded old Canucks T-shirt. "Hear me, planters, hear me now! Hear me in the hexameter from ancient Greece, cut with the poesy of Langston Hughes, based on a tradition of rhythm and blues!"

Verse about sudsey roses and potato drills, then shouting about mountains and big distances. He puts his hands against the ceiling and yells out, "I am fucking Irving Layton and Al Purdy, oh horrible test tube hybrid!"

"You suck balls, man. That was the worst poem I have heard in my whole fucking life!" Rico shouts out from the disgruntled audience.

Old Malonie scowls around the room, aware that he has about 1.5 seconds of audience patience before he must forfeit the centre of attention, so he promptly looks for the closest victim, which happens to be Gabby, and he decants the remaining drink all over her brown hair.

"Well, let's fucking go, then! Let's get to 'er!" Gabby yells.

The sax player's right in the middle of the scrum, salty dog number two, smashing his instrument against a table for some unapparent emphasis, until Carlos gets him in a full nelson, proving once again beyond a doubt his Hippie But Not Hippie status, and Gabby runs in and karate kicks the musician in the gut.

"How dare you insult Charlie Parker like that!" screams Old Malonie, jumping down off the bar.

Luke intervenes, grabbing Old Malonie by the neck and forcing him back into a throng of angry planters, and then out onto the dance floor. They push each other around in circles under the disco lights, like hockey players, or waltzing Matildas, trying unsuccessfully to end it with a head butt, more of a jousting of heads than an actual butting of heads.

"*Touché*," yells Grant, ramming.

"*En garde*," shouts Old Malonie, butting back.

These unfriendly overtures are waylaid by the barkeep, who grabs and pushes them both by the collars, admonishing them to go, "Outside! Outside, or I'll shove my toe up your ass so far you'll need a backhoe to dig it out!" But this serves merely to topple the two grapplers, as Old Malonie gets a heel stuck on the rug, sending them smashing into chairs, overturning a round table, releasing a waterfall of beer from overturned jugs. Fists flail, and arms blur like cats clawing in the air.

There is blood along with the beer. Blood above Old

Malonie's eyes, blood on the shins underneath Luke's cut-off denims, blood on the knuckles of the bartender, who's backed off to nurse a bashed knee while standing like a corrupt referee on the perimeter (the ref has taken a couple swings himself!), and it's a good old sloppy brawl and the barkeep lets them go at each other.

As the fight slows, Bazooka barges through the front door, panting. "They strip-searched me at the police station! They looked at my asshole and I hadn't wiped!" He yells with a look of horror.

Planter attention switches to the new spectacle. Bazooka has the crazed look of someone who has been abducted and released. This bizarre encounter turns out to be the last anyone really sees of the real Bazooka.

Luke ceases his thrusting as his opponent has become totally limp. Old Malonie is out cold. Luke stands up and slaps Bazooka on the arm and yells to the bar for another couple double rye and gingers. Trembling and grumbling inarticulate blasphemies, Bazooka flops down at the bar.

Old Malonie revives, raises his arm, pointing at them both: "There are strange things done in the midnight sun... Robert Service, cremate these cretins! Alive!"

Back in the centre of the bar, there are some diplomatic discussions going on between the salty dog musicians and the planters, as the jazz players pack up their now even more bent and dented instruments. "Sorry, it was supposed to be just an act. He's fucked, he's a poet."

They drag Old Malonie outside and leave him lying by his motorcycle on the curb. They pull some sod off the lawn across the street and lay it under his head for a pillow.

The police come in an hour later, grey under the eyes.

"We were dispatched about a fight in progress."

"No, there's nothing here, officer," the barkeep lies, not wanting them to come inside.

"Smells like dope," says one of the officers, confused.

"No, just pine cones, sir. Just pine cones."

The night has moved on back to the parks and inns.

MORNING AT THE KAP INN

The reception gives a wakeup call but the receivers are generally off their cradles and it's smooth sailing in the waters of early morning sleep, the blankets like these creamy lagoons of clouds and whoever you slept with a chiseled dirt angel beside you in the skank heaven of day off. Grant lifts his head and looks over at Luke who is lying there with blood-soaked cotton swabs sticking out of his nostrils. Grant reaches out and grabs the bottle of painkillers off the side table and blindly throws a few of the pills into his mouth and dry swallows. He pulls his pants on, and feels a breeze on his ass. The ass of his pants is missing.

Now Grant is stumbling down the hall that curves idly upwards by the Coke machines. He can feel cool air on his ass. He passes several metal doors with pistons that sigh as they shut. Out of an oddly-placed window he can see down into the parking lot. There's an old Chevy out there that's totally disintegrating, looks like it's been out there for years, the concrete sunk a few inches under each tire. Sometimes when he's hung over he gets these peaceful vision moments. He keeps walking along the hallway as it angles upward to the lobby, passes another metal door with pistons. He pauses when he hears the voice of a woman coming from outside. The voice is shrill, like a bird's, a bird scolding a fledgling.

At one juncture, hanging to his left, is another print of the Queen. She's smiling that vaguely Mona Lisa smile, and in the background is a peculiar character leaning against a chest of drawers, a man with his arms folded at his sides almost like wings. Similar, yet slightly varied, to the reproduction in Grant's room. Grant shudders, all these Queens around the inn are kind of unsettling. The character standing behind the Queen has a long sweep of silver hair down his shoulder, flowing over an ermine coat and a frilly cravat. Who could he be? The figure has a certain inner light — the way some portraits seem to possess something of their subjects.

Grant continues down the hall, and into the big lobby with marble floors. A chandelier of smoky glass nodules diffuses and makes patchy the light emanating onto the walls. Underneath the chandelier is a lady of some indeterminate middle age, positioned stiffly with her hands dangling at her sides. She is wearing thick, gauzy pantyhose and old-fogey black leather shoes with square brass buckles. As Grant enters, she turns and looks at him with very little expression, or at least nothing that he can interpret, then pivots woodenly and walks back out of sight behind a brightly-varnished partition, her heels clicking. The sound is not an echo of the click, but instead a crisp amplification in the petrified silence. She seems fascinated by whatever is up those stairs, whatever winds its way into those upper stories of the central atrium of this historical edifice.

Grant finds himself in the exact spot she had just been standing in, smack under the chandelier, light glowing on his bare head. He has a sudden idea of himself in the third person, standing there, in his assless pants. Everything shines faintly. Grant's stomach churns with a warmish nausea, and his nose itches. A peculiar hangover. He recalls a pillbottle. Reaching for it. The blurry label.

"Are you staying for another night?" The lady is now at the counter, behind the flowery ironwork wicket. Grant counts out money from his Outdoorsman wallet while she watches him silently from behind her trifocal glasses. It is very quiet. Grant pushes the money over the smooth counter into her hands and then looks up at her. "Could you tell me a bit about the history of this place? I hear they're tearing it down. Why would they do that?"

Her long, almost wand-like fingers, yank the till that is fixed into the marble-coated counter, and she sticks the money in without separating it. Grant notices the Queen, aged slightly compared to the other incarnations here in the inn, reproduced on the top twenty.

"Too many cracks." The lady lights up in animation, "cracks everywhere, they told the mayor that this place was officially unsafe despite the work and money the town has put into it. It is unstable. We did have an accident upstairs." She looks over Grant's shoulder, toward the stairwell, her eyes climbing them.

He looks at her eyes and notices something is walking across the triple lens reflection on her glasses. He turns around just in time to see someone move around the corner. Strange how silently they must have come down the stairs.

"Darn," she says. "I told them not to go up there."

"Who?"

"Lots of unsavory folk around these days. The North has become a hiding place for terror. Terrible people. Everyone decent heads down south." She pauses for a second, as if thinking, then seems to correct herself. Her face has taken on a strangled appearance. "You know what, I think it was you tree planters up there. One of them called himself a scholar, and he had a pretty one for company. A quiet one. They were fascinated by the Queen's room. They jumped the table before I had the chance to warn them about that room. Yes, a scholar and a lovely young woman."

A chill clings to Grant's neck. He feels woozy all of a sudden. He shakes a couple loonies from his pockets, then inserts the coinage into the juice machine and presses the zany fruit berry button with the back of his fist. A drink rattles through the system. He creeps back to his room, rounds a corner, and finds planters are out in the hall now, the folk boys jamming away on the banjo and the guitar:

And never would I go back... to north Ontario...

He feels woozy again and then he hears a woman's voice out the window, and it sounds similar but not quite the same as the till lady's — shrill, like some kind of anxious bird. For all he knows it could indeed be the same lady.

"Of course he will. People disappear. No, no, we must do what he asks."

And a man's voice in return: "The stink of it. Smell me, darling. What if they sewed her right open?"

Grant looks out the window screen. He sees cinnabar hair in a lampshade style, then the flash of eyes looking in the direction of the window where Grant is spying from. He moves out of the way.

There is silence, the creak of a hinge. Then he hears the man and woman speaking softly on the metal stairs.

"Yes, I agree, it must be the formaldehyde… we'll pickle the things like eggs."

Grant peers slowly out the window again to confirm the hazy words with the movement of human lips. With locked, fixed expressions, the man and woman are staring right into Grant's eyes. Grant lets his gaze drift away from them, in a manner which he hopes appears natural, down to the sinking Chevy, pretending that the couple is not what he's interested in. Then he takes off down the hall back to his room.

Their image is stuck in his memory. Tapioca suit too short at the wrists. A mustachio that swoops into a dull-edged goatee. Stooped and unclean, a coffee-stained traveling auto parts salesman or something, pant legs hemmed up too high. And she in this shiny mauve dress, polka-dotted with cherries, which seems to outcrop from her thighs as if supported by a crinoline. Grant continues down the tilting hallway.

Seems Luke must have left for breakfast. Grant wobbles his head around on the pillow in the empty room and looks up at somebody standing over him. All he can really make out are a bunch of flashing points of light and a circle of docile, blurry faces. People come and go from the room but he just lies there. At one point, two people are standing by the Queen Elizabeth portrait, discussing the figure depicted in the background. "Perhaps that figure is fictitious but everything else about the work seems historically accurate. Elizabeth's face is rubbed off. It's just a white blob. Interesting." In his comatose state, Grant can sense that their attention has shifted to him, they are observing him. "That's the voodoo." Grant lapses deeper but can still hear the debate about the figure standing behind the Queen.

"Well, actually, this is a portrait of Queen Elizabeth the First. You can tell from the collar, her ruff, the frilly fanciness and her egg head...." Grant passes out completely before he hears the rest.

He sleeps. He sees a sky full of stars and he hears a voice, which becomes the face of a man with a hanging mustache and ermine wrap. He resembles both the man Grant saw outside in the tapioca suit, and the figure in ermine behind the Queen. The long-nosed man opens his mouth and out comes the opaque phrase: WE END DIG GO WE. Then a high-pitched, almost electronically tweaked voice:

"The Kap Inn is the kind of place that you hear stories about, right, Grant?" asks the person with the shivery, squeaky voice. Walter, the anthropologist? It's hard to tell. It's hard to see.

"It's the kind of place kids are fascinated by. One of them says, 'You know what, Joey? That's a spooky house,' and Joey retorts, 'No stupid, that's a haunted house, don't you know anything?'"

"It's the kind of place where you will see someone in the top window."

Grant opens his eyes. Winger sits by the bed now. She is sitting there staring at him very intensely, as if she were some kind of physician. Grant recognizes that same intense feeling of being watched from his bedside when he was an infant. Vision zeroing in on him.

Grant's eyelids droop. He can still see Winger's lips move, but it is not her voice. It is the voice of a stern male, speaking in intellectual tones:

"But of course the comment will invariably reflect more upon the witness than on the actual object of perception…" Winger holds a photo album in her lap. Her hands have a kind of fur on the back of them. The intellectual voice continues. Winger's auburn hair hangs in a curl, just covering her cheeks as she looks down, moving a finger along one of the old photos.

"It's the kind of place you look up at, and you see that kid named Joey screaming in muted agony from the top floor, crying out the window, crying silently for your help, but you, as the skeptical witness, shake your head, rub an eye, look back to where you saw the tortured child, but there will be nothing there." Winger flashes for a second like an angel in a television snowstorm and then she is leaning in and either kissing or biting Grant on the cheek. Then she whispers in his ear again: "WE END DIG GO WE."

Grant flicks open his eyes. He smells burning onion and hears the sound of fabric being ripped. He is starving. He gets up, and he is buck naked. Somebody has written in marker on his chest, *Grant is the Breastest*. A blue piece of paper sticks out the breast pocket of his wrinkled day-off shirt. The note from Doug Colt. He looks at the clock radio. The numbers flash red. 4:00 PM!

He stumbles out of the room and finds Gabby and Luke outside with some others in the parking lot.

"Ah, poor Grant! You popped the wrong pill, mate!"

"Whatever."

Grant shows Gabby the note and she rushes ahead to meet Doug Colt on time, while Grant goes back to his room to find pants that don't have the ass cut out of them. The Queen watches him as he pulls up his pants.

Two biodiesel motorcycles are parked in front of The Chateau. Doug Colt is where he'd promised to be. There he is with his twitching soup-strainer mustache, his checkered huntsman's vest, and his pack of smokes square on the table. His mustache twitches ever so slightly when he notices Grant stumble into the lobby. He runs a hand up the tails of his mullet and shakes his head like an unlikely cover girl.

A maudlin love-rock ballad croons over the speakers, old fifties saccharine Chet Baker lounge combined with a certain eighties Alberto European Hair Styling brand of *amour*, while soundless horse racing plays on twin televisions which hang from steel angles in the top corners, seemingly giving hope to about ten old folks sitting there with their hand-held betting consoles, laying wagers.

Gabby and two other planters named Steph and Rea are sitting at the table with Doug Colt, passing delicate photographs around by their edges. Doug's wife, stately in demeanor and homey in manner, sits with them as well.

Doug Colt spreads his arms and stands to welcome the latecomer. Grant sits down with them and orders breakfast, a large coffee. He feels foggy. Doug Colt introduces his wife. He puts his arm around his wife's shoulder and tells the story about how they met in Hearst, the smaller town down Highway 11. Marguerite, his wife, had been, at the time, a young stripper looking for love and it just so happened (this, in 1972) that Doug had recently received a well-paying felling job, and after a successful date he told her, "Darling, I do want to do it in that there hay with you," and she said, "Forget the hay, let's 'it the timber. I want to ride your 'og." So the two fresh lovers climbed up on the big timber stacks out back of the railway and made true patriot love on top of the logs with the whole north laid out around. "I swear," says Doug Colt, looking at his spouse all misty-eyed and she looking at him with equal nostalgia, "w'en I saw my darling there wit' her w'oppers there, I knew she was a natural solution to every problem I ever did 'ave in this there life, *ostie*."

Doug Colt seems very proud of the tree planters, working so hard for the Clear Water Mill, but he is not so proud of the Terrorhouser influence. He presents the opinion many times over the course of breakfast that there needs to be some serious changes made within the industry. They are too fatigued to pay full attention to the details of the politicking but catch the drift of its seriousness, because at one point this man comes over to their table and says in a taciturn and pursed-lip manner, "Ah, Doug, always the agitator, why don't you let the planters do what they do without getting them *involved*. These city kids aren't ready for our brand of politics."

This seems to quiet Doug down a bit, as if he relized he was starting to say too much.

They switch their attention back to the photos. They're old photos, taken in a logging camp, starring big fucking lumberjacks standing by massive trees. For every picture, Doug has some detailed story to add, like the photo of this one lumberjack who was legendarily strong, and was jailed in Ottawa for assault, in a prison now converted into a youth hostel. The lumberjack was marked by history as a legend, just like all the supposed ghosts in the old jail and gallows, since, as the story goes, in a fit of hunger he put his massive hands around two iron bars, pushed one way and pulled the other, and bent apart the two bars in protest. This story is immediately believable just from examining the girth of the pictured arms. And then there was this guy Ted Horsejaw, to whose memory Doug Colt holds aloft another old photo, this one framed in brittle wood. He won't let them touch this one, so everyone has to bend in to see it properly. Gabby snaps a shot of it quickly with her cellphone. It is a sun-bleached shot of a bald man with the most tremendous eyes. According to Doug Colt, the depicted person was a famous railway rebel back in the thirties, a hustling hipster mountain man out for coin in the coin-dry depression days. This Mr. Horsejaw rode the rails during his youth, high-tailing it from the oil-drilling west to the copper towers and cosmopolitan clockwork of Ottawa, from small and puritanical Toronto to Fitzgeraldian crackup, post-swing New York. A real bad ass. A real brawler and player. Seems he got arrested in the early 60s in the act of trying to kidnap one Miss Knickers from an Upper Canadian dance club, a disturbed event of the kind common on the logging town circuit, involving a hot-wired truck, a couple thousand dollars worth of highly adulterated cocaine, a busted lumberjack pimp ring, and the eventual imprisonment of an off-his-rocker mechanic kind of guy known as Uncle Andy. Now, Uncle Andy was a close confidant of Horsejaw, with vital connections to the Meso Ontarian market. Unfortunately for anyone Horsejaw dealt with, Uncle Andy secretly spent too much time with local kids in Timmins, becoming close friends with them even at the age of 42, hanging out in tree houses and tutoring them on thievery and fighting tactics. This, in short order, drew the attention of the kids' parents, who found cartons of du Mauriers, contraband bestiality porn, and various high-velocity pellet rifles hidden in the backs of their childrens' closets. Initial suspicions led to covert community investigations, and the parents coaxed their kids into tattle-taling on Uncle Andy, who in turn ratted out Horsejaw under duress in the Timmins penitentiary, and both men ended up in some weird sixties rehabilitation program, part of the burgeoning Pierre Trudeau campaign of civil participation — the trippy off-headed sixties counterculture mentality having mixed with politics of the day — and soon Horsejaw and Uncle Andy found themselves way up near Crystal Creek or thereabouts, doing, of all things, reforestation (a.k.a. tree planting) as part of their community service. Inmates with duffle bags of saplings and overlarge shovels all heading into a little commune in the bush on some old junk bucket truck with weather chains around the tires, bitching, cursing, finding tree planting tougher to endure than jail itself, and finding respite to the agony of woman-less horror shows with no pay by masturbating each other like crazy whenever the foreman had his back turned.

So Doug Colt turns out to be a wonderful storyteller who doesn't mind being interrupted by a pointed question. When Gabby asks, "Who cares?" Doug explains to his small audience (first tucking in his gut and setting an elbow on his knee, taking a puff off his Export) that the tree planter is a part of this saw-toting heritage. "Damn it," he says, "looking at all you university kids, you silently suffering yout', damned if this isn't some kind of re'abilitation program, this sort of upper-end Siberian labour camp. I tell you, you are learning some lessons out 'ere, aren't you there."

They slurp their coffee with increased energy. Yeah, like they were all leaving the laws of life as they knew them — back into the animal kingdom, back each year to the green lap of Mother Nature to work for their allowance.

The whole organic paradigm: arboreal circuitry of the north; networks of places and people all linked together by a labyrinth of roads through the woods. It has something to do with timber stacked to the horizon and big cranes moving yellow and spot-lit at 2:00 AM across the horizon, with the saloon scene where strippers insert their own coins into the jukebox, slug their beer and proceed to jig around in a do-si-do with the metal pole.

PART II

'It's a wild road, mother,' said Paul. 'Just like Canada.'
'Isn't it beautiful!" said Mrs. Morel, looking around.
   — D H Lawrence, *Sons and Lovers*

"THIS IS VIMY RIDGE, BOYS. THIS IS HAMBURGER HILL."

Marching these roads, Grant can't help but lose it. Stumbling like an old elk through the misty maze of morning, circumventing a huge puddle that spills in the bend of the road where the tracks get deep and treacherous. The swamp machine clanks through the pond, its evenly distributed centre of gravity preventing it from tipping as it climbs almost vertically up the slash, the treads biting into, and finding grip in, anything. The treads like an early tank model. Water sweeps through these treads, forcing waves over the slippery, debarked logs — the runts piled along the edges of the roads dot-marked with orange logger's paint. Grant is hyper-aware of all this as he falls behind Luke, as if the more he thought his way into the wooded patches of supposed meaning, the further he got from his solid friend.

At a certain point, the watery line of planters turns off the FSR into the bracken where a big arrow has been fashioned out of flagging tape by Eliza to point them in the right direction. She went into the block early this morning and bushwhacked a shortcut. The line of grey forms zig-zags through the rough terrain of overturned root systems and dense brush.

Grant swerves silently away from the pack. Down the road a ways he stops to get his bearings. The winter blades have razed this area completely. It is a complete cut without any shelterwood. Sizeable curlings of fresh white wood are spread all over the uneven earth: cut this past winter. It looks like a metallic hurricane filled with razor edges came sweeping through, leaving tongues of soft wood licking the air. A fog coming in imperceptible tides. The metal treads of the swamp machine chugging through the fields of ooze over the timber edge in another section of the block. And what are these little flowers he sees? Blood-red flowers that his boots graze through. Like poppies. He can practically hear the bagpipes. He spits the mosquitoes away.

He looks back at the shredded stumps and slash; now he sees bodies reaching their stumpy arms upward toward the concealed sky, dead in the act of signaling to the heavens and all the minced body parts spread around on the ground. Again, his speed spade over his shoulder feels much like a rifle; his bags, bandoleers; his hard hat, the green steel helmet. He thinks to himself: I am walking through the battlefield of the mind. Bodies everywhere, stepping over figments. Stepping over mind bodies, bodies in the mind. One, two, three, hoe, one, two, three, hoe, hoe, hoe. The slash piles just masses of dismembered limbs sticking out, the neat stacks of thin logs like corpses spread along the tarmac in some sort of sylvan death camp — a dissected humanity of limbs and leers and glaucous eyes staring askance, hanging out of sockets.

"Grant, this way, man." Luke has emerged from the spruce. Grant shakes his head and they head into the trees to follow another path.

ANARCHY INSIDE

Plenty of disappointment and ennui in the hitchhiking world. So too in the fishing realm. Like the old carp that mouths the hook-embedded dough ball, tastes it, yet never really closes its mouth around the bait, but the tip of your rod bends nonetheless, such is the car that teases you by signaling, but then rolls by; or worse, the vehicle that actually does pull over onto the shoulder just down the road from you, and you count your blessings quick, running with your belongings not to mention your fragile sense of belonging, but just when you approach all out of breath and grateful someone gets out with a camera dangling from their hands, and you realize the potential saviours are actually not stopping for you at all, in fact they haven't even seen you because you are not part of their package, they are tourists stopping to snap a landscape for their coffee table album and they have no room for you. And you're so pissed you think, the hell with it, I'll just walk. You realize this fish-thinking is folly.

Archy also knows the opposite, the sweet ride that changes the course of events, that introduces you to a whole new bag of possibilities... which sweeps you to a town called Kapuskasing.

A VW rattles into camp. Out the side window falls a head with dark hair stark black like in some eternal hair moment, as if for that eternal second the hair was rendered bodiless, supported only by its length.

Archy!

He emerges from the sliding door and runs into camp, and planters who recognize him make haste to greet him, and so does a cloud of blackflies instantly alerted to the presence of fresh meat. Two older folk get out the front, looking around and smiling and pointing at the strange landscape, while Archy greets those who are greeting him.

Planters pop off a spud gun that's powered by ignited hair spray, to celebrate his arrival.

Archy introduces the older couple as Jim and Bertha. Gabby observes them intently, her nose ever-so-slightly twitching. She notices how strangely the godparents are dressed, and how they stand with a strange stillness. The woman has on a dress with puffy shoulders, and knee-high winter boots; the man is wearing a weird hoser hat. They must have stopped at Ten-Cent Annie's.

Tie-dyed Sphagnum bounces with beaming doggy teeth into the centre of attention, licking the noses, lips, and wrists of those who bend in and coo to her. She performs quick 360s of jubilation. Her colours are brighter than they were the year before, a razzamatazz, as though Archy were trying to actually make his dog look like the moss itself.

"Oh, so cute. You gave her dreads!" Stringy hair coils

hang off Sphagnum's haunches and the sides of her belly and Archy says they're natural, from all that doggy paddling in man-made prairie weed lakes.

Rico bursts out of the mess tent, spinach leaves hanging from his front teeth, hoists Archy onto his shoulders, and runs him around teetery, while Archy bellows with a lunatic smile on his lips, "Ahoy there mates, the tree planter is aback."

"Hey, if it ain't brother Archy, baddest mo' in the east side boreal," Shnogg hollers from the mess tent as he finishes spooning his mashed potatoes.

"I have a dream, Shnogg. I have a dream!"

His godparents bought a whole case of alcoholic cider for the camp. For some reason Biz is all chatty with them, and he invites them into the trailer. Gabby observes them walking away, and it suddenly strikes her what's so weird about that couple — they aren't swatting at the bugs.

Grant is up on the slope, stacking some unsafe logs, twisting out the rusty nails with a crowbar. When he sees Archy come into camp he chuckles to himself. He'll finish dealing with the unsafe logs, then go greet Archy. And the couple coming out... the couple? Their clothes... those colours... Grant blinks rapidly. All these couples, the cursed couples... Doug Colt and Bertha, The Queen and that squire character with the ermine... as though there was some essential duality at work, projecting variations on a primordial theme.... He yanks out a few more nails then goes to say hello. His leather boots scuff over the crabgrass. He turns the corner of the mess tent, then stops short in surprise. That couple is right in front of him and now he can tell who they are. Those eyes. Those plastic eyes. He remembers... *they stitched open the specimen... it must have been the formaldehyde.* The pistons sighing as the door shut. Outside the Kap Inn, outside the Kap Inn. Outside the Kap Inn! She speaks in a voice that sounds like it's muffled by wet foliage. *"The tropics, honey... the trunk, the biggest trunk body in the universe is in the tropics, underwater, the barracuda, the sharks... they are laying eggs in her mouth."*

Grant moves quickly the other way around the mess tent, tripping and then kind of fall-sliding around some old banana boxes. He bangs the crowbar a couple times against his thigh as he lies amid the dented boxes, trying to stimulate the old reality reflex. It doesn't work... reality is wigging out. The blackflies swarm his face, crawling into his nose. He inhales once and lets out an explosive cough when the bugs tickle his throat. Archy seems changed, despite the letters Grant's received, which he's been reading with almost delirious trustfulness, as the fatigue and the bugs have been getting to him like anti-logic beetles. But no... there is something... Archy seems wild, not really focusing on what's going on around him. Grant peeks at him over the boxes, through the screen at the bottom of the mess tent, which is swarming in horrid blackfly circles. Archy's once hippie-esque style has definitely turned to complete grunge, and he seems serious, uncharacteristically serious. Sphag too — she's barking more than she normally does, and is continually chasing her own tail. Archy and his pup have changed. Changed, maybe, for the worse. Maybe the peyote and his obsession with Marcos are not a good combination for him. He smells bad, even by planting standards, and his long hair is tangled, rough, and not shiny like last year. Something has happened to him.

"Grant, my man! Peace be upon you, my old friend! You been keeping it real, or what?"

"Hey, Archy," Grant says in a weary voice. "Thank wolf that you're back. Things are getting a little topsy-turvy around here."

"Yeah, man, we've got to talk... shit's going down."

The fatigued planters lift their shoulders a tad higher now that Archy's back.

Spice has prepared fatty lamb burgers as a welcome back meal, and someplanter prepared a whole thing of cranberry juice crystal mix. Archy chews on a bone and casts his eyes around, conducting a mental inventory of returnees. When he's informed that Bazooka has been arrested, he bends his head over his food and stretches his arm over the plastic protective cover of the table and clenches his fists. "Those bastards... those sky bastards..."

Biz storms in with an angered expression. He calls an official meeting for later that night. As the time approaches he honks a horn to get everyone out of their tents where they're hiding from a wave of no-see-ums.

Flaunting his specially brimmed hardhat and his clean khakis, he addresses the planters. The rumours are true, he informs everybody: Bazooka has left camp for what seems an indefinite period. He can't go into detail, but he assures everybody that it's not a good situation, at least not for Bazooka. The police got involved, and sure, everyone can probably put two and two together (in other words Bazooka's BC plantation was busted — a lesson against conducting business from a distance).

Biz has officially been placed in charge by the upper Tamponix command. He states this plainly in cut tones and quick assertive gesticulation. Production is down from its historical value, he says. There are no excuses. Even if you're so sick you shit your pants you still have to get out there and plant. And it isn't just production that isn't going well — quality has fallen below the 91% mark, which is the pay minimum.

Fucking Biz, Grant fumes. Fucking proud he can keep his shirts clean even working in the woods. Almost magical, the way he appears on the logging roads after delivering trees, with his tight white shirt immaculate and his expensive hiking pants made of the newest materials as bright as if he were coming back from the shopping mall. Eerie, you might say. His hair always trimmed too, and his jaw shaved. If someone has some kind of twisted agenda, it's surely Biz.

The fire sputters, smoked out with damp boughs, smoked out like the eyes of the planters who swat feebly at the hordes of bugs, lacking the strength to guard against the six-legged assailants any longer. Grant gets disturbed from his fly-swatting with the old could-I-talk-to-you-for-a-second tap on the shoulder, and Biz proceeds to shit on Grant, telling him that a first aid kit was missing from one of the vehicles, which should have been noted during the safety audits. Biz continues with a litany of Grant's failures: there is no more dehydration crystal mix, none of the potable water and no smoking signs were posted, and no safety meeting has been conducted so far. The regional manager had shit on him, Biz, over the satellite phone for not having the appropriate forms filled out and sent to the head office in Timmins, and he doesn't want to lose standing on account of Grant's neglect of duty. He just won't allow that to happen, not to *him*, not at the hands of *Grant*, trying as he is to prove to upper management that he can make it as a supervisor long term, not just interim. No more slackers pussy-footing around, this is *not* a summer camp, everything will be micromanaged now, production will run like well-programmed software without a glitch. Biz wants all the tents set up in a grid when they move to the next camp.

Grant's brain-pressure rises unhealthily as he thinks about this. He finds himself hiding out in the woods behind the shitters with a stack of laminated signs that Biz gave him, a ridiculous number of signs which Grant cannot recall ever seeing around a planting camp before. There's a sign to remind people to put the shitter seats down, in order to keep the mephitic fumes from rising out of the hole, and another that says *USE WET-NAPS TO AVOID FECAL CONTAMINATION*, and five signs that say *OUT OF BOUNDS*, which Grant has to post in certain areas along the circumference of the camp, because during camp parties certain groups of planters, namely Larry's crew, had taken to going on missions into the woods, and camp lovers had been seen scampering like bunnies back to one mossy spot during courtship. In fact many members of the camp are feeling an uncanny attraction to the spruce stands, and have entered the shrine of trees at night to listen to owls. Grant had been given a strange book by the anthropologist called *The Man Who The Trees Loved*, which was some freaky novella about a man who left his wife to go on long walks into the woods behind their home, and who had found there a security and mystery far greater than what he had cultivated at home. But then his time amongst the trees began to interfere with his marriage, and when he tried to spend more time at home, the trees actually started to come his way, to visit him by his window. It was a freaky story written in an archaic style and as Grant sits behind the shitters looking up into the canopy, which appears to be the latticework at the back of some obscure dream, he knows there is a certain truth to the story... the spruce hang around like monks... and the gurgles, whispers, and buzzing are like the music of prayer.

Grant nails up one of the signs on a spruce tree. There seems to be a sign for everything now, as he leafs through the stack. There's even one that says *AN EXTRA HOUR'S SLEEP LEADS TO GREATER PLANTING FEATS*.

Later, there's a group of planters building a curious platform near Biz's trailer.

"What the hell's that for?" Grant asks, as he hammers up his last *NO SMOKING* sign near the wooden structure.

"It's an elevated observation deck, so that Biz can watch, make sure Everyplanter's obeying the signs."

Archy bids farewell to his godparents the next morning. He gives them long kisses on the mouth region as he says goodbye. Grant takes a long look down the road after them as they drive away, and where the fork is he sees them turn the wrong way, the way that goes deeper into the forest.

Then it's off to work. It's a scorcher out there and the land is brutal. Planters get sunburned and sunstroke. Then it cools off in the afternoon.

After dinner — fajitas made with leftover chicken — Larry invites Archy and some others to his fish hut for a toke. It is solemn in the fish hut. The atmosphere is quiet and contemplative, what with Larry done up in his headdress. Larry's classical, perhaps to the point of being stereotypical, head attire, consists of an old coyote-hide bandana with osprey feathers wound in jute sticking out in an avian display from the back. Faux lambskin pillows are strewn about, like it were an Ontarian opium shrine, and there are all these photos of big bass and pike lining the walls.

"Welcome to the Shaman's lodge!" Larry is sitting up cross-legged on his foamy, packing his tomahawk. "And welcome back to the crew, Archy. For those souls who are ignorant, what I hold in my hand is a legendary peace pipe. We call it a tomahawk for lack of a better word. My great-great-grandfather, Black Tail, a fearless Mohawk warrior, wielded this in a fight with two Englishmen from Upper Canada in 1863. They met at Otter Lake, the British accusing my great-great-great grandfather Black Tail of stealing beaver pelts from a Hudson's Bay outpost. It was The Battle of The Wolf, as the tribesmen were dressed in wolf gowns. The Wolf Spirit proved a Power Boon beyond the Imperial Bond. This fine blade has been buried in the brain of an evangelical colonist. Holy blood. Check this." He holds up the thick iron weapon by the shaft for Everyplanter to see, points to a rusted streak along an edge. "Petrified blood, my friends, petrified English blood, fossilized Tory DNA." The head has been drilled through and a bowl of carved antler inserted, the shaft reamed out making a long passage for the air and smoke to gain momentum heading towards the mouth of the user.

"To begin, we shall smoke this tobacco twist. Then we will proceed to indulge in the holy herb." Larry removes a curled piece of tobacco, twisted, occult, something from a witch's handbag, and rips a piece off the end. "Cured in sugar cane extract, then left underground for three months, better than Cuban wet leaf, it is."

Archy gets the first go at the sacred tobacco. This biographical illumination behind his eyes: Archy at 16, fresh on the scene like a political Rimbaud; Archy at 17, expelled from school for involvement in a database overthrow; Archy at 18, handing out pamphlets protesting Iraq War #1; Archy at 19, getting into LSD-25 and west coast adventures of the most green-chai-sipping and thousand-mile-eyed variety; Archy at 21, launching himself in a catapult over a fence at riots; Archy with a Black Panthers tattoo fading on his forearm at 22; all of Archy swirling in the smoke coming slowly out of his lips, a certain lucidity that seems newly acquired, the vague nihilism of last year having been superseded, it would seem, by something more real, more powerful, more deep. Or so it seems now, as he fluctuates and exhales, his eyes almost backlit with fervour.

"That smoke is all together too righteous, wow!"

Still and quiet — outside a hawk owl hoots wisdom to the waking animal legions of night. Everything is wet and dense and frog-chirpy and night-birdsongy and lunar, zeroing down into the dense little society of humans.

Once the tomahawk returns to Larry he has a bud ready. He packs it carefully in the hole. It is, he explains, part of Bazooka's new crop, fresh from the vernal valleys of the BC interior. If there is someone who knows weed, it's Larry. He's partial to only happy, calm herb, herb that is organically grown. If there is someone who knows how to grow good weed, it's Bazooka. So the two of them work well together. This herb was passed down through good hands and it shows in the quality of the product, the effect. "Fire in the hole!" A hand with a lit twig reaches in and blazes up the herb. That was Bazooka's old saying. Apparently his legacy will remain in the weed.

Gabby is uncommonly quiet, observing Archy the whole time as if processing gossip data. She leans forward when Archy starts going off on this rant.

"Okay, guys, so our prospects aren't exactly peachy, but really, (cough, cough) I have this idea, or no, I would probably call it more of a theory, now, let's see, just sit down, 'cause I want to introduce you to the 'The Cock Arse Hierarchy', copyrighted right now (cough, cough, you won't get off unless you cough…)."

Everyplanter snuggles into their dirty little pillows to listen to Archy.

"We are, according to my Western Ranch reckonings, being raped by big fat hairy cocks and balls coming from the executive branch of the cubic hierarchy. The first cock in this perverse hierarchy is the profit cock. This is a downwardly wielded cock saying 'work harder for less pay, six days a week.'"

He makes stabbing motions with his fingers squeezed into the tubular formation of a cockprobe.

"The next cock comes, again downward, from the forestry engineers, who select the land and determine what the specs are for each block. The spacing. The bidding prices. All that. We practice planting a tree one way and then we are told to replant by someone else, because some moron in that upwardly mobile office position who hasn't planted a tree since his Boy Scout days decides it will be better for the forest he's never seen with his own eyes. They make decisions based on aerial maps photographed during the winter, then come spring it floods and it takes us an hour just to wade into the block. And of course we have to suck it up because, hey, this is a tough company doing a tough job and everybody has to take it like a man. Bend over! These are professional cocks reared downwards, like, we're way at the bottom of this massive chain of cock command coming from the cities. Cocks, massive cocks blasted downward, and we, at the bottom, bend over and open wide."

Larry holds up his palm. "Now wait, wild one, we are performing the necessary function, reforestation. If it weren't for us, all the land would be sown by crows, the land, dear Archy, would belong to the dead."'

"Okay, sure, like we're the necessary dirty fingers of one of the industries. But Larry, no offense, you've never been one to understand reality. So let me continue." Larry is obviously put off by this as he bends his chin down into his chest. The osprey feathers quiver above his head.

"Now, hell yeah, the third cock — the tractor driving cock. This cocky sweaty sticky balls category is comprised of the people who scarify the land; machine conductors who are supposed to facilitate our job, but who instead, either due to imbecility, or because of some malice, (come on now Gabby, you agree with me), fuck over the workers. This, my fellow planters, is horizontally driven cock. It's cock from a fellow bush worker, is what it is — these skidder and bulldozer drivers all dozing off, or drunk, or disgruntled, driving their prep machines in loop-di-loops, creating frigging labyrinths of corridors and patchy scarification and we're supposed to be planting quality trees in that, for eight cents a pop!? And then there are reverse cocks, hell yeah, horizontal dicks thrust remorselessly from one planter to another — the incestuous cock — like your planting partner sluts out the front of your piece and it wasn't that they didn't know it was yours, it was that they didn't give a rat's ass — they just wanted the easy trees. And let's not forget all those unclassifiable cocks — unavoidable fuck-ups like augured vehicles, repo, etc, as well as the environmental cock that is indifferently driven by Mother Nature herself, part and parcel with any outdoor job. Grant, you are experiencing Mother Nature cock. The rain, the big rain cock blasting down your trailer. Freaking celestial cock, darn primordial cock."

Pause.

"Let's overthrow this shit, let's hack down the cock-hierarchy with androgynous wooden sabers. From the chaos will arise a new, unique system, a new tribe starting a new something or other. Who's in? We'll save the geese and string them to our chariots, and we'll soar through the northern skies!"

"Archy, Archy, my man, my man, you are crazy as per usual, my crazy wavy friend Archy," Planter Without a Name says as they manoeuvre through the bio-smog of the camp back to the tent area. The night seems to be a warm-lipped creature, and the bugs mostly at bay, hypnotized or abdomen-rubbed to sleep by the warm and cool currents alike.

"I swear," says Archy, "I swear… you know, have you read the subcomandante's Manifesto? No? Well, there is a spectre haunting North America, that's what it says, and now there is a spectre, a spectre of a different kind I say, a spectre haunting the wooded communities of the true north strong and free, but it's different, it's not the same old, same old. It's spectral cosmic plurality! You with me?"

"Not if you're going to badmouth sodomy like that," Planter Without a Name says. "Some of us like joining cock-in-the-arse hierarchies… it's in the Chuck Norris Kama Sutra Book, unless, as you say, it's some kind of ultra-sadistic corporate cock hierarchy, in which case, that ain't cool at all!"

"Fair enough, fair enough… to each their own… everyone is welcome… we're moving away from the cock model, I'll just put it that way…"

The next guy pushed to the front of the school bus says his name is Ralfka. Bosso sticks the barrel of the rifle between this guy's teeth for a moment, then pulls it out.

I am of mixed descent, Ralfka admits, looking pleadingly over to us who sit at the kiddy-sized seats like unwilling jurors. Things just aren't right in a lot of ways and I always felt I wanted to get those things out of the system. I used to be a nihilist, but now I am the opposite. I stand for the reinvigoration of enviro morality. For a rebirth of a happy totalitarianism… I… I… I… am… (He starts blubbering profusely)

— What are you scared of? Tell us now or forever hold your peace in the bottomless grave. (Bosso narrows an eye down the cross hairs of the rifle)

I am fearful of my own capacity for destruction and chaos. I am haunted by the sound of batons smacking shields: the rhythm of the opponent's system. At the protest in Quebec City… the Mounties in formation. Clack. Clack. They moved forward in robotic display like they were the mouths and we were the poutine… I mean, phalanx. The horrible contrast between —

— *Say it now! Speak now!*

Between my friends: drunk on dépanneur king cans, whipping rubber bricks and teddy bears from a catapult over the fence at the Robo-Mounties; our bucket drums, the urban tribal sounds, the hockey organ beats, the whirling bottles, and the cameras, digital cameras everywhere... the planes, the fucking planes crashing into my home; the Mohawks at the front lines waving their clan flag, inhaling the tear gas like it was mist; the determination, the snake-like unraveling of the police regiments forward, always forward — the complete mastery of reality or... or rationalism... displayed by our opponents, and the chaos, the chaos of... us... that's why we need a computer commander...

Bosso's face is cobalt. He glares at Ralfka through his Oakleys. The left lens is worn down in the middle so we can see his eyeball. There is hardly any light in the school bus, but we can see every detail.

— *Now get off this bus or I will blow your head off, Ralfka. Bosso shoves him down the steps, out the side door. We all look out the flinty windows; we see Ralfka run, tears rushing down his cheeks, to the side of the dirt road. There is a man standing by the woods, dressed in military uniform, waiting for him. The man clutches Ralfka by the shoulder and hauls him toward the woods. Then the school bus lurches forward. Looking back out the kidsafe windows, we see Ralfka disappearing into the undergrowth, followed by the military man. Then Bosso shrieks, and our heads whirl back to the front.*

— *All right, who's next? Who the hell is crying? Whoever's crying, it's your turn to get up to the front of the bus.*

Biz holds another meeting. He's got a projector hooked up to the generator and is doing a PowerPoint presentation in the mess tent.

"We've organized the remainder of the contract like this, you see...." He runs a hand through his hair and points with a laser pen to several photos projected onto a shitty old roll-up screen. Various cream shots. Biz's presentation is like an Italian porn shoot of sexy land.

"This, my planters, is why we've lowered the tree price.

There's just way too much cream to go around, ladies and gentlemen. Doesn't it make you want to do something improper?" Biz clutches his cock through his clean white pants. "Yeah, baby..."

There's some ogling and even moaning from the planters. 400 hectares of pure cream!

"There will be more than enough," ensures Biz, with a satisfied smile. "More than enough for all of us to do our share of pounding.

THE GOOD OLD BLOCK SPANK

The idea of revolution excites Grant. He strains to convince himself that Archy is normal and that everything is normal, and that any sinister complexity is just a superimposition of his own fancy upon the rather boring and eventless environment. But the peculiar behaviour and corroborated observations of others would seem to contradict... perhaps out here everything becomes a group fiction, small things take on the power of political import.

The sun and wind have burned and blown the bugs away, leaving a green and happy day. He decides to whip his dick out, partake in a good old block spank, aiming his phallus over the greenery of his piece. Whacking off feels as if he is fucking nature in the abstract. A week's worth of spunk in the bank and the sun shining on the idea of a different tomorrow. Here's my own little contribution, he says to himself, zipping his fly... then, after letting the sun beat on him, just standing still for a second, he continues to plant slow, pondering the big fiction. He plants along, just humming away, observing the odd bee, and thinking all these little happenings — his mind leaping from one to the other.

It's like he's the captain of this trunk ship, which has a streamlined, space-friendly bark exterior, and control panels made of mushroom buttons. Super cool, he thinks, as he descends onto a new frontier. Like he's the little prince flying on a burning tree through the solar system of his imagination, searching for a planet to land on, and slowly descending through a purplish atmosphere, and he sees the green and blue planet rising toward his descending trunkship. And now he swoops over oceans and forests, looking for somewhere to land. He sees in the outlines of the continents the green body of some huge lady, and it is upon the open landscape of her body which the trunkship lands. On clear-cut landing pads, and then deep, deep, sinking into the tropical waters.

Groucho injecting his arm with steroids. Biz watches, wetting his lips with a nervous tongue. Now Biz and Groucho driving down a road under the bizarre sundog moon, which looks like a huge eye, for the sun is somewhere below the visible horizon but nonetheless illuminates the moon with intensity. They are now by a thicket of trees, and the trees are wagging their hips, and he can see the lips of Biz and Groucho as they stand now, beside their truck, talking to one of the trunks... and Grant realizes he is seeing this for real, it's happening there, in the distance, way down there where the road emerges from the timber edge.

And he sees two planters a few hundred metres into the horizon, shrubbery sticking up around their genitalia, as fig leaves, and now another of Biz's crew, an up-and-coming crew boss, he's barking angrily at the naked planters, commanding them to put their fucking clothes back on.

And these voices... the voices of Biz and Groucho... and they are talking to somebody whose voice sounds like it's coming through a synthesizer.
Who are you?
I am another Xylophloe, how do you do?
Fine. You wanted us to meet you here by this tree, and now it turns out that maybe you are this tree.

How is the planting of the experimental trees coming along?

Grant's mind skips.

And there is the anthropologist, with his binoculars... looking... looking in Grant's direction from a raised area on the other side of the block. And he has white things on his feet... some bright, beautiful socks which are radiant in the sunshine... *hey, my fucking socks*.

... fucking socks... *YOU GO INTO THE WOODS AT NIGHT AND YOU FIND ONE, WHAT IS IT?* He was picking up all these transient waves, kind of like a super sensitive radio...

He wonders where Murielle is planting. He is wondering if he can ever love someone out here. He knows that love is like the sun on the rise, coming up over the horizon, warming everything like a giant alien ember.

Murielle finds the toads are different out here than in Montreal. For one thing, they are more reddish-brown than the mud toads in the city. And these forest toads are quicker, stealthier and more guileful.

And the bugs in this part of the block are fuckered, which explains why there are so many toads, which in turn shines light on the origins of the booming snake population. She spits and slaps and still, bugs get in her armpit and under her chin. That makes her twitchy. So do all the hopping toads darting about. They play tricks on her eyes. She keeps thinking she sees little flashes of movement on the forest floor. As if she perceived words being created; as if sentences came from this forest and at night little fireflies flashed like the first sparks of thought. The operetta of tiger frogs is the first glottal pronunciation.

She muses at the mind's tremendous capacity to create

what it expects. It is expecting toads, so it mistakenly apprehends them... it expects stairs to rise through the leaves like this was Mount Royal... it visualizes her father in the streets of Montreal, her eyes filling in the details of a stranger's face with the pigment of memory.

She sees a toad that looks like it has a piece of live wire attached to it skittering through the brown leaves. The wire is a snake. It is engorging the leg of the toad up to its spotted thigh. The toad's eyes are open wide, gold motes surrounded by tadpole-black, and with its forelegs it is struggling to wrench itself free — failing to grip, pulling against the serpentine tug of death. The gardener snake's jaw dislocated, hanging wide open.

Murielle's eyes shine in hatred for the predator. She knocks the jaw of the snake with the side of her shovel, and it releases, strikes at her, misses, and slithers into the seams of the forest.

She sees the forest through Grant's eyes, understands the mutterings she has heard him utter in his sleep. How it is not always pretty out here. Not at all. How there is something large, inexact, that swims through the swaying trees, swarming into the black holes of the cuts.

And for some reason watching the toad getting swallowed makes her envision a birth. She remembers where she came from.

LOVERS IN THE MULCH

"My parents were part of the francophone move west," Murielle says, turning on her sleeping bag. They are naked and their bodies are pale and pimply yet still super beautiful. Celestial aura of her tent. Folded open beside them is her Fertility Regularity Chart with that day's date checked off in red marker.

"My mother, she was beginning a French school board in Calgary when I was not born yet. She was meeting my father out there. He was running a fruit picking company. They were big hippies, I think. Yes, I am sure of this. They went to the hot springs in 1982. You know how hot that water is, how do you say, full of *soufre*? That is when occurred the little reaction that made me. I was conceptualized in the hot springs."

She puts her little hand on Grant's rough jaw and swivels his chin so his eyes are directed into hers.

"You don't mean conceived, do you?" Grant says, observing her planet-like irises.

Murielle shakes her head on the pillow and her hair rustles against the blue pillowcase. *"Oui, c'est qu'est ce que je vouderai dire."*

"Je ne comprends pas. Speak in English, please." Grant sits up and sips some water from a whisky flask that he stole from Luke, and groans. He isn't drinking these days. No tobacco, no alcohol: the straight edge. "You're crazy, you know that, Murielle? I can't believe you enjoy this. It's the worst contract ever!" In mid-sentence Grant starts hacking and it sounds like he's going to cough up a lung.

"You are the crazy one, *monsieur* Grant. I am with it. You are from the trees, Grant… or a tree… that is probably why you are coming back here every year to plant. You will meet a tree princess one day and you will have many tree babies."

"Murielle, I want *you* to be my tree princess."

She doesn't respond. She's turned her head and is cupping a fly between her palms and letting it escape out the bottom of the tent flap.

"Fuck, Murielle, quit saving bugs already!"

Jean Michel is implicit in the buggy silence that ensues, as Murielle references her *chum* in debates over the ethics of celibacy. Her basic position on the matter being that as long as nobody finds out the specifics, it's all good. But she doesn't realize, Grant argues, that someone always finds out, and someone will always get hurt. She plans on getting back together with Jean-Michel after the summer, Grant's gathered that much. He's baffled by Murielle's ability to divide her love in two like this.

"But I know this is a bad company," she says. "Afterwards I go out west to pick fruit and then I go to Africa."

Screw you too, then, he feels like saying.

They dress and head for the stream.

"Come here for a sec."

She hops over to him like an inquisitive kitten. He dips his fingers in the stream and dabbles water into the corner of her eye. It's somewhat puffed up from the bug attack.

He's dirty-faced, but he doesn't feel self-conscious about it. That sort of thing just doesn't faze Murielle.

"Nice evening."

"*Oui, c'est vraiment agreable dehors.* The weather is very hallucinating."

"Hallucinating. That's a good way of putting it. What do you mean by that, though?"

"I mean it's changing like a chameleon."

The day is happier-faced now. They pass planters washing in the main brown pool that is only waist deep.

"I feel like we screwed first, and had foreplay later. Would you have an abortion if you were pregnant?"

"*Non.*"

They squat next to each other by the pool and splash hand cups of water onto their faces to wash away the DEET and salt.

"Will they shoot the bear?" Murielle asks as she dries her face on her T-shirt. "Luke would not do something like that, would he? Biz and Luke had a gun, did you know this, Grant? And they said the bear trap wasn't working."

"No, they just want to scare the bear." Grant keeps his eyes averted and just keeps staring into the rippling water. Then he lies sideways with his head propped up watching the little golden ghosts of the water ripple, aggravated by the rush of currents over obstacles. The dirty water froths brightly none the less. It feels as though the whole thing were coming apart before his eyes. His arms heavy and hurt but the sun coming over him like a great balm. He actually falls asleep. He wakes up with her head nestled under his shoulder. The sound of her voice, like her tea, wraps him in the gentle folds of sleep. He has a thought in the twilight between waking and sleeping: That Luke will walk through halls of stone. Grant, to the trees and mountains. Murielle will grow wings like a dryad.

"Tell me the story of how you hit her," Murielle says.

ARCHY HAS BEEN CONFERRING WITH DOUG COLT

Community Dairy: the beauty of northern cuisine with service that calls you "dear" and the best breakfast in town. The cook works behind the counter whipping the cream and preparing the pie.

Doug Colt pops up and seats himself on one of the stools, and flips through his checker's cards for a bit. They can see his motorcycle outside, with Princess in the cargobox, panting in the summer sun.

"Have you paid for your breakfast yet? No, well it's on me... or wait now... Sally, these planters are doing big things soon, how 'bout a freebee?"

"Anything for those sexilicious tree planters," says the waitress.

"It's a little reward for planting such great quality," Doug beams.

"Let's cut to the chase," Gabby prods.

Doug gets serious. "I don't know if you heard, but the workers —"

The waitress puts pieces of key lime pie in front of them.

"The uprising of 1991. Yeah, we knew this was going to be something related to that."

They eat away at the pies.

"The town of Kapuskasing, the workers. We owned the mill collectively for three some years until Terrorhouser bought us out and gave us stock options or big cash. Well, see, I was one of the ones who spread word about the original buy-in. I know people up north, we're trying to do some things up here. You ever 'eard of the 'emp strain called Rooteralis? Northern weed, my tree planting friends, and northern paper. It grows like stink in Russia. It's all part of the evolution."

Gabby cuts in. "Depending on how you want to look at it, right? I mean, there's fact, then there's bullshit. To call what happened in the early nineties a revolution or evolution or whatever, might be taking liberties with the truth, wouldn't it?"

"All I can say, missy, is that what the people did 'ere in Kapuskasing was unprecedented in Canada and maybe even all of North America. Call it a revolution or not. We seized ownership of the mill."

"That shit doesn't happen anymore," Grant chimes in.

"I was the union representative at the mill, and it was through my initiative that the right papers were signed, and I also did the publicity."

"So it was a throwback."

"To Marx —"

"The days of…"

"Revolt."

"That's exactly what it was. A brief period of up'eaval followed by change. The dialectiques of the forest. I come from a long line of shit disturbers. D'ose pictures I showed you, well that there guy Horsejaw was my uncle… this stuff is hereditary. But dere's some things you should really watch out for, things that will totally…"

His attention is distracted for a moment by something outside. He runs his fingers through his mullet.

"I want the tree planters to follow in the footsteps of the town. I see you guys, lots of you studying forestry, culture. All these great things. All these smart kids…. Get a list… a petition… win that contract away from Tamponix… we'll save the North."

They munch their pie with whipped-cream ideas about some great new camp in the woods. They'd still be serving Terrorhouser logging, but Doug Colt seems to think they might not be around for much longer. In the event of bankruptcy, the contract would revert to the Ministry… and the planters could start other initiatives. He has ideas about retraining displaced forestry workers as hemp farmers.

Later Doug Colt vrooms into the traffic circle wearing a Clear Water hat, and two other motorcycles idle behind him with some real tough dudes sitting there. They have large muscles and visible tattoos and shiny golden teeth, but in a positive kind of way, as if instead of badass they were "goodass". Doug Colt collects the petition from Archy. There are tremendous puffs of smoke or mist wafting through the traffic circle, and the community bells at church are ringing slow, deep, from the hospital behind the Kap Inn.

When they were tearing down camp to move it down the road, the sky had been cloven by oppositional clouds and colours — on one side showing off ridiculously huge idyllic clouds all lit up like cream puffs trailing off into white fences and a vortex of rose and red — and at the furthest perimeter, the tempest, darkness cracked with heat lightning.

The quitters line up with their beaten up gear scattered on the grass. Some quitters even left their tents back in the old camp. Ghost tents billowing soiled and ripped in the empty wind.

Luke overhears Benito on the pay phone explaining how he wants to leave with everyone else.

"You ain't just going to give up like that now, son." Luke says into Benito's free ear

Benito cups the receiver in his narrow armpit. "Listen, I came here for economic reasons, not political reasons, alright, Luke?"

"Listen, I'm talking about duty. It's our duty to finish this contract."

Benito looks offended. "Why is everybody acting so

fucked up? Even you've gone insane, Luke. Even you, the coolest guy in camp. I'm getting the fuck out of here…"

Benito slams the receiver and runs for the quitters' bus, but Luke runs him down, grabs him by the lapels, and bellows in his ear, "No, you are not! We're bound together in this, son. We're going to the furthest reaches!"

"Fine, fuck! Fine."

"We need you for the new generation of woodland youngsters," shouts Archy, overhearing the dispute. "Hey, Grant, you gonna take the helicopter ride with me? Biz says he needs someone to show the pilot…"

"Where is Biz? At the tanning salon?"

"He went back to camp early, I think."

They can hear the sound of the helicopter coming, so Grant grabs his garbage bag full of clean laundry and his guitar and heads with Archy over to the field.

The copter sounds erratic as it descends, blowing toilet paper out of the bushes. The cockpit is one of those plastic bubbles — an old bush model, a discontinued version of the A-Star. After it sets down and steadies its runners the pilot swings open the side door and steps down off the landing skid. He's got a spherical white helmet that's very chipped and he looks kind of wobbly at the knees and all helter-skelter and blue under the eyes like he just woke up, and he's waving, yelling, "GO, GO!" — Archy and Grant and two other veterans run and put their stuff in the back compartment then jump into the passenger seats, Archy in the front seat.

The pilot grimaces as he takes them above the green. Not surprisingly, the cockpit is full of crap — old Styrofoam cups and crumpled cigarette packages. Grant's flown with this pilot before; the guy was fired a few years back from a commercial gig in BC and must have been given a last chance in old Ontario.

"You guys like roller coasters?" The pilot croaks over the intercom. The pilot's grin devils up before they can respond, and he pulls the steering stick into his chest, making the helicopter arc nose first into the blue, and up, up, hearts heavy with the G force and then right when the pilot reaches the apex he stalls the engine for a split second and the nose tips sideways then points straight down and they start to freefall — plummeting toward the big fields of evergreens down below, now a green sea, and they all scream. They can feel their organs being pushed back against the seats.

"That was a jackhammer," says the pilot once he rights the helicopter.

"More!" screams Archy. "Come on, more!" And he's jumping around in his seat, pawing at the windows with excited hands.

The view is quite amazing, and they can see where various industries have carved the land into factions... and they descend to a lower altitude now, skimming along, and Archy is asking the pilot about the different controls. "If we're going to start our own company we're going to need to know how to fly a helicopter," he says to Grant, swiveling his head to look in the back. He looks ridiculous with his big helmet and flowing hippie hair.

"Look at that — " Grant sees something down below in a clear-cut.

"What is it?" Archy asks, still turned.

"A backhoe. What's a backhoe doing down there?"

"Could we do a fly-by?" Archy asks the pilot.

"Sure thing." The pilot pulls sideways on his control stick and they circle the clear-cut, hovering about the tops of reserve patches.

"This is near your old camp, isn't it?"

"Yeah, that's what's so strange...." They observe the backhoe in the clear-cut, which is part of the block system they just finished planting.

"Looks like somebody has some pretty major stashing plans."

The rest of the camp has been packed into the trailers, and the procession moves down the road deeper into the bush.

The forest is ashen, cloaked in dust.

Past kilometre 68, the old camp disappearing behind them. Biz stands at the front of the bus counting heads while the bus rattles along. The clay road becomes smoother for a while and presently they chug past a murky-edged, silver lake. The road bends, following the contour of a river. And there is another planting camp there, planters sitting on the top of their buses, feet dangling off.

It gets dark and they pass oil trucks, or mining trucks... tankers with red stripes and high beams digging cones of light from the darkness, convoys from deeper down the FSR.

The camp of tree sluts is sent with every planted sapling deeper into the arboreal mind. Everyplanter is as green as thoughts emitted by the earth — consciousness of the camp forming one larger, omega-consciousness of the forest itself. The idea of a calendar has dissolved. They are skinny Australopithecus.

The trees undress from their leaves like strippers; the marten slink through the folds of the disappearing forest. The bug swarms follow the carbon dioxide trail of the bus, like an omnipresent, atomized intelligence, as if they were psychic particles, mini holographic figments conjured by the ailing mental health of the frustrated planters.

Finally, on Biz's command, the buses turn down a nondescript dirt road and come to a stop. The planters get out and stretch, and the bugs descend. It smells different here; mold or slime. The new camp is hardly a campsite at all. Ray says that it's probably Block Z, the zone where Terrorhouser moved in without the Ministry's consent.

They hold a meeting and it's a bug fest.

"Welcome to the creamshow," Biz smiles. "It's right outside. The camp is on the edge of the cream. Block Z, my planting friends. Block Z." Some planters look into the darkness. It looks flat because the stars come down flush with the horizon line. The corners of Biz's lips twist upwards slightly as he watches their pleasure. "Just look out your tent in the morning and try not to jizz or wet yourselves."

"Are we going to be planting that tomorrow?" One of the highballers asks with a look of lust.

"Aha! A question. Now, what did I say last time about questions? This will be the final answer to any question. Answered as follows: we need you boys and girls to finish the other blocks first. We must. The Ministry is making us do it, through the recommendation of Northern Cloners nursery. We have to finish the chemical treatment blocks first... with the experimental trees.

The chemical land is super tough. The alder boughs are cock-stiff and the dead grass forms a layer which is difficult to punch through with their shovels. They get helied to the new blocks. They pound the day away in blistering heat — athlete's foot for everyone involved. The land is rocky, but since nobody is going to come back to this distant cut for a long time, the quality doesn't matter, so the day turns into a bit of a slut fest.

All day, the old heli shuttles back and forth, carrying slings filled with boxes of trees, and dropping them in strategic positions. Everyplanter is financially happy by the time the helicopter comes in to start picking them up at the end of the day.

Styler's crotch is horribly chafed after pounding six thousand trees. Luke gives him some Silver Soak Man's Powder. He pours the white talc into a palm, pulls back the waistband of his quick-dry jogging pants and powders up. Then the helicopter comes and he's comfy the whole way back to camp. SWALLS be gone!

Everyplanter is momentarily happy because they made some cash. Grant sees Murielle in front of her European Blue Gaz stove, aglow after having surpassed her personal best that day. Flames licking the travel pot she's using to brew some celebration chai. When Grant passes again, he notices Murielle sitting behind Groucho, and if his eyes are not failing him in the dim light, she's giving Groucho the massage of a lifetime. He watches, voyeuristically. Her delicate yet muscular fingers knead into Groucho's back muscles like dough. The camp turns into an open forum for spying and eavesdropping. Grant lets the jealously burn to an ash in his heart.

Later that night he appears from the shadows and shocks Murielle. "Boo," he says. "Hey Murielle, I want to tell you the story about how I hit her."

"Alright," she says slightly reluctant now.

He feels like he can finally describe to her what happened and finally release all the problems that this personal history engendered.... It was this unwritten understanding between them, or perhaps it was in some way etched into the very skin of the landscape: you have to get back up and face the day, and for Grant it was to look that thing in the eye which he had been evading, through the trips down south and the hiking and partying, that feeling of having done wrong to the great pristine thing, femininity, nature, that if he didn't, or couldn't, or failed to face up, those root memories were basically like a consciousness virus. He had to kick closed that final hole with the bruised eye staring up out of it, or he'd become a very bitter person very quickly and live alone in the woods. He had to make peace with those mistakes. And now he's sputtering out the words to Murielle, how it was a very real trial involving a quite real ex-girlfriend testifying against him on battery charges. He'd really been "fucked up" back when he did those things, he'd let the darkness, or the negativity, or whatever it was, cloud his judgments. Maybe he'd loved her. Maybe she'd loved him. But slowly things had become really fucked up. She'd treated him nice though he considered himself a creep, and he really was one, because he was going through psychological growing pains. She'd worn her long range vision goggles and he'd lost even his short range contacts and couldn't think a day ahead. They'd begun the kinky practice of dressing up in costume — he in a bunny hat, she in a huntsman's vest, and they were certainly experimenting, willfully blurring the boundaries of the real and unreal. Then they'd started bringing each other down in life, and cheating on each other, and ignoring each other, and fighting louder and louder until one day, smack! They had taken it too far, or maybe just in the wrong direction... falling short of real freedom. Those strange pills had something to do with it, the ones handed out at the parties they went to held by people wearing track suits with fanny packs full of what seemed in the moment of epiphany and peaking to be philosopher stones.... A bad decision to take those pills maybe, and maybe they amounted to that final turn of the screw, perverting the most sanctimonious laws of the mind, a painful descent from a lofty summit of epiphany scaled without having to climb.

Yeah, he'd punched her out, and that was pretty much it, for the relationship that is, but it marked a new beginning of another kind, this time between Grant and the law. The law which you don't know you are breaking until it is broken and the cuffs come around your wrists. She'd hit him first, but for some reason that didn't matter. Battery charges, incarceration avoided by some weird plea bargain, then community service at the local garbage dump where Grant got to stare for 200 hours at heaps of waste. He recalls muttering to the probation officer, while he was high on garbage fumes, something about women never going to be equal unless they learn how to take a punch. "You beat the shit out of her, didn't you?" the officer had said. Murielle raises her eyebrows at this and looks disgusted, but Grant tells her how it was this dark demon phase he'd gone through and he'd overcome it and meeting people like Murielle, so full of life, how it made him see things now through different eyes and now he's almost planted enough trees to offset the past abuse... having planted more than one million trees is good for the judgment day balance sheet. He has practically accumulated enough carbon offsets to buy a personal jumbo jet and commit a mass murder. He feels okay about the past now, he's fucking suffered enough and it's time to see the humour in it, right Murielle? But she seems silent on that matter, and asks him about what happened to this girlfriend, is she okay? And Grant asks if she would believe him if he said she never really existed in the first place, and Murielle shaking her head and swatting the bugs... and they both look out over the horizontals, the verticals, the outlines, which are as they are — and having no judgment about them beyond how they are outlined by the rods in his eyeballs, Grant realizes that this place had taken on the dimensions of his girlfriend, she exists here in some insanely abstract way... the abused land... and now that she has passed from the landscape it is as though she's forgiven him, which is another way of saying he has forgiven himself, and then, as he tells Murielle, in the most pathetically fallacious display, the sun comes out and lines up the crystal water drops on a spider web in a portal geometry. He can't help but admire Murielle as she sits with him, swatting at bugs and looking over at the tents like she wants to leave the shale pile and trying to understand what he is saying. Would this bring them closer together or drive them further apart, neither of them knew, neither could think clearly enough to know...

Nobody ever would have suspected her to be a torturer of innocent creatures. She seems, of everyone on the bus, perhaps the most innocent. Bosso chuckles at her revealing confessions as he holds the gun to her head. She is saying: on one hand, I loved those small and perfect creatures, but on the other hand I wanted to torture them. I was camping on this island with my two friends and there were these dragonflies metamorphosing, emerging in prayer positions from the shells of waterbeetles clinging to the trunks of blue spruces. Next to a rock by the water there was this lone mephisto flower with marine blue petals. Everything on the little island was so beautiful, but then after a full day we became bored and we took out our aerosol DEET which we hadn't used so far because there were no mosquitoes on the tiny island and we sprayed the meta-

morphosing drgonflies and they writhed in chemical agony and we picked all the petals off that flower and destroyed the symbol which centered the beauty of the island. We used to cut the fins off of fish, as well, and shoot birds that were mating during springtime with my brother's BB gun. I was an evil tomboy. This whole time I have been walking around with something nagging me... the secret that lurked behind my... and blaming my brother for bringing me along... she trails off and then suddenly she lets out a loud ow! and holds her forehead as if it hurt deep inside her head. All right, shut the fuck up, get out, Bosso says, snapping out of any sympathy he may have felt. We all look out to see where she goes in the lit night and there is this huge whale floating in the trees and the fronds of the trees splashing around, and the whale looks like a scrimshawed humpback carved in a huge tusk. She peers pleadingly through the window. We will all be seeing each other again, Bosso says. Then a tree limb snatches her by her arm and starts pulling her in. Before she disappears into the brush the big humpback observes her with its large docile eye and the moon beats like a heart and the silhouette of the standing twin spruces in the Milky Way frames the sky and everything becomes dark outlines inside the bus except for Bosso's grin. Straining ahead toward our uncertain destination with salix dancing out the left and owls curling on the right. It is the perfect opportunity to jump him, with his gun fallen to the floor after we hit a bump, except we cannot rise, so tired are our muscles, no matter how much energy we try to muster we cannot rise. We are stuck behind him, imprisoned in our seats, and clouds of mist disperse across the big rectangular window and his face is militant in the hard oval mirror. At one point we look out the windows and there are scenes from other countries. Explosions and wailing, and people squatting in circles. And we are all screwed up. And then we look out and we see a huge tree, the biggest tree of our whole lives. So large we cannot wrap our minds around it.

THE DECLINE OF WINGER

The highballer gets brutal land all week; she's losing it. She becomes a pounder gone wild, a monomaniac. On the bus she disappears into her headphones and smokes big joints all by herself, blowing fat clouds sucked out the open windows. She doesn't socialize with anyplanter except in this psycho sort of way. Planters bitch about her behind her back. She is the unpopular woman. The land is all rocks and Winger curses as her shovel pings. It's a lesson in geology out there: conglomerate and diorite, schist and gneisses, the minerals split along fracture lines revealing crystals and fossils. Lithospheric complications. Winger flails away, totally slutting her trees. Eliza has to have a "quality" talk with her. The checkers are on her ass and Biz gives her a written warning.

Everyone is twitchy; Winger in particular. She's hanging out with Walter the anthropologist all the time, and when waiting in line for supper she swats furiously at the bugs like she was a crazy woman. Even after dark she swats like mad while she froths her mouth up with Danny's Natural Toothpaste. Somebody has to remind her that if she stayed still for a second she'd notice the bugs had gone to bed. That she would be so crazy is partly understandable because the bugs adore her. One day she shows up after work with a scarlet wave down the side of her forehead where she got chewed by the blackflies. Another girl's face puffs up, too. It usually happens to fair-haired planters for some reason, this bug-ravaging. People start calling Winger "Puffy".

One morning they wake up and discover that the camp is badly flooded. There are runnels and rills purling between tents making the campsite look like an archipelago. Winger refuses to get out of her tent that morning. Eliza tries to coax her. With production down they need Winger pounding to her full potential. When Winger finally does the old okay all right fine then and emerges from her tent it is head first, and Eliza sees that she's shaved off her beautiful Madonna hair, and she has a moon hennaed on the back of her scalp. She informs Eliza that she's growing potatoes and that they will shoot right up in no time, just watch and see. Better than P.E.I. potatoes, she promises. "Where?" someone asks her. "In my Queen's garden," she says.

Getting out of camp that morning it is as if everything is jinxed — Everyplanter slept through the breakfast horn including, uncharacteristically for such a dialed-in camp cook, Spice, so it's a cold breakfast of various cereals, then the bus gets a back tire stuck on the deceptively soft shoulder so they attach a tow rope to the front and yank the International bus out with one of the Fords, but the Ford gets stuck too, even worse than the bus. The wheels on the ditch side are sunken to the top lug nuts and Sil jumps out foul-mouthed in a waterfall of fast food wrappings, belly sagging underneath a soiled white shirt, slapping bugs, and they have to go to Biz's trailer. "You want to use my truck?" Biz says with a troubled blankness as he finishes folding his clothes. Outside, planters are all digging at the wheels and laying quad ramps under the wheels for traction, and Everyotherplanter is pacing around camp and swatting bugs and sipping coffee or is in the sloppily and loosely set up mess tent, waiting, hurry up and wait! Eliza can see some planters hovering around the stuck truck as if some intangible force in the air has stripped them of their powers of concentration and stupefied them into shuffling around in a slug-like mass. So Biz gets out there, finally, and drives to the front of the tow line, this time in reverse, and tries to use his winch on the first Ford, but the winch cable is all frayed and it snaps at full force. Holy shit! The broken cable whips back and takes out his front windshield, kablammo! Biz ducks, then sits up again, covered in glass shards, with a holy fuck expression. So they have to call in a grader. The grader: huge-wheeled, big-bladed, towing out Biz's Ford and Sil's delivery truck, and then the International bus. And as a consequence of all this mucking around the planters don't get out until midday, and hardly make fuck all.

Smallmouth bass and sunfish somebody passes us through the window. The juices surge and swish in our mouths — Canuck-style sashimi. The salt and protein rev up our fear-numbed bodies. All the living symbol thingies everywhere have convinced us that we are actually in a dream or somehow sucked into a program. That everybody on the bus has somehow interconnected together into a group nightmare. But then why does it hurt so much whenever the bus goes over a big hump and we smash our heads? Then we see the huge tree again, as we come down the other side of this extended gradient — Bosso looks out there and as though we weren't supposed to see it he whispers, "Shit, the Tree of Life." There it is, detonating into the sky, and under it, lit more plainly than anything yet, a couple strolling, hand in hand.

PROMO

To the isolated camp come few visitors. Yet lo, there appear two headlights in the fog, from the eyes of a rattling all-wheel-drive beast. A short man who nobody recognizes hustles back and forth through the ghostly shafts of those lights, from his trunk to the mess tent with armloads of high-tech shovels wrapped in plastic.

"I planted 300,354 trees in 54 days with a Workwizer shovel," says the shovel sales dude. "That's an average of 5,562 trees per 9 hour working day, 618 trees an hour, 10.3 trees per minute, a tree every 5.8 seconds for a whole week." He's on a ten camp tour... he's here to max the North's production.

He even challenges Luke to a shovel duel after a number of beers.

"You see... great shovels for medieval dueling as well... one challenge, then I'm off to the next camp..." They clank shovel/swords, parrying back and forth to the laughter of Everyplanter watching.

About 10 planters take out advances and purchase the new shovels. And their production rises… a little bit.

PRODUCTION DREAM PHARMACY DREAM

Murielle is unable to sleep in the sick warmth of summer humidity and mosquito air, but is copping some second-hand sleep by watching Tammy, jealously observing her moon-softened features succumb to the twitches of her dreams. Murielle tries reading by headlamp, but the novel she's working through, *Le Voyeur*, is a bit too brainy for her fog of stupidity, the bane of the mid to late contract, and then Tammy blanches, moans woman moans, and if Murielle could see first through the nocturnal topaz and jade of the tent in the starlight with the branch shadows stroking, and then through Tammy's forehead into her dreams, she would see Tammy going through psychological transformations. She would see something like a glass blower sees when at work.

Tammy is inside a pharmacy lit with thousands of vanity lights on a no-name dream street, Tammy feels like she wants to be outside the store in the shadows because inside the pharmacy there are no shadows, but she's inside, wearing a tight mini skirt and a bra which presses in her boobs and her lips are dry and her eyes feel baggy and she's moving wanton down an aisle frantically filling her fuzzy purse with all sorts of perfumes, powders and creams. Part of her wants to leave and be naked and mossy, but the other half desires beautification… more, more creams. Dry and chapped, eczema-pocked, saggy skin, Tammy's clothes disintegrating, her body disintegrates, and she starts popping off the lids and spreading the creams and oils on her face and neck. Popping lozenges in her throat, she spreads and spreads ointments, and in the mirror she can see her bones, and puts on foundation to cover the caverns, and powder over all her body, down all her cracks, her womanly parts, because they're so dirty and swallows mouthwash because her breath stinks, and she is weak and falls to the white tile floor, she is so bone skinny, no strength anymore it's all sapped, her hair has become no more than orange fluff from all the bleach, and now the dissolved molecules of her bones and flesh are absorbed back into the shelved products and she stares at all the customers from the vantage point of the products which contain her, she is staring from the labels into the eager eyes, which used to be her own, which are beautiful and natural and imperfect, the eyes of people who are reaching for the boxes and bottles. Then the dream loops and her wrists slither together between her thighs and she relaxes as her dream deflates. All she needs is a little mascara this time, she is much more composed in this next dream, with Murielle watching, or more listening, to her friend's moans which don't sound like pleasure anymore, sees Tammy's eye twitch open… seem to focus on something and then close, elevator slow… and Murielle has to leave the tent to pee but she doesn't want to. She snuggles against the big pod of Tammy's sleeping bag.

The wind gusts through the tent city of dreams, the inner walls of the tent balloons in, blown by the east wind, a thwapping and snapping of fabric, like the sound of polythene ripped taut. It is such a relief from the humidity. Murielle's incredibly restless; like the whole camp were rocking from some inner turbulence, keeping her awake. She looks out her tent flap, staring into the dark wind. She's lying on her boxspring in Montreal. She'd been somewhere just then; she'd been out on an open street, feeling the panic of disorientation, no points of reference. There was something imperative, a plan, and the whole anxiety was a result of being unable to remember what that plan was. Slowly, the faint walls of the tent resolve back into the assemblage of things as they usually are, and she realizes she dozed off just for a second and is now awake again. The tent is being forced onto her, the tent is closing in on them, the whole top squished downward by the frantic bluster, poles like multiple fishing rods, and she the fish getting gang-fished by the night, stars glaring through the screen. Her stiff hands clench the hem of her sleeping bag and her heart beats like a mouse's while the structure flattens and a knocking, a knocking comes at irregular intervals. All sorts of trumped up thoughts assault her imagination as she lies there trembling with her eyes wide open in the dark, and she turns to look at Tammy — how desirable her position! Her friend sleeping through it all, such bliss amidst the bedlam!

True what Hippie But Not Hippie was telling her, how the body can only absorb about two cupfuls of water at a time. Her bladder feels like her tent, pressed down — the whole world, inside and out, feeling like a vice, forcing her to act, get out of the accumulated heat of her sleeping bag and do what must be done, which is to go outside and pee into the wind and rope down the tarp tighter. She lies still and attentive, waiting to see if the alive sound ceases, but it does not. She figures that perhaps it might be better to catch whatever it is in action; the fact that it's making noise means the creature is occupied, so she has a chance to see it before it sees her. She would risk her life to pee at this moment. She wishes briefly that she possessed a male member. With a male member she could easily just pee in a bottle (she saw Styler come out from his tent one morning with a two-litre bottle full of what looked like pink juice, all puffy-eyed and triumphant, and showed everybody and they responded, "Oh, dude, there is something seriously wrong with your bladder. You're pissing pink, dude!").

She pulls some sweat pants over her boxers and slowly moves out from under the flap of the tent. The warm wind surprises her skin. Her little bangs are tossed back like a bouffant in a big blast of wind followed by an immediate stillness. She crawls out a little way, using her hands to guide her.

The alive noise seems to be issuing from a wooden plank

somebody pitched their tent on across from hers, partly obscured by patches of brush. On one of the stems of that particular patch of trees is attached a rope that leads to one of the supporting platform planks. This creates an inadvertent pulley system; the wind blows the trees, which forces the platform up a couple of centimetres, then drops it with a thud.

She pulls the sweat pants down and pisses into the long grass which tickles her thighs. Just as she's about to dive back into her tent she looks across the way. There is something standing under a grey pine. She squints at it. It definitely wasn't there before.

"Bonjour? Est-ce que quelq'un la?" She poses the question to the silence in a loud whisper. Whoever it is acts inanimate. Then it seems to shift slightly, like a moose, or a loose heap of branches. She dives back into the tent and snuggles in even closer to Tammy. She curses under her breath when she remembers that she forgot to pull the rope away from the trees but the knocking has ceased for some reason and soon she hits the stratosphere of sleep and her consciousness is a blank stretch of ozone layering off, off.

At one point during the night she has a nightmare. She sees a creature with a heart of ice and eyes of fire, singing with a deadly beauty, and Tammy follows it into the bush, and then come these terrible biting and ripping sounds.

She opens her eyes. A human voice. She pulls open her tent flap a bit and peers out with one tired eye and sees Spice, naked save for flip-flops; the cook's soft voice a gentle alarm, as if speaking through her thighs. Two planters jabber about the noises of the night before; it seems Murielle was not alone in believing that the world had been ending. There had been a bear watch all night long, so it couldn't have been a bear. So it was nothing, one of the many things that seem as if they might become something, yet never really materialize as such.

IN A GUN-CRAZED MOOD

Grant is happy to have the gun. The decision to entrust him with the Defender seems stupidly in his favour. Everyone yearns for that ultimate responsibility, the power of the steel. Now he has it, a pocket full of blanks, and a mission.

Winger still hasn't noticed Grant standing there watching her brush and spit white semi-phosphorescent gobs of milky toothpaste onto the ground. She wipes her mouth on her shoulder and puts the toothpaste back in a plastic cylinder, then turns to Grant with unfocused, smoky eyes, the swath of puffy bug bites giving her a bestial appearance. She doesn't appear surprised to find him standing right behind her, and seems unfazed by the surprise of his touch. Grant muses how even caught in bathroom acts she's attractive, like a wildcat dressed in a negligée. But she looks more like an Egyptian cat now. Once revered, now merely mummified and abandoned to museums. The tattoo on her shaved head lunar… and Grant's head now partially grown back like a clear-cut from his initial pre-contract razor job, but still they suit each other, a bald couple.

When he tells her he's got a gun she gets excited. "You want to go bear scaring with *me*?"

Grant touches her on the shoulder. "Yes'm. Such a starry night, Madame, figured maybe you would accompany me on a little sojourn into the glades." He imitates the mannerisms of the anthropologist.

Winger's face grows distant in the starlight. She seems mildly amused, casting her haunted eyes in the direction of Walter's trailer. The spruce trees behind the trailer sway like slow dancers against the yellow mist of the horizon.

She links arms with Grant; off his other arm hangs the gun, barrel split. They head out of camp, attached in this way.

"I cannot *believe* you put in five thousand yesterday. That was tough land." Grant flatters her.

"I have been inspired. Do you have a light?"

They stop and Grant lights her up. She puffs smoke over the flame.

"By what?"

"I don't know, maybe it all started when I saw the photo on Gabby's phone. The photo of the photo of that famous lumberjack. And, I don't know… I guess I've learned a few things. When I went upstairs. You know… the treeliens are always upstairs. Because it's closer to the sky."

"Pardon me?" Grant laughs at her. She's gone crazy alright.

They cut off down a trail to the interior of the forest. The moonlight comes in through the gaps between the spruce. After several strides through the mysterious forest she pulls up and points to the mud on the ground. Paw prints, absolutely massive. Testament to an exceedingly huge creature having passed this way. They exchange glances, then follow the tracks inward.

"It must have headed that way."

At the main road Grant shines his flashlight into the darkness and it lights up a wire fence. On the other side of the fence writhes a swarm of aspen shadows. He uses his thighs and boots to press down the springing stalks of bush as they work their way into the understory. Delicate white creatures flit through the blue light. The littlest creature gives the sonic impression of a monster out here; there is nothing visible, the rays illuminate only empty plants. Grant and Winger gulp in unison. Grant holds out his head lantern — long-lasting halogen, the light it emits not the warmth of old filament bulbs, this is the light of crystal caverns, of blue sunlight refracted through glacier fingers. Winger bends down and pokes the edges of the bear print.

Then she turns her strange erotic face towards Grant.

"Grant, give me the gun please, I want to see something."

"Are you okay?" He asks her, as she reaches around him toward the stock. Her eyes have that hollow look once again.

"Well, actually, I'm a bit pissed off. I want to take a turn with the gun. Why are you the only one?"

Grant can come up with no reason why he shouldn't give her the gun, other than that he is the safety officer and thus in charge of resolving, in this case through avoidance, potentially unsafe situations. He pushes the length of the gun into her grip, keeping the barrel pointing toward the ground. He tells her to take it in both hands.

She takes it firmly in her hands. They walk down the road under the twittering stars. The halogens track blue outlines through the sharp trees — the spruce sticking up like jagged daggers. He looks at her and she has this smile.

"Are you *sure* you are okay?" he asks. Winger cranes her neck towards the stars and she opens and closes her mouth in silent utterance. The shotgun is limp at her side.

He tippy-toes around the side of her, in the hope of getting position on the rifle in case she totally loses it. Perhaps this is his most pathetic of fallacies, assigning meaning to the expressions of this woman and the expressions of the landscape. Eventually the imagination runs disturbed like a polluted stream — becomes fatigued until common sense sleeps.

"You stole my possum fur hat, didn't you!" Winger shrieks suddenly. She is turning on him under the stars, under the black trees that seem to sway just slightly though there is no wind in their needles. The gun is erect in her hands and searching for a target.

She stands in an athletic pose with the gun pointing alarmingly close to Grant. He jumps back, heart leaping.

"Winger," he says, in a high voice, taking half a step forward, then stopping when she raises the gun, "you're starting to freak me out a bit."

"Look out! Don't you want to know the secret? Look out!" She has raised the gun and is charging Grant. He crosses his arms and raises a thigh to shield himself. She fires the gun. There follows a big crashing noise.

Grant lowers his arms, and with wide eyes traces the

sound into the darkness.

There, Winger, and behind her, as if it were her shadow, the bear, lunging through the high grasses, scared shitless. The bear is the most opaque of all the shadows in that roadside, baring its brute flexors and haunches into the brush, then galumphing up onto the road in full view of Winger and Grant, ten metres down the road. It swings its dull eyes toward them.

"Let me," yells Grant in fearful excitement, reaching for the gun, but Winger jerks it away, her eyes will-o'-the-wisp. And again, to his confused horror, she is turning the gun on him... and not the bear.

"What the fuck?" He shouts in her face, grabbing the muzzle of the gun. He manages to wrench it away from her, then reaches out to punch her but she steps back a pace. Meanwhile, the bear struts across the road and turns in the direction of camp. Grant pushes Winger away with one arm, raising the gun with the other, and fires the flaming blanks. He charges the black bear from the side, in order to angle it away from the path to the camp. He pumps the gun and fires again.

A truck roars down the road toward them from camp. Jiggling headlights. Silvester's Nightranger Five Wheel Drive skids around the corner out onto the main road, plowing right over the grass corner, tires spinning in the dirt. Sil slams on the brakes and rolls down the window.

"Biz is coming with the 303," he informs them, spitting through his buck teeth. He smells like rye and looks coked up. He wears his black leather jacket with the burning skull on the back and the long tassels, his substantial one pack paunch hanging out the front: there is Sil, in all his glory. He heaves something hurriedly out of the back seat. A chainsaw.

"No! Stop! I want to shoot it," screams Winger, running from Grant to Sil. Sil is yanking the start cord. "Step aside, please, little missy. This is no time for heroines."

Sil follows the bear, pressing the throttle and shaking the saw. The bear moves slowly away — accustomed to having its way at the top of the food chain, master of its territory.

"If ya know what's good for you, Mr. Bear, you'll make like a rabbit…." Sil slices the air with the metal teeth, but the bear doesn't care. Suddenly it stops and flops down on its big ass, and perks its ears.

But then Biz pulls up in his company truck with his 303, and, sensing that this new presence is deadlier than the amateur buffoonery of its present assailants, the black bear lunges away into the shadows. Biz jumps out of the truck with his gun. It is obvious from his expression that it isn't blanks he's about to fire.

Silvester and one of the Terrorhouser checkers haul the alpha carcass and leave it for a few planter volunteers to drag and roll it up the ramp onto the back of the flatbed using two quad winches tied to its paws.

Folks stand around bitterly in the mist, drinking their coffee and staring balefully at the bear carcass on the flatbed.

Grant secretly fills up a thermos of the management-fresh Brazilian coffee, which he considers a little thank you perk for dealing with the bear. Grant tries to explain what happened the night before to Everyplanter as he sips the coffee. Everyplanter had heard the shots, but didn't know the details.

"It was a psycho bear," Grant explains. "Nothing you can do about a psycho bear… they're funny in the head." Then he hears someone clear their throat. He turns around to see who's standing behind him and gets punched in face. His coffee spills over his Tamponix hoodie, the new one Biz gave him recently, because, being safety officer, he gets some of the management perks.

It is Murielle's fist that catches Grant on the side of his nose.

"You have betrayed both me and yourself." She spits at his feet. He chases after her with a hand over his mouth and nose, cupping the blood which drips between his fingers. Murielle's running legs take her into the big creamy clearcut surrounding the camp. The slash piles are stacked perfectly, the soil free of debris. Grant grabs her arm behind one of the slash piles and starts kissing her, forgetting about the nose bleed....

"Sorry... I'm sorry Murielle! It all happened so fast. Can't we just screw out here in this beautiful land..." He falls to his knees underneath the huge sky as she runs back around another slash pile and disappears back toward camp yelling at him: "You're the psycho, Monsieur Grant... *fou*... *fou*! Blame it on the bears!"

Murielle's anger and sense of loss reflect the emotional consensus of the camp. At five hundred and fifty pounds, the dead bear is a whole lot of wasted cuteness.

Groucho drives the bear off on the flatbed, destination unknown.

"Hopefully to the bear burial ground," Tammy comments.

"Probably to the dump," Eliza corrects her, spitting into the bushes.

"Don't worry, the French are emotional," Gabby advises.

"Yeah, I suppose so."

"Anyway, do you *realize* how big this is? We're going to fucking overthrow this camp. Nationwide gossip! The killing of the bear is going to sway the disbelievers! Did you see their expressions? They hate Biz!"

"Yeah, and now they hate me because they think I was involved in the bear killing! Remember what Walter was telling us about mass murder, well... you should have seen Winger... I think she's going to —"

"⊥ fuck the horror story, Grant! We have a revolutionary story. There are no ghosts, there *is* no haunting."

"Sometimes I wonder if there isn't something haunted about revolutions, like Archy said. Think about it, the same architect who designed the Kap Inn also designed the lodge in Kubrick's *The Shining*, and James Cameron was fucking born here. Where do you think he got his ideas? From the fucking woods. He was haunted from a young age. It's always in the woods where people go crazy and claim they had out-of-body experiences and shit. This whole place is creeping with something, *evidence*, *proof*, *arrows*, all pointing at each other! I think Doug Colt's a frigging fable. I think we're in a fucking fairy tale."

Gabby stares across the marsh. She pinches her lip, picking at the chappedness. "I think we should pay a visit to Walter. That freak will know what's going on."

"That fucker? He sabotaged my trailer!"

"What?" Gabby sneers. "C'mon. How do you know that?"

"I saw him wearing my missing socks!"

Gabby and Grant walk down the little path and into the clearing where Walter has set his trailer. Gabby knocks. They hear Walter rustling in the bush.

"Excuse me, I was just listening to the birds." They hear Walter aheming. "Many grackles in these glades. A feisty bird! Intelligent, chipper, and not afraid to peck the hand that feeds it. Such are the birds I fancy." Walter's voice is apparent before he is. He pokes his head around the side of the trailer, looking toughened, like brown bread compared to white, his forearms rippling, the intellectual flab around the gills almost entirely burned off by the Olympian-level workout of tree planting.

"How's your research going?" Gabby pokes.

Walter sighs. He beckons them to sit on a stump. "Oh, I've moved away from my main principle somewhat. I have less energy for my studies these days, I must admit." There's a mosquito drawing blood from his forehead, distending its crimson abdomen, so Gabby smacks it for him, and the blood blotches the anthropologist's high forehead.

"Maybe you can help us out. We were wondering why

everything seems to be a little on the weird side... Winger, for instance..."

The anthropologist gets defensive at the mention of Winger. He motions toward his trailer to indicate that she is present inside.

"So you want me to tell you what I know of this?" He arches his hand around the whole circumference of sky and earth and camp and birds and bugs. "I've been doing *some* research," he says sourly. "You two *do* know that every situation is a nexus of uncertainty that, once made certain, will bring an entire dilemma into focus. Such is the Oedipus complex. To unlock the mystery of the mother solves at least part of the riddle of being."

"Does this have something to do with the painting of the Queen?" asks Gabby.

"The Queen, oh yes, the Queen!" He picks up an axe, grabs a chunk of pine and whacks it in half. Then he hacks one of the chopped halves into two more sections.

"I am most certainly into the potential harmony between the earth and the sky," he pontificates, chucking the kindling in a loose pile, then returning his intense eyes to Grant and Winger. "We must dance, as it were, to the rhythms of the earth, not those of the heavenly bodies. We come from the earth, my friends. We are born as grubs and flit as butterflies between the ethereal heights and the quagmire of the below. We all try our hardest to break free from the sky, to feel the cold damp of the grass in the morning, the sludge of humus between our toes, the natural rush of serotonin from an orgasm... the sinew of the root... oh, I could go on, I could. I will!" He has one leg up on a chopping block, triumphantly, his gaze cast upward and away.

"Gabby, was it not you who first asked about that unidentifiable character in the Queen Elizabeth portrait? Well, I have completed my dutiful research and discovered that this painted figure is no less than the most famous courtier ever, Sir Walter Raleigh, the poet and secret love of the Queen, who was ultimately beheaded when James 1st succeeded her, as punishment for nefarious trade in Spain. He was the finest of Renaissance men, and a marvelous courtier; a writer, an explorer, a gentleman. For instance, it is said he once laid his coat over a mud puddle for his lady."

Walter cuts off the history part when he sees their eyes glaze over.

"Now listen up… the *key* here is, on one hand, music, and the other, dance. Back in those Elizabethan days of yore the most nimble and graceful court dancers were said to be most in tune with the music of the spheres. Out here in the northern bush, as I say, this sacred dance is reversed. The planters held in highest esteem are those who master a relationship with molecules of filth. Everything is mimicking the movements of the earth, and whoever is most in tune with the earth is the best mud courtier and will win the esteem of the Bog Queen and plant the most trees. It is my belief that what we are undergoing is the subtlest of hauntings with the most cosmic of consequences. What we are after, my fellow planters, is a key. If it is true that we are undergoing a haunting by the intelligence of the land, the intelligence of history, and the intelligence of what I call treeliens, then we must do what we can to circumvent the problems and achieve a fresh harmony with the land. Let me quote Sir Walter Raleigh: 'History hath triumphed over time, which besides it nothing but eternity hath triumphed over.' That's from his *Historie of the World*."

"This has nothing to do with the planter rebellion, does it?" Gabby crosses her arms and Grant fires up a cigar.

"Oh, it most certainly does, young Gabby! I beseech you recall the conundrum: 'You go into the woods at night and you get one and presently you look for it, but you cannot, for the life of you, find it… so you leave.' Now, this riddle has been haunting everybody, has it not? A whole camp has been flown over the cuckoo's nest trying to answer this most logical question. Oh, I know… I've seen the planting partners mulling over possible answers. It has plagued your waking and sleeping minds, and to solve it would lift a great weight off our *corpus callosi*. Perhaps this riddle, and its answer, is a prophesy, and within that prophesy lies a code. T'was with Winger we first saw that riddle. Scribbled in a wild calligraphy it was, next to the Queen's room at the Kap Inn, in the room marked *Xylophloe*. The day you were on drugs, Grant. *YOU GO INTO THE WOODS*.... Doug Colt? Well, I assure you that he is a very haunted man. Ask him about that riddle. And look at these people."

Walter removes a small leather-bound album. Inside it is a picture of two odd persons who look very trashy and slutty, and Grant's eyes widen in surprise. Looking out the window... peering down... those same eyes staring at him from the parking lot!

"Archy's godparents!?"

"No, Grant. They are witches. Witch-like. At least they are bewitched. They exist, however, not in the way that most things exist, not how one would expect them to exist at all. *Ha ha*! At the Kap Inn, at the Kap Inn, at the Kap Inn!"

Grant scratches a bug bite and blows smoke.

"Are you on acid?" Gabby knocks Walter on the noggin. "Witches are a product of the narrow-mindedness of psychotic societies, to scapegoat people and shit. Enough with this retro bullshit, Walter. Are you really an anthropologist? If you are, then I recommend you catch up on the last century of human history..."

Walter looks at Gabby abashed, offended, flabbergasted at her cheekiness.

"No, Gabby, I am not on drugs, I am on history. Plain and simple. Don't you see? You are awaiting the moment when reality bends. You are all looking for some sort of beloved human meaning in a world where belief has been rendered entirely inhuman. But know this: the spirits reach you in code, cipher, sign, gas, beglittered surfaces. There exists in this universe a hierarchy of consistencies: they reach for you through a string of moments, they drift for short periods through the lightest of hierarchical elements. These symbols come as sign, flame, cloud, smoke, radio waves, dream images, patterns of oil over water, through numerals and letters, like a virus in circuitry, my dear Grant and Gabby, and finally a violence comes. They are beseeching you to listen, for they have a most important message, for you and only you."

Gabby shakes her head at Walter as if he were a lost cause. She's tried to bring him into the planter cool, but he just wouldn't fit, he's way too much of a tool. "I just don't know about ghosts, your logic about the spectres seems strange. How, exactly, does Walter Raleigh fit into the Canadian north? I just don't see the connection."

"Well, boo! Like a ghost, say! Like a ghost! Boo!" Exclaims Walter, jumping up and down and clucking. "*I* am Walter Raleigh! Ho ho! Frogs bow at my feet! Behold! Yes I, eee, I, eee." He grabs a robe hanging on a hook off the side of his trailer. Royal white — the same ermine as Sir Walter wears in the portrait with Her Majesty. Grant and Gabby gasp as Walter flings the ermine over his shoulder, staring at them both as if he were a massive bird of prey — glory devouring his eyes.

Grant and Gabby are backing away as they would from a bear.

Walter follows them, spitting and speaking profusely. "You like my fur, you like my fur! That day you saw me with the binoculars, Grant... I was not planting, I was hunting... hunting small rodents for their soft pelts! And my Queen is no other than Winger! I've been feeding her pollen... her abdomen is swollen and soon we shall all swarm together, my planters! Aha! Now you get it. Now you get it. You shall all live together in the bogs under our rule and you two will be the courtiers and dance in the mud. And Murielle, that French biatch, will be with the *grenouilles* where she belongs!"

At dinner (pork chops in mushroom sauce), Winger is rolling around with lettuce stuffed under her armpits and crying toward the stars and Walter is talking Grant's ear off. Bad luck of the draw. The only seat happens to be next to the psycho.

"Pack life, Grant!" says Walter. "To enter again the domain of the primitive! We needed this. The family went against this. Changed? Yes, it has. Of course, the Utopian dream has always been the human dream, and the human dream has always been the absolutist dream, and the absolutist dream has been proven to be the phony dream. But to consider the man who coined the very term, Utopia — Sir Thomas More. He conceived of an English society where there existed a working communion between the farmers and the urbanites. The denizens of the city would go out to work in the fields for part of the year, and vice versa, you see, in this utopian version of England."

"Listen, would you fuck off?" Grant interrupts as he moves away from the dinner table where Spice is dishing out food with a fake smile. He has to step over Winger who is performing a bizarre interpretive dance on the dirt floor. She jumps up and dry humps him for a second and Everyplanter laughs. Her previous murderous attitudes toward Grant have strangely lapsed into carnal attraction. Walter eyes her with mild annoyance.

He's got some things spot on, Grant thinks, reluctantly agreeing with Walter. How nasty, short and brutish, how dirty and unwieldy everything has become. How fucked up. How really unreal. How tainted the dream has become, by fungicides, by shotguns, by diesel fires, by social politics. So wrong! So distracting! Living in an age where everything feels polluted, even one's own semen, the fruit, the fish.

After dinner Larry pulls Grant aside, puts his arm around his shoulder, and strolls with him out to where the northern lights are illuminating Block Z beside the camp, the stars hanging over a vivid blue haze.

"We're going start planting the cream tomorrow," Larry says, pointing out over the flat, moist, sandy expanse.

"How the fuck?" Grant is shocked, but at the same time horny, in the way he gets looking at opportunity.

Larry relates his meeting with Biz that evening, how he'd approached Biz in his trailer. Apparently the bugs were horrible in there. Martens had chewed out the screens on the windows, trying to get at the Coca-Cola inside, so Biz was having a hard time staying in there with the appalling number of mosquitoes.

"Listen, Biz," Larry had said, "things have been going shitty this contract, for my crew. They feel like they haven't been treated properly. Some of my rookies, they're making negative dollars after camp cost and equipment. Not good. We aren't getting any of the cream. Eliza has had several cream blocks, more than sixty hectares. We've had barely twenty. Things aren't going too well around here, Biz — "

"My camp? Moving out of sequence? I must disagree." Biz had combed his hair and folded a white work shirt for the following day, pausing to slap a mosquito. "The formation is going as planned. Pyramid, the eternal pyramid." He had stared at himself with a feverish smile in a mirror streaked with bug guts, wings, and blood. He'd slapped one that was penetrating his neck. "Like clockwork… just like clockwork."

"So in that case, you don't mind if we plant some of the cream just off the inside of camp?"

"Cream is there for the taking… so take away." Biz had said, seeming strangely detached.

Larry slaps a knee and laughs through his twiggy beard as he tells Grant. "Looks like I got him on the right night!"

That morning they go ape shit. Grant's going for it. He feels like a kid again. A kid with a huge tub of cookies all to him and his friends. They slut in thirty-five thousand trees along the horizon of Block Z. And keep very quiet about it.

They both wear hand-knit sweaters. The girl draws attention to big, colourful leaves falling from the branches of a huge maple. They focus simultaneously on one leaf. It is the last leaf on a bare upper branch in the ochre, almond, cashew sky. The abrupt whoosh of the leaf releasing from its stem seems the depletion of the pinkest of lungs; the exhalation of an emblem, slowly revolving, turning like the palm of a hand, towards the damp hummock below. And the couple sees as they are wont to see, with the evenly hovering sense the forest incites — present in the hypnotic gyre and grace of this leaf's passage through levels of gravity and wind and coolness — the slow gentleness of the country as a whole. More than in any history book or heritage moment on television, they feel a timeless progression downwards, backwards, inwards: directionless yet coherent.

The couple twine their hands into a mandala of ordinary sprigs, their eyes like transparent fungi sprouting from the matter in their brains, luminous toward the sight before them.

We watch this while we eat our sunfish and drive slowly over bumps and Bosso keeps saying, no, don't look, no, nothing to see out there.

Roused from their stupor by the sound of an engine, the couple peer up from their amorous knot-tying and see a yellow/green vehicle bouncing along the dusty road. On the side is written the name WE in huge lettering. The couple looks back at the falling leaf.

The leaf keeps falling. This maple leaf tumbles from such an altitude, and so succulent is the current upon which it is borne, that it falls and falls from the source. Everything holds around this loopy palm; it is the focal point of all other movement. For one moment the couple think the leaf blows toward them, that one might pluck it out of the air and place it in the other's hair. But such is not the case. It is whisked over their heads into the anonymous fiery leaves on the forest floor. They turn and kiss each other daintily on the lips, and it is a kiss only partially human. Their lips mate like amorous gentle slugs. As the bus rolls by, the tree recedes and wilts, and they begin running toward the bus. The couple is running toward our bus in leaps and bounds.

STUCK IN THE BUSH

Biz holds a meeting concerning the weather. A tropical storm is approaching, he got word of it on the satellite phone. Something about pacific winds. He looks deeply pained as he paces in his clean pressed carpenter pants and ironed white shirt. He confers with Groucho, both of them clean shaven, having put on their best clothes to face the weather. He's aware that Everyplanter needs a day off but the camp isn't producing up to standard, so they have to push on. Groucho speaks up as well, saying that he just got back from a scouting trip up the Swanson II and he found it was flooded out from the risen bog. He doubts the school buses could make it through, so they are stuck for a couple days anyways, so why not just plant? The trees from the latest Northern Cloners reefer are the final 50,000 of the contract. The experimental trees. Projected to be deposited within four *big* work days. Biz says he has one more thing he wants to mention.

"I've lately heard the term 'planter revolution'," Biz says. "I think it's really just an elaborate form of bitching and complaining. Guys, this is really unprofessional. I mean, don't strike. When you get your paycheques it will all make way more sense. Please, I know we're all at our wit's end, but let's just cool our jets a bit, put our heads down, and work."

Everyplanter wonders what Biz has been up to. Those sharp-featured shadows bucking around in the windows of his trailer, the late-night engine noise, his increasing tendency to drive off somewhere — somewhere to confer with Terrorhouser techs, everyone assumes... and he is always, always talking about those experimental trees.

The morning is eerie. The clouds look unusual, small dots on the horizon moving quick. Someone says it's the beginning of the storm.

By the time the buses are ready to go and Groucho and

Eliza are sounding the hurry-up horns to get their crews moving, some planters still haven't emerged from their tents. Biz runs around screaming, "Okay, get out of your tents. You shits, don't abandon the rest of us here! I told you last night! Some of us want to finish the contract! We have the experimental trees to plant, and we're going to get an extra half cent per tree for those ones. Probably for sure."

Archy has emerged from his tent. His eyes are puffy but fierce.

"We're striking, Groucho, and there isn't anything you're going to do about it! You're not finishing the contract! You're not coming back next year! *We're* coming back next year, you supercilious autocratic mo' fo'!"

Biz puffs up his chest. "Alright, then! None of you fucking strikers are getting paid in full for this contract. I'm going to make sure each one of you gets fucked individually in your smelly little communist asses."

The land has been sprayed with a selective herbicide called See Clear that destroys anything green so the spruce can grow unobstructed. Blue-grey alders stick out everywhere like dead hair on a balding, tumour-pocked scalp. The land is a synapse system drenched in acid: the birds that once were fluttering thoughts have been burned away, except for the odd grouse with its little nest on the bleached ground in dead yellow grass. A shovel scares the last grouse and it shits white goo all over its clutch of eggs.

The Terrorhouser checkers have unloaded bins of what they say are the experimental trees. Straight from Northern Cloners nursery. As directed by the head grower over there. This new stock seems exactly the same as the older stock, except there is a peculiar odour. Biotic and fleshy. And they shine preternaturally. When asked what the difference is between the old trees and the new experimental ones, the Terrorhouser checkers only say they have, "certain transformative preconditions." The fruits of their international bioprospecting program. Someplanter swears they could feel one squirming in their hand for a second as they were planting it, and some other planter gets peeling skin on his hand, some bizarre reaction to the experimental pesticides.

Rico and Shnogg, not into the whole striking deal, stride down a summer road through this cancerous landscape — the big troubled scenery welling up around them with harpy wings.

They keep on slogging, feet brutalized by the hard clay ruts. Twisted ankles. Rico fingering his incisor tooth, Shnogg carrying his shovel through the back straps of his day bag.

Rico uses his shovel for a crutch. "My feet are falling off, brother."

"This be badass winds and bugs. I haven't seen weather like this since forever."

"Let me harken you back, brother. 'Member how we got into this. This digging. These long dying days of chemical. We've lost the rhythm, just like Walter be saying… no resolution in the luxury of them stars. Like we be homeboy angels lost in the gutters of a criminal universe."

Between short bursts of extreme wind, a trickle of heat permeates the haze, and green deerflies whirl around like miniature special-effects vultures.

"I be hearing you, homes." Shnogg squints into the horizon. The sky is like neither of them have ever seen before.

"Let me drop some knowledge on you. This fucked-up place is our ghetto."

"Hold strong, bro. People will learn. See. Nobody be knowing what really be going on. But we know, we know like the black, black rose, the rose of all our days. One day they will learn, Rico, that the new millennium is our turn."

"Yo, bro, don't get all Mansony now."

They pass through a stand of tall, pop-up poplars, rushing and laughing in the wind. Their mouths are dusty and yearning for fruit. And then the wind comes blasting over the open cuts.

Shnogg walks along the road where it bisects the stand of trees. Rico stops to piss, sticking his shovel in the ground, and hobbling to the side of the road.

"Give me the binocs, Shnogg."

Shnogg passes him the little binoculars.

He stammers, his jaw drops. "It - it - it's…"

"The Tree Of Death," chirps the junko hopping along branches.

Swaying up there in the savage heavens: the colossal tree. Wilting fast as if influenced by the whim of some unnatural autumn, a dark technotronic pounding issuing from the shadows at the centre of the branches and leaves, swaying at an accelerated pace, the objects within the leaves and shadows eclipsing themselves, becoming afterimages. The thick upper limbs growing through the bars of the sky as if it were a chain-linked fence. Growing taller, even as it perishes.

The clouds subdividing, becoming layered horizontally across the sky. The wind booming through the tunnels of the forest accelerates in invisible waves over the cleared areas, blowing with open lips on old maps.

Now the leaves are curling, like used chrysalises, and tumbling away, leaving another layer of glittering leaves. These are falling away in the blasts of wind, and the loons are taking on statuesque stances, tumbling through the brush into what seem to be mangroves or banyans (tumbling away into another country?) and the leaves are turning blue and red, and shriveled.

Under the tree, a merry couple are holding hands and twirling, twirling at the base of the tree that is thick enough for a highway to pass through. But then the dancing couple are fading like a photograph dissolving into a background, and black light replaces any warmth of vision with a faked purple fuzz.

The two homeboys make haste over the soft floor of the inner sanctum and down a draw where water ekes through. Above them the trees stretch very high, as if they were old growth, but this land has been harvested several times over. The narrow road ends, and they bust through another stand, chickadees pesking about in the gossamer of thin branches. Shnogg grabs Rico by the arm and hiss-whispers him to hold up. He points across the road. And there is this huge black man with dreadlocks and army fatigues with snow camo patterns, creeping across the road with his wide back turned to them. Then he turns his head around in their direction, surveying each direction independently. When he notices Shnogg and Rico he puts a big finger to his lips and shushes them.

"See through me," says the black man.

"But it's good to see you, bro."

"See through me," the black man says again, sneaking into the woods.

"Wait. Wait! Come back here! Who are you? I love your hair. Come hang out with us, bro!"

"Who the hell was that?" Rico squints because the wind is blowing shit in his eyes. The storm comes on, over the treetops.

"It's the person I always wanted to be!"

"Well, that was just weird. I thought we'd seen everything, Shnogg…" They continue along the road, keeping their eyes peeled.

The walk seems never-ending… and then another surprise — Groucho — strange because his crew is planting on a totally different side of the block. He's holding an experimental tree in one hand and looking out over an opening. His Tamponix fleece is blown open, and his clean-shaven face shines like his eyes, which are directed upward and away across the opening.

"Maybe he's back here to whack off," Rico whispers as they watch the foreman through some alder boughs. They are about to yell something when a second figure emerges onto the road. The second person is running in a crouch through the long grass towards Groucho. Groucho raises the experimental tree above his head towards the sky. Across the clearing an eerie mist swirls over the trees and the wind rushes. The second person has stopped and is squatting in the grass, holding a shovel menacingly in his hands, as if waiting for Groucho to make a move. Shnogg and Rico watch from the top of the hill.

Back in camp, back an hour, the strikers have moved into the trees to get away from the wind. The revolutionaries sit on logs and in the moss: laughing, snorting, playing pop fly with a rock and a shovel. Archy scribbles in his notebook, pausing to slap mosquitoes and look down the road to see if Luke and Eliza are on their way back from the spy mission he sent them on. His Pocket Marx rests open on his lap and on the ground are some other books, beat up from all the travel.

Archy is working on *The Art Of Crew Bossing*. Part of a Book of Knowledge which he plans to disseminate in the planter-owned camp next year.

It is better to be slightly feared by your crew members than partially loved, since true love of a leader is impossible in the harsh, unfair conditions of the bush. Partial love leads to deceit and lack of respect for the seriousness of the crew boss's demands. The leader ultimately dissolves his leadership with this love and the term boss is phased out.

No hierarchy. Power is a grid of four-dimensional distribution.

If the truth is cool, run with it. If the truth is demoralizing, then withhold it. Of harsher truths: let the crew figure these out on their own. Frequently the crew will fail to notice how bad things are unless they are reminded. What sucks goes without saying; saying it only makes whatever it is that sucks, suck worse. Avoid the verb *to suck*.

Instill the working philosophy of "the complete planter", who works not only for the greater good of the forest but also for the prosperity of his planting brothers and sisters. When conditions become exceedingly challenging and the urge to go "on the take" arises (ie: slutting trees, and/or quitting, and/or vandalism of camp or forest), that planter will have a firmer purpose (or goal), and will refrain from carrying out destructive fantasies.

Create a mythical paradigm to guide the crew on their planting journey. It is not just a clear-cut, it is a legendary war zone. It is a zone of challenge, of tomorrow's victory. For example, it is not a forest, but Lothlorian forest; it is not a boulder, but a boulder that was once a person who was transformed into the boulder as punishment for not planting enough trees. Myths lead to belief and intrigue, which lead to inspiration, which increases crew production. The myth of big money must die.

Always be one step ahead. When your crew is walking into the block, you are in the block already, figuring out where you are going to put each planter, taking into consideration their skill level and performance over the past week. At night, when the camp chores are completed, examine maps so that the next day you will know where you are leading your crew. Think, if only for a couple of minutes, of the next day.

Although you will always have marijuana on the block, it is not for you to smoke. It is for your planters: for menstrual cramps, for guys frustrated by their testosterone.

Always have a lighter. Always have wrapped candies on you. On a shitty day hand out these candies. A lighter is always handy on a wet day when a planter's fire source may have become dampened.

Never criticize your planters behind their backs. Nothing kills loyalty like the suspicion that one's leader is conniving or unscrupulous. In the morning, stand on a stump and address your crew. Address problems to the pack, or, if the problem concerns a certain individual, talk to him or her in their land. People take criticism better when they are in their own territory.

Foster alliance and friendship amongst crews. Do magic mushrooms with your crew on day off, and bring them into the forest with their flashlights.

Stay cool. Coolness and foresight save you from running around too much.

Pay attention to detail. Keeping the details in check ensures that the big picture gets painted in smooth strokes.

Archy's brow crinkles pensively as he strains to remember Larry's words. He's in the process of transcribing all that Larry's told him over the years, like Plato scribbling down the wisdom of Socrates.

Today is the day that Doug Colt told Archy he would come into camp with the "back-up brigade," whatever that entails. The savage storm could be an impediment, depending on what sort of vehicles Doug has at his disposal. All this goes through Archy's bugging-out brain. One third of the camp putting down their shovels was more than he could have asked. Almost all of Larry's crew... some of Eliza's.... Since Biz has announced the end of the contract, it is imperative that the official overthrow happens either today or tomorrow. If not, everybody will go home, become apathetic during the off-season, and end up returning to Tamponix Reforestation.

Groucho drives a truck into camp to fill up a jerry by the grove where the strikers are hanging out. He glares into the trees. "You fucking pussies! You know you will never get hired back next year. Even you, Archy!" He vrooms from camp too quickly for his own good.

"What an idiot, what a huge penis," Archy looks up again from his *Art of Crew Bossing*. "Groucho thinks he's the man now that he's fill-in crew boss for Biz's shit show. The cocks are climbing up the hierarchy. Cocks will rehire anybody, that's how a bad company works. Even after organizing a strike they would still hire me back. Cocks need more cocks to get longer." The other strikers are lying around with blank expressions, and he isn't sure if they are listening or if they even care.

Negative Aspects of Marijuana #1: Apathy. The occasional smoker uses weed to wake up and see life in a new light. This is an energizing high. Too much can lead to bone-deep apathy, especially amongst teenagers, becoming a problem… because reality just seems dull…

Then a shout from down the road. One of the strikers, Ned, is knee-up around a corner of trees. Archy immediately recognizes something in his fellow planter's expression and he runs past him and down the Swanson II.

For a despairing second on the arc of infinity, direct light shines on the coloured little bundle of fur lying at the side of the road. Archy gently lifts up the limp neck. A big orb of a tear fills up Archy's right eye, reflecting, it almost seems, some trip down memory lane where a spry puppy chasing cottonwood fluff through wisps of horsetail, catching its first tennis ball between its teeth; little Sphagnum hanging out with all the skater dogs and punk hounds in the hard Knox summer tenements in a town called Cadillac and someone saying, "Were you high when you named her? Isn't she getting high now with all the second-hand opium smoke everywhere?!" Sphagnum splashed with all the tie-dye hues of heaven. Now here she is, lying on her side with twitching paws on the logging road with red flecks dribbled from her nose. Blackflies cling to Sphag's nostrils.

The wind ruffles her coloured fur and breaks the teardrop on Archy's cheek. He looks up the road, his eyes now full of menace.

"Groucho just drove off. He was backing up," Ned says, from behind Archy. "He backed over your dog, guy. There must be some fucked-up shit going down on the block. He just ripped away with a fresh load of experimental trees."

Archy casts his hard eyes down the road. He grabs his dead dog up in his arms and cradles her back to the glades where the strikers are hanging out, and lays her on some moss. He jumps on the back of the quad.

Spice opens the door of the cook shack, sees Archy. "Biz told me not to let anyone take that! He's going to behead me if you take the quad. Archy! Archy!"

But Archy is off, roaring down the road the way Groucho went.

Walter the anthropologist comes running out of the timber edge. "Doom, doom. Wendigo! Wendigo!"

He runs to the cook shack. "Let me use the radio," he demands of Spice.

"No, Walter, you are not supposed to. You are too messed up for technology."

Walter pushes her aside and grabs a walky-talky and starts yelling into it.

Murielle sprints out of her piece and into the forest. She hears the human caterwaul of somebody apparently in big trouble, blown on the tropical winds from a great distance — airborne agony.

Why did Tammy go into the woods? Where is she? She'd been chasing those bees. She'd always mentioned seeing these bright orange bugs, and was convinced they were a species yet undiscovered by entomologists. Before the tropical storm had gotten really fierce, Tammy had spotted one of these peculiar bugs, glowing yellow and blue, a fully mature specimen with horrendously long legs, a cross between a hornet and a bumblebee, and she was positive that this strange bee creature was the product of one of those little mutations that occur beyond the range of the see-all eye of science, and she chased after the zoomer wasp with a jar open. Murielle couldn't believe it: Tammy, who had been frightened of worms when she arrived, chasing a mutant bee! Putting the first year of her biology degree to good use!

Murielle finds her planting buddy lounging on this big bed of sphagnum moss that looks like something out of *Alice in Wonderland*. Tammy sits there with her empty jar cupped in her forlorn hands, obviously upset that her mystery bee got away.

"I don't get it. Usually they chase me. I think they see infrared."

"Come, *tout de suite*!"

This wailing. It sounds like the banshee herself. Tammy starts running, following Murielle.

They run together into the roaring wind, branches cartwheeling by, tangled clumps of sticks rolling like boreal tumbleweed. They fight side by side through the wind toward the source of the scream. Their bodies kites on the verge of taking off. The wind funnels and muffles the noise, luckily no rain on that wind, but it's difficult to tell exactly from which dingle or glen the screaming issues.

They can see the Terrorhouser trucks with their fiery red logos pulling around corners and then disappearing into the inner reaches of the forest. They spot a figure way out there in one of the clear-cuts, so they sprint on over. The person is stuck underneath a fallen spruce.

It turns out to be the guy from Israel. "It blew on top of me," he says. "Ah, get it off of me, ahhh. I can't breathe!"

Murielle and Tammy pull away the branch, their terra cotta muscles bulging around the shoulders. They hear the screaming again.

"Was it you who was screaming?" asks Murielle.

"No," the Israeli yells back, wincing in pain. Now freed, he slouches on the clay and twigs.

"But I thought, *mon dieu*!" They hear more screaming, with a gurgling this time, coming from further up the hill.

Tammy jumps up. "I will run to the next screaming!"

"*Bon chance*," yells Murielle after her. "I'll stay here, until help comes for him."

"Okay! After this, I'll never call you a stupid French girl ever again. Promise!"

"And to me, you will no longer be the Torontonian princess!"

Tammy runs away, leaving Murielle tending to the injured Israeli. She fishes out her emergency whistle and begins blowing, but the sound is drowned out by the winds, and the continued howling from deep in the woods.

"Did he tell you to go this way?" Luke yells ahead after big-hipped Eliza, as they scamper toward their destination.

"Yes, yes... if we hurry we can cut him off. The road's so shitty it will actually be faster on foot."

Luke makes noises of obstinate annoyance. He's got a camera, which he examines to make sure it has battery power, then he continues running with Eliza. He can't believe how absurd it is getting involved in this adventure. Tree planting should be about planting trees, not entering, physically, into mysteries and conspiracies of reality! And here they are, in some good-guy-versus-bad-guy movie, chasing Groucho, to some location where, apparently, he's supposed to meet Biz for some massive tree-stashing plan. Archy had asked/ordered them to head this way, to spy and be witness to the unfolding atrocity. Biz's last chance to maintain any hope of an empire... by burying the remaining trees.

"Jesus, Buddha, Allah," Luke curses multireligiously to himself as he looks into the gravel pit. Eliza is certainly in no need of verifying on her map that this is the place, as the backhoe is there too.

"This is un-fucking-believable," she says.

There are all these trees running around on their root legs. Luke and Eliza watch in semi disbelief. Biz is operating the backhoe, pit-digging.

"Looks like Biz's treelien bargain fell through. Shame on him," Luke gasps. He now understands what Grant has been saying with regards to Archy's letters.

As Luke and Eliza watch, Groucho chases down a few escaped treeliens with his defender, blowing them into fragmented lumps of bark and sap.

"Well, now that we're over here, I really don't know what to do. Should we stop him? Maybe it's best if we let him finish burying those freaks of nature," Luke says.

They watch as Biz throws the last treelien box, which is painted metallic green and says *Northern Cloners* on the side, into the pit.

"Fuck you, you freaks!" they hear Biz shout as he pours diesel onto the tree boxes. He gets into the backhoe and dumps more soil onto the hole, then gets out and lights the whole thing ablaze in a huge wax-fueled inferno. Tree formations of smoke rise in the sky, which is getting windier and cloudier and crazier, blowing bright embers into the timber. The winds from the storm act as huge celestial bellows.

"Burn, darlings, burn!" they hear Biz shout, standing in the smoke, his supervisor fatigues getting tarnished for the first time. "Looks like we forgot one of those son-of-a-weed-trees," he growls, reaching for a lone treelien he's found. It squirms around in his grasp, its little twiggy arms waving, its bark lips letting out a shrill sound of discontentment. "Let's kill it!"

"Biz, it's going to attract the damn trunk ship again," Groucho points out.

"Listen," Biz says, his blue eyes bright with idiocy. "Listen, Groucho, you're going to have to go through with the original sacrifice… it's the only way to make them think we planted the seedlings."

Groucho, big, bearded, bald, and depressed-looking, withered from all the pesticides, can only grunt in response. "Uhhhhhh."

"You know what to do! You remember the alpha! Now go, Groucho, go! Sacrifice that treelien… it will get the trunk ship to leave, finally, and they won't bother returning. They'll figure out we've sabotaged their earth nursery operation and the deal's through. Treeliens have no revenge instinct. They are forgetful, daydreamy bastards. They don't hold grudges. This deal was bullshit to begin with. Earth soil isn't right for these freaks of nature."

Archy squeezes the quad brakes. The trees along the road are thrash dancing. His eyes are all deviled up and his long hair lashes á la black stallion. He follows an orange flag line into somebody's piece. Peering into the growth he spots two planters working away in the ferns and the taller blueberry bushes.

"Where's Groucho?" He yells at them.

They glance at each other, then simultaneously point through the shelterwood. One of them shouts back that Groucho had passed that way not long ago on a quality check. He had an experimental tree in one hand, and a spade in the other. The other planter does the cuckoo circle with his finger. A sound of a radio comes from a stump.

"What's that?"

"Oh yeah, Eliza left her radio with us in case of emergency."

Someone is saying something. Archy grabs the radio, presses it into his ear to hear above the wind.

"... *pzzz... pffzzzz*... Mayday, Mayday... the day of the Xylophloe treeliens is upon us... alert to the sacrifice of Northern Cloners trees... the official offering... first of the new breed planted, ready for the first live crop, with aquatic Central American and African projecthood."

Archy puts the radio back on the stump and then looks into the timber edge, his eyes dark and hollow with introspection.

"Are you going to plant, or something?" One of the planters asks Archy, looking at the shovel that Archy holds clutched in tightened fists. He must appear just as fucked up as Groucho. He doesn't answer, but instead steps forward, stumbling on branches, plowing on through the winds, leaving the two planters looking at each other with mule deer concern. They bend back into the wind as blueberries thrash around them like little wet dots.

Archy goes through the back of another piece — more planters from Groucho's crew, all of them wanting to get the hell out of the tropical storm, all of them wondering where their crew boss has fucked off to. He asks some dog fuckers if they'd seen Groucho. A blast of wind sends a hardhat flying into the bushes.

"No!" one of the planters yells. "But if you see him, tell him we want to go back to camp. We shouldn't be out here!"

"Will do!" Archy keeps struggling up a slope, through another flag line, into another shittily planted piece, ducking to avoid an uprooted juvenile pine that sails down a hill. It lands on Someplanter at the bottom of the hill. He pauses, looking down at the wounded planter, then moves on. A casualty of revolution.

Then he sees Groucho behind some ghost trees, by a clearing. He crouches and runs through the helter-skelter brush. Groucho stands near the edge of a big curving rock. Archy raises his shovel to one side, ready to whack, and moves towards Groucho, his eyes full of the peculiar gunmetal will that Larry once said drives the revolutionary, the killer, and the clown.

We are yelling to the couple that they might save us. We bang at the bus windows. They dance in the fibrous and emerald-shimmering core of the tree, the grass tall and weaving around them, their eyes huge and luminescent. Bosso is gunning the bus, trying his damnedest to get away from the couple, but slowly the wheels of the bus are skidding backwards and he's cursing, running the wheel this way and that. Not them, he is saying, every year the couple has to ruin my plans, but hell, this is all part of the plan, hell, oh hell, but my time has come, and he looks hollow and scared now and hasn't reached for his gun, as if he were giving up. Five years, he is saying, five years I've been the emissary of We End Dig Go We and now it's time for me to go, oh, I am going back to the place where riddles come from, oh. But never forget I am Bosso, I am the Boss of your confessions in the business of penitence and redemption, oh remember that as I disappear into these shadows of lost industries. Bosso says something into his radio and jams the brakes and opens the door and tells us to all get the fuck out of there fast, and we are out, bounding through the long grass into willows and dark ocean-shadows and the deep damp of the forest, looking back, seeing other trucks pulling up around the bus and the army men with guns again, the couple sashaying through the trees as we run, and their voices, like birds of freedom, are calling on us to spilt up, split up, only a few will get away.

THE KEYSTONE SCENE

Before the "tropical storm" started moving like batons across the sky, the day seemed to Grant like an artist's rendition of happiness, the glades humming with so much chemical potential beauty — the power of a new forest — a new generation of plants just raring to go. The green force. Leaves quivering in glee; frolicking in their photon bath. There is meaning — he saw it glimmering in the surface of little pools and shining in the cups of the wildflowers surviving in the tiny crevices. And it was the simple meaning of existence, the will of the present encompassing everything.

Sunburn? Bah to that. Grant doesn't care. He yearns for the direct contact of the rays that releases something in his nerves and muscles same as a good roll in the hay.

The rain from the night before has made everything moist, the earth receptive to his initiatives. The branches touch but don't whip and strike back, and the flesh is left unscarred. He is working with the land, not against it. All these years it took him to learn that lesson.

The tumescent cumulonimbus is starting to speed up on its route through the framework of branches, from easy breezy beautiful cover girl sky, to Pollack pacing through a Monet. And those same clouds become Janic symbols through which high-flying snipes soar and disappear and make songs with tail feathers in the wind.

The little saplings shine green in the bright sun. And what a huge piece he's planting today. He hasn't even made it to the back yet. Tree planting is like taking a pleasing walk in the forest on days like these. He has been thinking positively. The contract sucked but he's still made a few grand. He has a tan, he's burned some belly. It's practically over. Half of his earnings will fund, well… they will fund whatever spurs him… whatever spurns him… The rest of the money will go towards the Doug Colt project. 60% of everyone's season's earnings is the amount Archy and Doug Colt have tabulated. That will be commensurate with a 55% initial share of the new company, with the Clear Water Mill holding the rest of the shares at first, with a complete planter buyout slated within three more years. And then they will phase out money altogether.

And yet again this mysterious buzzing comes from a patch of brush bisected by a huge fallen poplar. In his stupidity, Grant thinks it's still too early for wasp and bee nests, as he associates them with the late summer contracts when there are about four nests per hectare. So he continues his methodical daydream planting.

He wants to build a shack in the mountains, in a permissive milieu of some sort, a place where wanderers settle down. And there he will work on a letter to his family, telling them that he wants to visit them, that he is coming home to visit after his stay on the mountain. And maybe another letter, a letter to fellow wanderers. But his pleasant train of thought is disrupted by an ember scorching the side of his hand. His mind is seared out of its dreaming; his mind farts and fucks up. The first things he sees are tendrils of smoke rising from the hollow of a log. Smoke with wings. So there are some bees this time of year! He sees one bee hover above the pack and rotate its armoured head, point his way, then accelerate and bury its stinger in his forehead. He drops his shovel and tweaks the bastard, crushes it like a fly. Then he bounds away to a safe distance, about thirty feet from the nest. He raises his hand, touches the burning spot where the bee nailed him. He feels something still stuck in his forehead and squeezes and pulls at it. For some reason this intensifies the pain. What the fuck? Then it hits him: venom sack. He has drained the last dregs of his assailant's powerful scourge. Then the dreams dissipate and the sky grows doomful like it was brewing weather patterns into some sort of mandrake root stew.

The winds strengthen. The back of his piece opens up into a huge pocket surrounded with rocks that look like the backs of whales. He begins planting out the pocket and it is then that he hears a distant scream.

Almost at the same time he sees an instant totem in the moment, a massive, larger-than-life bear head snarling upwards, which becomes, in the next moment, a twisted piece of wood, sticking from a charred burn pile.

That scream is definitely not safe! He pretends that he can't hear it. The screaming stops and he pretends it didn't happen. The bear did not appear. The scream was a typical planter scream, he reasons, just someone venting their frustration. Everyday stuff. The bear a glitch of the eye, the same glitch which inspired the art of the continent's first people.

He's about to walk back to the road for a bite but he hears the scream again. This time it sounds different. Someone else screaming now. It's coming, again, from somewhere back in that mossy pocket. Grant drops his bags. Keeping his shovel clenched in his hands and spread across his chest, he lopes toward the back of his piece, heart pumping under his collarbone.

Then he trips up, falling into the skeletal hand of a cedar branch, his shoulder cracking, aromatic needle tufts batting his ears and the edges of his nostrils. His thumb and wrist twist painfully into the mud. He struggles to his feet, wipes mud from his face, and pushes on to where he thinks he can pinpoint the screaming. There is somebody over there, near the shelf.

The scream comes again, softer, more plaintive, cutting through the light. Grant's eyes become cameras, zoom in. There. Somebody, a raised arm. Somebody blurry. Somebody screaming there. Some figure twisting in pain.

Grant kneels, holding his head steady. Yes, those are Groucho's eyes, big Groucho, lying on the moss, screaming.

And bleeding. Eyes stuttering. It's as if all the emotion Groucho never could plumb and dredge from his life was finally bursting out.

Grant's mind flashes back to a thousand imprecise moments. Grade two: his friend tumbling face first into the brick wall of the school yard. The monitor, Miss Birch, ran to the rescue. Grant remembers seeing the blood and then rushing frantically inside to find his teacher. Miss Birch — what does she end up doing to help? No tourniquet — only in war movies. Apply pressure. Send for help. Apply pressure. Except, where is Groucho's wound? The wound is low. In the groin area.

Groucho's eyes are tortured, squinting up at Grant, dark around the rims like smeared mascara. He is clutching his groin. Why is he clutching his groin like that? Grant's worst suspicions come true. He surveys the bench of rock. Those high whale-rocks from which Groucho must have plummeted, just like the trailer plummeted, just like the tree-price plummeted. There is a stick at the bottom of the shelf, sharp, coated with coagulated blood. And the broken end of a stick protruding from Groucho's... out of his... and suddenly in Grant's mind, the answer to the anthropologist's riddle... you go into the woods at night and you get one.... you look for it... you can't find it... *a splinter, a splinter.* And so you get the fuck outta there.

Groucho squirms back and forth on the bed of moss. His frothy lips open in a contorted vowel shape, and he screams again. A huge splinter, magnified by the situation.

"Rest his head on something," Tammy says, kneeling beside Grant. She's come out of nowhere. Grant stands silently by while Tammy grabs hold of Groucho's white wrist for a pulse. He's totally pale and his hands have moved down to his sides, revealing the stick. Then he reaches feebly for his wound again, like a dog trying to lick its stitches. Tammy coaxes his hand away from the wound and feels the side of his wrist again and feels how slow his pulse has become.

Tammy and Grant crouch on either side of the fallen Groucho and peel down his pants. They are pulling his pants off, working the waist band around the protruding splinter while he shakes in a paroxysm of shock-induced pain.

"We need to take this thing out of him. We need to stop the bleeding."

The only material they can think of using are clumps of sphagnum moss. Sphagnum is growing everywhere in the lush pocket. They pull clumps of it from the succulent beds upon which they kneel. They press these makeshift poultices into his wound and Groucho looks strangely peaceful as they apply the moss to the gaping slash between his thighs. It is as if he now had a woman's genitals. This moss, his tampon.

"He's trying to say something."

"Nature," Groucho sputters. "Look… the experimental tree."

The little sapling worms around like a homunculus beside Groucho. Like a freak of nature. Then it just lies there like any normal sapling would. Groucho touches the small tree gently with his bloody hand like it was a child or pet. The sky then becomes disturbed, the clouds sucked through an inward funnel, penetrating underneath the storm clouds, lighting up their skin and the birches with the same pale light as the sun behind the clouds, as if something were taking off back to where it came from, leaving a vacuum, quickly filled by whatever remains.

We have no trouble sprinting through the grid of the mathematical forest. It feels natural and free which is strange considering the fact that we are running for our lives. The spruce and pine trees seem perfectly distributed, too grid-like to be natural. The couple is leading us — but they've told us to split off. Suddenly I am with nobody else. I am all alone. I am there and I keep hearing the voices of the others. "This way, this way." I hear somebody yell, "Hey, where did everybody go?" I want to get back to the group. I keep seeing little *perforations in the path, ways that seem evidence of previous passage, but I do not know which way to go, and it is angling in an updown direction, the path that I am making, and all I can think is that my name is__. It is 1915. I am German. I'm in Kapuskasing. I'm stuck up to my balls in mud. I'm a POW digging away. Now I'm just an echo in this huge arboretum uphill — I should be out of breath except that I am breathing with the pulmonary power of a blue whale. I keep looking back at the Tree of Life — but it is a poor reference point, and keeps shifting along the horizon every time I look up. I am trying to find me: I am a place or a time, or a hovering fluid-sac of consciousness. My name is Treeve, comes a voice, and now the woman who is leading us is small, and naked, and sitting in a hole in some old growth stump. Kiss me, she says. Kiss me and we will begin again. Then we will move beyond the beginning for the first time. And her eyes get shiny, like she's yearning for the skin-on-skin unification of our souls. Her lips enwrap me. Will you sleep forever with me, touching my lips against your white eyelids? And then, abruptly, she looks at the sky: go, go back with the others. She has a tiny hint of mustache and her pit hair is sprouting just a bit. I keep running through the spaces between the trees and I come out, ducking under a cross of trees onto a promontory of grey stone. A breeze is cast over the long and far horizon. Evergreen and evergreen and evergreen spruces extending, a rolling farmland, ships made of bark with wooden propellers scud over the vast landscape, and then blasting from grass-like tubes, a purple fire which burns the trees... now looking along the ridge, there are the others. They're all staring out over the landscape of crazy dirigibles burning the crop. We sit together on the ridge just staring over that bending horizon. And this nymph is flying around saying: My name is Murielle, my name is Murielle. A huge path is opening up. And Murielle says: many different paths, but they are illusions created by the desire for a path. There are many paths, c'est vrai, but they all become one big path going straight through the centre of things. You are a pack, they say run as a pack but remain individual, each unique! What you have seen is what you must ensure will not be...*

alongthehorizongrewanunbrokenlineoftrees

— (landscape: 1 / bpNichol)

"You're fucked, Grant. You don't have your first aid? I'm going to sue you and your hopefully rich family, just watch and see. You signed a contract that swore you were fully trained with level 3 first aid." Biz comes on like dark water smashed on jagged rocks. "We're going to take you to court, safety officer. And Archy, too. I saw it all. I saw it through my binoculars! I was there, on the other side of the clearing. I saw Archy knock Groucho off the ledge. I witnessed your negligence."

"Listen, Tammy was there. If you saw everything, you must have seen Tammy helping me administer first aid. And *she* has her level 3."

Biz stares nervously out the window of the office trailer. They are expecting the planters who were stuck on the block to be back any minute. The ordeal of the last hour is still freshly budded in their brains — strapping Groucho into the rescue helicopter, his eyes hollow and his groin blood-soaked. Getting his butt cheek pinched in the stretcher by mistake.

The storm ravaged pretty much every aspect of the tree planting situation. All the saplings at the master caches were scattered from overturned bins, and the bundles blown into the trees — the remaining experimental trees were swept away into the bogs. The weather haven was finally wrenched from its supports and blown into Block Z. That clear-cut became a huge vacuum sucking in all the manmade fabrics. Personal tents flap on the horizon where they are stuck on slash piles, blown there like kites.

Spice and some of the disconsolate strikers are still out there cleaning up sleeping bags and tent poles, and carrying them back to camp, bundled haphazardly in their arms. Biz is hiding in the cook shack, struggling with the satellite phone, trying to get the thing working, but the sat universe is shocked by some sort of signal storm.

Eliza is sitting on an apple crate smacking gum in her big lips and blowing bored bubbles, even a storm and a rebellion can't rattle her, she's seen worse. She finally speaks up. "What Grant and Tammy did with that moss was, seriously, probably the best thing they could have done. The paramedics said that the moss stopped the bleeding and cooled the wound."

Biz fiddles with the sat phone. "I am contacting the Regional Manager again. I'll tell him about that moss all right... shoving that moss into Groucho's... your perverse negligence, Grant, and I'm going to let them know that. And those sick jokes about Groucho having a vagina. Something went very wrong this year, and we're going to make certain that the instigators get the punishment they deserve. I'm going to ship them to fucking Siberia!"

"Oh yeah, then whatcha have to say about this?" Luke waves the digital camera and flicks the review button, giving Biz a quick look at the backhoe pics.

"Cute... cute... rabbits dressed up as little trees, running around posing as some sort of outer space freaks, and there, is that an actor posing as me? Then who do we have in this photo... Groucho... superimposed, blowing one of the tree rabbits to shreds! Who do you imbeciles — technically wizardlike — but imbeciles none-the-less less, think you are? Stanley Kubrick? James-mother-fucking-Cameron? These photos are baloney."

"Yeah, well, we know that you know James Cameron..."

"Oh, and now let me guess... you're going to say that blah blah the Kap Inn is haunted, I heard that one before. You're going to say there was a freaking Wendigo in camp or something. You're going claim — I know because I've heard it all — that we were planting tree humans which were engineered by Terrorhouser through Northern Cloners subcontracts, actuated by Tamponix, because the treeliens had tons of perfect counterfeit greenback bank accounts or something, and that me and Groucho were the first ones to make contact with the treeliens last year when they descended on the clear-cuts which they had assessed from space to be perfect landing pads and procreation sites, and that they hid their queens in upper chambers of buildings like the abandoned Kap Inn so they could retain a signal lane with other trunk ships, and that it was there that they planted spores in Winger's brain and gave her a queen complex which she sexually transmitted to the anthropologist, except that for him it became masculinized into a courtier complex, and that for instance the main trunk ship is in the Caribbean somewhere parked underwater, or at least was until this tropical storm... I know, believe me, you'll say all this, and some freak like the anthropologist is going to back it all up for you with some theory of connectivity... well, let me inform you... you're full of shit. You have over-active imaginations. Plain and simple. When will you learn to be content with reality?"

Their little tiff is interrupted by the sound of the buses chugging back into camp. They sound louder than usual. Biz pretends to be distracted, then makes a grab at the camera. Luke steps back, though. "Tut tut. Don't be stealing the evidence now, Biz." Eliza sticks her head out the door to see what's going on out there. So does Grant.

They are shocked to see motorcycles cruising like dolphins beside the school buses. Bikers with black goggles straddle low-rider choppers and behind them a Clear Water van with a shiny bumper powers along like a shark. All those wheels rolling slowly, determinedly along, palpitating on their shocks. Shnogg and Rico recognize the good ass dude, who's now on a motorcycle too and wears a doo-rag with a Jimmy Cliff design. A whole lot of polished stainless steel glints down that road from the motorbikes. The strikers have come out of the trees and are jogging along, their arms raised like happy branches in a desperate celebration. They have tied lengths of flagging tape to the back of the school buses and it streams out behind. It's like a whole team coming slowly toward an invisible victory line.

Biz's jaw practically drops like the bone chops of a swamp donkey skull. He reaches instinctively for a shotgun, but Grant forgot to put it back there on the rack after his last bear watch. Biz curses his stupid safety officer and clutches his hands into even tighter fists, punches the air, nose twitching. He opens a little closet and pulls out his 303, then runs out onto the road to confront them all.

The three motorcycles grind to a stop and Doug Colt gets off one of them.

"Biz, you're done like the dodo." Doug Colt steps forward. Backing Doug Colt are the two other bikers. Doug's wife, Marguerite, is beside him on her own bike.

One of the male bikers peels of his helmet. It's Old Malonie, the old Canadian poet from the bar fight.

Biz makes a move forward. "Now, Doug, let's see what you've got! Come on, a big biker like you. Let's see your weapon!" Biz takes another step forward toward the rebel pulp mill worker.

"Now, Biz, we recommend that you put down that rifle." Marguerite has unstraddled her thighs from around the body of her bike. "Let me handle this, Dougy-poo," she says, and Doug steps back. "Now, your poor friend there," she continues, "Grouchy is his name, isn't it? Too bad about him, but I still have to tell you… from all our eating pie with your workers and chitchatting with them on their days off, it does appear that your company treats their employees like animals and you do a poor job reforesting the boreal, and, well, your time is up here. Kapuskasing has spoken."

Biz lowers the rifle and asks to see the filibuster contract. Doug Colt comes forward with a clipboard. The contract-busting agreement, signed…

Grant Hackwood.

The name *Grant* trembles on the edge of Biz's livid mouth. He grabs the anti-contract and he scans it quickly. He wields the gun to where he expects to find Grant, but his safety officer has moved in among the strikers.

"As safety officer I have the power to close camp," Grant says. "This is officially a mutiny. I invoked the mutiny clause."

"But we still have twenty-nine thousand, two-hundred and twenty-two trees to plant!" Biz looks like he's going to cry. His gun wilts to the ground. Some of the inner-circle goons have made it up the road and are backing him, but they are outnumbered.

OUT OF THE BUSH

Counting the kilometres backwards. The flatbed is loaded down with gear and the planters are riding on top, dangling their feet like Kermit the Frog legs off the side and it's all sunny. Sun-bleached hair squiggles across foreheads, and Everyplanter realizes that summer is upon them a rush of solar power, and they're looking back and forth like curious and tongue-hung dogs from one part of the sky to the other, and then across the land, the long grasses sweeping, it's apparent to Everyplanter that "She" is overcoming the chemicals. The pain is lost in a sea of regrowth, the persistence of whatever it is that presses against the forms of things, making everything buoyant and full of potential. The procession of planters drives through the seams of this coming-together. The sun diffuse over the shaved bush of what they see.

Back in town, they scramble to get rides home, some planters discussing staying in town for ice cream and sleep, others want to bust right out on hard-core canoe adventures, some are hitchhiking home... but having stuck out this surreal contract was the best thing they could have done... they have regained some sort of lost version of themselves. And next year the operation is theirs! But so much planning on the off-season... who will supervise? People are a bit leery of the prospect of Archy running the show, but he seems to be the one with the most ideas and the most drive.

"So Archy... some people think you pushed Groucho off the cliff. I hope you have an alibi. If he dies from his wound that would be some serious manslaughter."

"Shnogg and Rico are my alibi, right boys?"

"Fucking A, bro. Fucking A. We were at the top of that shelf. We saw the whole sabotaged situation unfold."

"And what happened?"

"I don't know, it was as if Groucho was sucked off the edge. He was holding up that tree, homes, it was crazy. He was holding up that tree and the sky was dark in one spot and shit, I don't know bro... I don't know... all I knows and I'm willing to testify that I know is that Groucho fell off before Archy even reached him. Archy was angry... sure... but... I don't know... it all feels like a dream, homes, like I was a character in someone else's nightmare..."

The regional manager seems strangely empathetic with the planters. At least he doesn't go wild. He seems resigned to a sort of managerial levity. With a little pressure, he is forced to submit and go to the bank and give Everyplanter who stuck out the contract the maximum Tamponix advance of 700 dollars.

"You want a job as tree-runner next year?" Someplanter jokes. Surprisingly the regional manager responds with excitement. "Actually, I do. I'm sick of being the head of state. I find power restricting."

Everyplanter has a pocket full of bills but don't really feel ready to head back to the city. It's like a big family now. A big stupid family. But the city seems like a ferocious prospect. It all seems to possess this symbolic magic — every billboard or display case, all the new smooth architecture — like a system of emblematic portals; free passes into the logic of some global tragedy; a fantastic network of glitz; a virtual destiny which digests you then spits you out. Like a megalopolis cow, an eight-stomached *bovidae urbanus*. And this false promise at every turn: all that is technological, and graphic, seems to possess a coherency, while everything human is in a state of paradoxical disconnect. They want to bring the lessons of the woods to bear upon the city.

One after another. One tree at a time. Still planting in the soils of the mind.

"Holy shit, what's that!" Benito says. He'd been up at the front of the bus, talking to Eliza about how his season had gone from bad to worse, and now finally better, brilliant, anticipating the next season with glee, when he spotted two figures up ahead on the road, which he at first thought must be wildlife, but which, as they approached, turned out to be human figures now disappearing into the spruce trees.

"That looked like Walter and Winger…" He and Eliza say at the same time.

"Those freaks… those freaks are going to try to live in the forest now, like two bees starting some heinous colony of insanity…"

"Leave them be," says Larry.

All the small roads forming one big one heading right through the centre of things. The bus rolls into the parking lot in the old Kap Inn. And Grant remembers how all the weirdness seemed to begin on one of those first day offs, when Benito and Winger had first gone up the stairs…. Benito had seemed immune to whatever was up there, and Winger had gotten all fucked up, and then Walter, and now both Walter and Winger are off spinning nettles or something in the wilderness. It's as if there was some connection, historical and continual, between hauntings and extraterrestrial visitations, maybe more than their proximity on the movie store shelves… he remembers what Walter said about a "nexus of uncertainty…" But… no… no use thinking about this now, the contract, the contract is over, broken, gone… those thoughts will stay for now in the woods with the splinters, in the house, and in Moon Beam.

"Hey Luke, make sure…"
"Make sure what?"
"Make sure you send me an email or something."
"I thought I'd see you in August, at the festival?"
"Yeah. I'm going home for a while, though."
"Ball deep, man, balls deep."
"It's all over… no more soakers…"

This is Larry and Archy, and these are the days of their planting lives. It was the best of land and it was the worst of land. It was the grey jay flying in-between, desiring neither for its nesting ground. Like saplings into the ground, so are the days of their planting lives. The days when they lost their sanity in a swamp… on an ill-advised acid trip… and found it later in the company truck, with a bottle of Fireball. These are the friends they made and shared everything with, including their herpes. Yes, these are the days of their planting lives. The creamshow and the shitshow of their days. Like strips of duct tape slowly forming a duct tape bikini, so are the days of their dog fucking, as they plant for eternity. And now with tree and man working so closely together for all, will the human race find a new place? Or shall new species rear their freaky heads, and finally, the tree, its roots freed from the ground, find a new equilibrium, with the human growing from its permanent place in a computer chair, and now, reversed, the tree plant humans, and make swings to dangle from their human arms? Only future seasons shall know… the future seasons in the endless cycle… of the days of their planting lives.

(Historical Tree Planting Note: In May, 2007, The Kap Inn was burned down by a kid from a broken home.)

ACKNOWLEDGEMENTS

I warmly appreciated people listening to my recitations from the early MS; who commented, and unwittingly influenced this version of *We Will All Be Trees*. Special thanks to those who scribbled stuff in the margins: Adam Roberts, Meagan Gough, Mel Massey, Ryan Casey. Thanks to Sasha Bukowski for saving an early draft from the morning dew. Huge merci buckets to Maya Merrick, editor, who initiated me, and helped this book lots. Finally, another huge *muchas gracias* to publisher Andy Brown, who persevered through trying personal times to make this happen.

The Planter Rap by Tammy on page 131-132 was written by BC / Ontario planter Kim Rapati. She had this to say about her rhyme: "i kept singing it all day cuz it went with my planting rhythm... and i thought i was planting perfect 7s the whole time but i'm pretty sure i checked after and it was 10s or something and made myself replant. but at least i got a funny song out of the day."

— JM

Josh Massey's prose and poetry has appeared in magazines across the country and abroad. Often based in Ottawa he has planted in four provinces, and over the last few years has earned his living doing forest and wildlife inventory. He composed *We Will All Be Trees* on a portable typewriter in Guatemala, Montreal, and Northern BC.